"You're a beas rms.

"Aye, and that t I've told ye before, desp perate men." He paused, then stalked purposely closer to Zoe. "And desperate women, I'm thinkin'."

"What are you jabbering about?" He was directly in front of her again, close enough for Zoe to smell the wildness of him.

"We both know why ye ran when ye did. Why ye kissed me in the rain."

"*You* kissed me."

"T' my recollection 'twas a mutual act, that near t' sent the rain about us sizzlin'."

"You mustn't talk like that."

"And ye mustn't be such a hypocrite, Zoe." The back of his fingers skimmed across her neck. "Do ye think I can't see the way yer eyes turn t'silver when I kiss ye." He stepped closer. "Or when ye think I might."

"You mistake my illness for passion." Her breath was coming very slowly.

"Are ye tellin' me ye're sick again?"

"Yes." His mouth was only a whisper from hers. "I ache."

Zoe didn't wait for him to close the distance between them. With abandon her hands reached up, grabbing fistfuls of thick, wet hair and pulling his mouth to hers.

It was no gentle kiss. His open mouth hungrily devoured hers as Zoe's fingers tangled deeper into his hair . . .

Books by Christine Dorsey

TRAITOR'S EMBRACE
WILD VIRGINIA NIGHTS
BOLD REBEL LOVE
THE CAPTAIN'S CAPTIVE
KANSAS KISS
SEA FIRES
SEA OF DESIRE
SEA OF TEMPTATION
MY SAVAGE HEART
MY SEASWEPT HEART
MY HEAVENLY HEART
SPLENDOR
THE RENEGADE AND THE ROSE

Published by Zebra Books

The Renegade and the Rose

CHRISTINE DORSEY

ZEBRA BOOKS
KENSINGTON PUBLISHING CORP.

ZEBRA BOOKS are published by

Kensington Publishing Corp.
850 Third Avenue
New York, NY 10022

First Printing: September, 1996
10 9 8 7 6 5 4 3 2 1

Printed in the United States of America

One

April 16, 1746
Culloden, Scotland

The pipe's haunting tones echoed across the mist-shrouded moor and sang through Keegan MacLeod's blood. He was a Scot, by God, a Scot. As were his ancestors and the clansmen with whom he stood shoulder to shoulder.

He'd nearly forgotten. The gaming halls and perfumed boudoirs of London could do that to a man. That life seemed far removed from the icy sleet and chaos of this April morn on Drummossie Moor. Yet it had been only a fortnight ago when he'd cursed the summons of the MacLeod to return to the Highlands . . . to return home.

Cursed yet complied.

For his father wanted all his sons beside him when he fought for his Prince. Charles Edward, grandson of the last Stuart king had returned from exile in France. He'd landed on Eriskay determined to put his father upon the throne of England. The rightful heir, many thought, including the MacLeod.

Personally Keegan didn't much care who sat on the throne. At least that was his opinion till now.

But generations of Jacobite blood flowed through his veins, and so he'd come.

His brothers, sons of the MacLeod, were here as well. Angus, the eldest, his red hair plastered to his head beneath his bonnet, to the laird's right. Duncan, with his soft blue eyes and pleasing voice beside him. Keegan was to his father's left. And finally William, fresh from his tutor, and restless with anticipation of the battle to come.

They all wore the white cockade of the Stuarts, five bows of silk in a large knot. Their plaids were kilted, then tied high between their legs. A silver pin bearing the MacLeod crest held the drape free of their sword arms.

" 'Tis a fine day for a fight I'm thinkin'." Angus stomped his feet and flexed his beefy shoulders. He was broader than Keegan, though nearly a head shorter, but he swung his broadsword with an ease Keegan had long admired.

When his father made no reply Angus continued. "I know you've a problem with the field, Da, but—"

"I'll not be second guessin' the Prince . . . or what happens this day," the MacLeod countered, clasping his free hand on the shoulder of each son in turn. "Nor shall any of ye. We'll stand together as MacLeods, and proud we'll be of it."

"When will they be comin' do ye think? Or will the English bastards turn tail and run at the sight of us?" Arrogant words from William, whose cheeks looked more like the downy underbelly of a lamb, than like those of a full-grown man, Keegan thought.

But all he said was, "Soon enough we'll be knowing."

As if his words were prophetic a loud chorus of huzzas sounded from the ranks. Across the moor to the northeast, silhouetted against the dark sky, the enemy's first scarlet and white standard topped the rise. It was followed by another, then another. And then the Duke of Cumberland's infantry came into view, three columns of blood red uniforms coloring the gloom.

The shouts and taunts continued, interspersed with the yelled commands to "Close up ranks!" It seemed as if the British troops would do nothing but stand, their numbers stretched across the field, their regimental drums pounding like one giant heartbeat.

Keegan gripped his broadsword, and stood, waiting for the order to advance. He stood thus when the first volley from the British exploded over the field, striking down William at his side. It was as if part of himself was blown away as he watched in horror when his younger brother crumpled to his knees, then fell face first into the heather.

"Will!" The collective lament roared around him as Keegan dropped to the ground. He knew before he rolled his brother over that he was dead, but Keegan tried anyway to revive him, calling his name and rubbing his palm over the smooth, whiskerless cheek.

It was Angus who took charge, wrapping the body in his plaid and charging two of the clan's humblies to carry the laird's son to safety.

But there was no time to mourn.

"Close up ranks! Close up!" The officers' shouted orders filtered through the thunder of artillery, the screams of the wounded.

All around him men were falling, clansmen and fellow Scots, mowed down like so much harvest wheat as they stood waiting for the command to attack. Waiting. When it finally came, Keegan leaped forward, a hoarse cry of "For Will," rushing from his dry lips. His father and remaining brothers were at his side as he fired his musket, then ignoring the grapeshot hurled his way, yanked one of the claw-handled dags from his belt. But it was the double-edged broadsword he longed to use. To feel the weight of it slash through the faceless soldiers who had killed Will.

The smoke burned his throat and made it near impossible to see. He guessed he was within twenty yards of the enemy, though only infrequently, when a gust of wind cleared the air could he see the wall of scarlet uniforms. Keegan pushed forward, halting only when he tripped over a body. Falling to his knees Keegan blinked, then found himself staring into Angus's lifeless eyes.

"God no!" Keegan scrambled to his feet, wiping his eyes and searching through the mist and smoke till he spotted his father's grizzled head. The older man had lost his bonnet in the foray, yet he still stood, as did Malcolm. But the Rebel losses were devastating. Dead and dying covered the field, winnowing from the clans their best young men.

Fury swelled in Keegan's breast. He hurled himself forward, swinging the broadsword like a man possessed. For Will. For Angus. For his fellow Scots littering the moor.

He fought and slashed and somehow avoided the

deadly stab of the bayonet, but there was no pene-
trating the solid wall of the English battalion.

The retreat was called, then called again, and still
Keegan ignored it. It was as if another man had pos-
session of his movements . . . of his soul. Not until
he felt Malcolm's hand grabbing his arm did Keegan
hold the relentless swing of his broadsword.

"The laird," Malcolm screamed at him, and Keegan barely heard above the din of battle, though his
brother's muddy, blood-spattered face was nearly
touching his own. "Da's wounded."

Swinging about, Keegan reached for his father,
catching him beneath the arm as the laird's knees
crumpled. "Take this," Keegan screamed, shoving
the bloody broadsword toward his brother. Angered
because of Malcolm's hesitation, Keegan opened his
mouth to repeat the order. That's when he noticed
the glistening fluted tip of a bayonet protruding from
Malcolm's chest. Blood gurgled slowly from his
brother's mouth before the English footsoldier jerked
forward, forcing Malcolm's body to the ground with
the heel of his boot.

Keegan had no more time to mourn the passing
of this brother than he had the others. He was the
only one left. He who had not wished to fight—had
not wished to interrupt his life of fun and debauch-
ery. He who had counseled against supporting
Prince Charles more on selfish than patriotic
grounds.

These thoughts flitted through Keegan's mind in
that briefest of moments when his brother crashed
to the ground. Dipping low, Keegan grabbed up his

father, tossing the laird over his shoulder, then stumbling away from the English line.

Bodies were everywhere, the dead and dying. Keegan tried to close his mind to the carnage. This was not the time to think on what had happened. He must get his father to safety. Yet two days with little sleep and but a few oatcakes to fill his belly were taking their toll. As the sounds of artillery exploded around him, Keegan could not stop the faces of his dead brothers from flashing before him.

Hot pain tore through the arm that dragged his broadsword and Keegan knew without looking that he'd been hit. Yet he pushed on. He would carry his father to Castle MacLeod if he had to. He would.

Yet it was a dry-stone fence that caught his eye. Bordering a sunken road, the fence held momentary shelter. After he caught his breath he'd take his father to the bothy on the rise to the right of the road. This was Cullen land if memory served him, and they'd be proud to treat the laird's wounds. Then they'd be off for the hills of home.

Home.

Though in the years since he'd been grown he'd done his best to stay away, the word rang, a litany through his heart, as he plodded on over the body-littered moor. As gently as he could, Keegan lowered his father, resting his back against the limestones. It wasn't till he straightened that Keegan noticed another using the stone wall as a refuge. It was a soldier dressed in the uniform of an English dragoon. Despite the chill air, sweat poured down his back when Keegan saw the pistol pointed his way.

Lifting his broadsword Keegan ignored as best he

could the pains shooting through his arm. The two men, one wearing a scarlet surtout, the other garbed in plaid, stared at each other without moving. The English soldier was the first to speak and when he did his words were colored by an Irish brogue.

"Be off with ye," he said before letting his head fall back against the rocks. The pistol's muzzle dipped toward the ground.

"I'll be resting my Da if it's all the same to ye." Keegan lowered the broadsword, then dropped to his knees beside his father. The laird's wounds were numerous, but none appeared mortal. At least that was Keegan's uninformed opinion. But it wasn't safe to stay here, even if the soldier to his right hadn't the strength or inclination to shoot.

"Come on now, Da, we'll be heading home. Give me your—"

At that moment a great huzza came from the direction of the English. Keegan realized the artillery had stopped, but he could still hear cannons from the ships in the bay echoing off the mountains.

"They'll be coming now," the wounded man to his right said. "They're claiming the field as their own."

Keegan stared at the Irishman, then back toward the line of dragoons. As predicted, amid shouts and cheers the soldiers began marching across the moor. Then they were running, bayonets fixed, stabbing at any of the Scots that moved.

Keegan grabbed for his father, but in that instant knew it was too late. The wound on his arm dripped blood as Keegan lifted his broadsword, placing himself squarely in front of his father. He thought he heard a mumbled, "Save yourself, lad," but ignored it.

Then he could hear nothing but the clang of tempered steel as he swung the broadsword, fighting off the first three soldiers who came at him. One, then another, dropped to the ground at his feet. But the third soldier had moved to flank him. Even amid the chaos, the click of the pistol hammer sounded frighteningly loud . . . the report almost anticlimactic.

Keegan waited for the pain to consume him, for it was the wounded Irishman's gun, he was sure. But there was nothing. Jerking around, Keegan saw the third soldier crumble to his knees, then slump forward, blood blossoming from the front of his jacket.

"What . . ."

Turning, Keegan's gaze met that of the man with the pistol. Their mutual stare held, and for just a moment Keegan could swear there was some sort of link between them, though he was equally sure they'd never met or crossed paths before. Still, there it was, a feeling almost akin to friendship. Shaking his head, Keegan again reached for his father. For whatever reason the Irishman had saved his life, now it was up to him to get his father away.

But there was no escape. More soldiers were bearing down on him, laughing and killing any survivors as they came. Keegan was soon surrounded. His father and the fence to his rear. Scarlet-coated soldiers blocking the front.

Damnation, he would fight to the death.

Keegan raised his broadsword, sweeping it in a giant arc, daring the footsoldiers to come at him.

Fury raged through him, drowning out the fear. This was to be his death then.

"Halt!"

The shouted command caught the attention of the English soldiers as well as Keegan. He looked up to see an officer, astride a magnificent chestnut horse. Beneath a gold-trimmed hat, the officer's face contorted in anger. The tip of his saber pointed toward Keegan but it was to his men he spoke.

"I'll have no more senseless killings."

"This thieving rebel is the murderer," one of the chastised soldiers countered. "We be just tidyin' up the field a bit."

"You'll be doing no such thing while I'm about." Now the officer turned his attention toward Keegan. "Surrender your sword."

"And be cut down like a cur? I think not."

"Foolish words from one just seconds away from that very fate."

"I'll die a free man, protectin' my father from the likes of ye."

For the first time the officer shifted his focus to the old man slumped against the stones. "You'll do him no good with your defiance."

"I'll do him no good by surrenderin'."

The stallion sidestepped, obviously anxious to be on his way. The officer seemed to share his mount's feelings. "Hand over your sword and I'll see that no harm comes to your father."

"And I've an Englishman's word upon that," Keegan spat, his voice full of contempt.

"Aye, you've Lord Foxworth Morgan's word upon it."

* * *

A word he should have never taken.

With but a few steps Keegan paced the length of his cell, then back, slamming his fist against the heavy wooden door. This is what believing Lord Foxworth Morgan had earned him. A spot in New Gaol; a date with the hangman.

And the memory of watching, helpless, as the soldiers tortured and killed his father.

Keegan shut his eyes against the pain. Four soldiers had grabbed Keegan, pinning his arms to his body, the instant he handed over his broadsword. Their laughter still rang in his head. They'd used their bayonets on the laird, stabbing and slashing till naught but the bloody plaid remained recognizable.

"Nay." Keegan sucked in his breath on a sob. He would not cry again. Better he go to his death cursing the man he'd cursed as the British had their sport with his father.

Lord Foxworth Morgan.

Keegan slid to the floor, burying his face in the lee of his bent knees. How much better it would have been to die on the battlefield. For his father. For himself.

Keegan spit into the vermin-infested straw on the floor. In the months since Culloden, Keegan had railed against God, against the Fates, against himself and even his father who championed a cause destined to failure. During those long, lonely days he'd made peace with himself as best he could, with his father's memory and the God who watched over him.

Forgiveness and acceptance. With one exception. Lord Foxworth Morgan. He should have used his broadsword on the English officer rather than taken his word on anything. His last regret in a life filled with them was that he couldn't take the British lord to hell with him.

And if he ever had the chance again, by God, he would.

Keegan's laughter was harsh. He had no more chances. No more options. He'd been judged guilty by the English courts and as soon as the sun rose over the Thames he'd—

The metallic rattle of key against lock interrupted Keegan's morbid thoughts. He pushed to his feet. So it was time.

"Can't even wait for the dawn, eh?" he said as the thick-lipped jailor motioned him from the cell. The man carried a lantern in one hand, a pistol in the other. He said nothing as they walked the corridor, past the spot where a sentry with his fixed bayonet usually stood. Keegan's cell was on the third of four stories. He led the way down the stairs into the darkness.

At the bottom he was nudged to the left, down another corridor. Keegan kept walking till he came to the door that marked the end. The silent jailor motioned Keegan aside, then slipped a key ring from his belt and unlocked it. The portal swung open to the blackness of night. And just as quickly Keegan was shoved through the doorway.

"What the hell . . . ?"

The door slammed shut, the jailor disappearing behind it.

With Keegan on the outside.

Slowly he turned, trying to focus in the darkness.

"Hurry, Monsieur Keegan. I have paid the jailor well, but he's obviously not a loyal sort, so we can't count on—"

"François?" Keegan could hardly believe his ears.

"Oui," came the little Frenchman's response. "Now we must—"

"But how? Why?"

"I am your valet, am I not? It is my duty to save you. Here." He thrust first a pistol, then a sword toward Keegan. "We should leave now. I've arranged for a boat to take us to France."

"France?" Keegan who had been following his rescuer came to a halt. "I'm bound for Scotland."

"Non, non." Keegan could see his valet's hands fluttering. "That is not a good idea."

"But my clan is there."

"Non, non, you must go to France." His voice, high-pitched in tranquil times, became even more so.

Arguing with François was futile. Keegan had learned that over the three years the man had worked for him. When they came to the end of the street, François turned one way; Keegan another.

"Monsieur, where are you going? The docks are this way."

"I thank ye for savin' me, but I'm goin' home." Keegan paused and clasped his hand on the valet's bony shoulder. "I'll always remember what ye've done for me. If it were in my power t' reward ye—"

François shrugged. "I used the last of your money to procure your release."

Keegan was surprised there had been any coin left at all. But then he'd gone from his rooms so quickly when he received his father's summons, he'd hardly had time to tell François where he was bound. He'd refused the Frenchman's offer to accompany him then, and he shook his head now as the words were repeated.

"Ye're better off on yer own than taggin' after me." But even after he said it the Frenchman continued to dog his steps, pointing out how dangerous it was for him in Scotland, and how he should get himself to the continent with all haste.

"François." Keegan finally stopped, ducking into the shadows. "I'm goin' t' Scotland." He lifted his hand palm out to cut off the valet's words. "And I'll hear no more on the matter.

"But before I go," Keegan continued, his expression turning hard, "there's someone in London I must see."

His father's death would not go unavenged.

Two

September, 1746
London

"Oh my dear Lady Zoe. Whatever are you doing out of your bed? Reading again? Did not the good doctor say just this morn how important your rest was? And goodness knows it is the very bowels of the night. The vapors in this air alone . . . Well, one simply can't be too careful." Margaret Phelps, life-long nurse and companion to Lady Zoe Morgan rushed toward her charge. As she crossed the library she swished her plump hand, sending invisible evil vapors scurrying away from her ladyship, causing the candle she carried to flicker.

"And an open window too." Miss Phelps's chins quivered as she made a "tsking" sound with her tongue. "Goodness knows this will set your recovery back a fortnight." She put aside her candlestick and taking a deep fortifying breath, stuck her head out the casement window and pulled it shut. "Whatever was in your mind, child?" she scolded, turning to face Lady Zoe. She straightened her ruffled night-cap, took the leatherbound book from Zoe's hand, then shook her head again as she glanced at the

gold-embossed title. " 'Tis beyond my under-
standing what you find so interesting in these books
you read."

Zoe opened her mouth to speak, to explain to
Miss Phelps how reading about the world, about
those souls strong and healthy enough to explore
the far reaches, made it seem as if she were not
housebound. Her mind could travel and see new
things, even if her poor sickly body could not. But
before she could utter a word, Miss Phelps bustled
on.

"Now let me see what harm has been done. 'Tis
a good thing I'm such a light sleeper else I would
never have known you weren't abed." She pressed
her palm to Zoe's cheek. "Oh my, just as I feared.
You're feverish."

"I do feel a bit warm, though I did before I came
below stairs," Zoe finally dared to say.

"All the more reason to stay behind the curtains
of your bed. Oh, I do hope this isn't the death of
you." Miss Phelps wrung her hands before taking
one of Zoe's and stroking her pale fingers. "Tell me
dear, where is the pain? Your head?"

"No . . . well. Perhaps." Yes, there was definitely
a slight ache behind her eyes, Zoe decided. "And I
do feel a bit light-headed." Leaning back against the
cushion, Zoe allowed her forehead to be stroked.
Her grey eyes slitted open. "Do you really think I
may die this time?"

"Not if I can help it my dear Lady Zoe." Miss
Phelps brushed aside loose curls of brown hair that
had escaped her mistress's thick braid. "Oh dear
me, where is your nightcap? Here, you must take

mine." Snatching the ribboned and lace concoction from her own head, Miss Phelps draped it on Zoe's. Too large, the ruffles nearly covered her eyes. "There now. Tell me what else pains you. Your chest?"

"No . . . yes." Zoe pressed a hand to her heart and took a deep breath. "I *can* feel my heart racing."

"Oh dear." Miss Phelps shook her grey head. "What of your limbs?"

Zoe pondered the question. Till a moment ago she thought she felt fine. How lucky she was that Miss Phelps awoke to show her how wrong she was. Though Zoe wasn't eager to return to her room where the fire in the grate put off more heat than needed on this September night. The outside air had felt pleasantly cool. It was a shame the vapors were so bad for her.

Zoe sighed, sending Miss Phelps into a flurry of activity. She rubbed Zoe's hand, then lifted her lady-ship's feet off the floor, stretching her legs along the settee.

"Should I awaken one of the servants and send them for Dr. Owen?"

"No." Zoe shut her eyes. "I'm sure tomorrow will be soon enough for him to see me."

"You're quite certain, dear Lady Zoe? We simply shouldn't take any chances. Not with your health as it is. What if you should succumb this very night?"

Oh dear. When Miss Phelps put it that way, Zoe wasn't certain. Would she simply expire here on the settee? Or would her death be a gruesomely painful affair like the many Miss Phelps had described to her? Zoe took a shallow breath. "If I could have a bit of tea, perhaps—"

"You needn't say another word. I shall return as quickly as possible." The older woman took up a candle, then hesitated. "You will be all right without me, won't you?"

Listlessly Zoe lifted her hand palm out to her forehead. "Please hurry," she moaned. When she was alone Zoe let her arm drop onto her chest. In and out, she counted each breath as she took it, hoping it would not be her last. She was so weak, so—

A loud crash made Zoe leap to her feet. She squealed, her eyes torn wide, as she stared at the wild-looking man who'd just burst through the library window.

He stood amidst broken glass, his dark hair long and loose, a beard covering most of his lower face, wearing clothes a rag picker wouldn't want. And he seemed almost as surprised to see her as she did to see him.

Yet he was the first to regain his composure. With a flourish he lifted a sword, larger than any Zoe had ever seen, pointing it her way.

"Where is he?" His demand was thick with rage, colored by a Highlands accent.

"I . . ." Zoe couldn't make her voice do more than squeak. "I don't know who you mean."

"I know this be the house of Lord Foxworth Morgan. 'Tis he that I want." The man's eyes narrowed, studying Zoe from the top of her beribboned nightcap to the slippers peeking from beneath her robes. "Who are ye? His mistress?"

"Certainly not."

"I thought not." He took an aggressive step forward, then another. "You'll be accompanying me to his Lordship's chamber if ye don't mind."

Zoe tried to back up but the settee was in the way. Besides, he was quicker than she, grabbing her arm and twisting her around in front of him. "Unhand me. I won't go anywhere with you." Brave words but alas untrue, applied to the wild man who was dragging her toward the door to the hallway. "He isn't here. Fox isn't here," Zoe finally managed to say.

This announcement made the wild man pause.

"I've it from a reliable source that he is." True, it was a fortnight ago during his trial that Keegan discovered Morgan had returned to London, but he'd hoped he was still here.

"Well, you're mistaken. He left." Zoe turned to stare into the man's eyes. Their intensity made her look away.

Keegan was reaching for the brass doorknob when the door opened.

"Oh my dear." Startled, Miss Phelps dropped the silver tray she carried. It hit the floor with a clatter, spilling tea and biscuits across the carpet. Then the older woman realized what she was seeing and let out a loud scream.

"Hush yourself unless 'tis yer wish to see the lass cut to ribbons." Keegan lifted the edge of his blade.

"Oh goodness me, don't hurt Lady Zoe. Please."

The broadsword inched down. "Ah, Lady Zoe, is it." He stared at the older woman. "Morgan's wife?"

"Good gracious no. Lady Zoe is his Lordship's sister. She's a dear, sweet girl, prone to—"

"Sure I am that she is." Keegan pushed past the

old crone who seemed on the verge of fainting. God save him from vapid females.

"Where are you taking her? No don't!"

The old woman latched onto his arm, her hands like a vise. "What the hell?"

"I won't allow you to hurt her."

"He wants Fox," Zoe managed to say. The sword nudged higher with each yank Miss Phelps gave her captor's arm. "Tell him he isn't here."

"No, no, he isn't. He's gone to the—"

"Miss Phelps!" Zoe's words stopped her nurse midsentence. "We don't know where he is," she finished.

"Aye, and I'm the king of England. You're a pair of liars unless I'm missin' my guess." Keegan shook the old woman off. "Now grab up that candle," he ordered the younger of the two. Ye, old woman, into the library with ye and be quiet if ye don't want yer sweet charge here ravished by a mad Scotsman."

"Oh my, dear no. Don't touch her. She's—"

Keegan slammed the door, shutting out the whimpering protest, and faced his captive. "Shall we?"

"I won't tell you where he is."

"Is that so?"

The sword veered toward her throat and Zoe stifled a scream. She wouldn't have stifled it had she thought screaming would do any good. But even if the servants could hear her, which she doubted, there wasn't a one who could face this barbarian and win.

Zoe tried to ignore the candlelight shining on the long length of polished steel. "I demand that you leave my house."

Zoe thought she noticed the corners of his mouth lift. One dark brow definitely did. "Ye demand now, do ye? Seems to me, I'm the one to be makin' the demands around here." He lifted the end of the braid that had fallen over Zoe's shoulder to emphasize his point. "Come here."

None too gently he yanked her along behind him as he headed for the stairway. At the bottom he stopped, and pulled her in front of him.

"Lord Foxworth Morgan," he yelled so that the sound echoed off the walls. " 'Tis Keegan MacLeod. I've yer sister here. If ye're anythin' but a snivelin' coward ye'll come down and face me."

His challenge was met by silence.

"Ye cowardly son of a bitch."

"I told you he isn't here." Zoe could hear her captor's harsh breathing, could feel the force of his anger.

"Then where is he? Ye . . ." Keegan yelled to a group of servants who'd awakened during the yelling and were now huddled at the railing near the third floor steps. "Ye with the candle, step forward. Unless ye wish to see your mistress die by my hand, tell me where his Lordship is."

"They don't know." Zoe spun out of his grip, facing him, their eyes clashing. "Fox often goes away for a fortnight or more. He could be anywhere."

"And I'll be tellin' ye now, I don't believe ye. He's yer brother and ye're sayin' his whereabouts are unknown to ye?"

"Yes," Zoe gasped, for he was now slowly guiding the point of his sword up the front of her nightrail. When it reached her chin he paused.

"I'll be havin' the truth from ye. Now."

He was going to kill her. Zoe could see it in his eyes. She tried to breathe and couldn't. Tried to think and couldn't. The words that finally escaped her mouth were more instinct than rational thought, more truth than lie. "He's in Scotland."

"Scotland?" He shifted his stance but not the sword. "I was of the impression he'd left his unit."

"Briefly, yes. But he returned." Let this madman try to find Fox amid his regiment, if he was there. For in truth Zoe wasn't certain where Fox was. But if he was in Scotland the brave men of the king's finest would cut out this knave's heart.

Hell and damnation. Keegan lowered the sword. He'd hoped to find Morgan here, to dispense with this before he returned to the Highlands. All he wanted was Foxworth Morgan. He didn't even plan to kill him. Not outright anyway. He'd allow the bastard his sword and give him a fighting chance which was a hell of a lot more than the Englishman gave Keegan's father.

"There, I've told you, now leave." The fact that the steel no longer flirted with her throat inspired her words.

"I'll leave all right, but I've a wee bit of doubt about yer veracity."

"He's in Scotland, I tell you." Zoe was already planning how she would send word to her brother, if he had returned to his regiment.

"So ye do. And so he may be. But Scotland's a vast land, and I've a wish for yer dear brother t' come t' me."

"That he will never do."

"Not on his own perhaps." Keegan lowered the broadsword. "But with a bit of incentive, I think he might." Keegan made his decision quickly, grabbing the girl and dragging her back toward the library.

When he burst through the door he found the old crone perched precariously on the edge of a chair straining to reach one of a brace of pistols decorating the wall above the fireplace.

Keegan ignored her—he seriously doubted she knew what to do with the weapon even if it were loaded. He did give her a message. "If Lord Foxworth should return here, tell him that Keegan MacLeod has his sister."

"No! You can't be serious. I can't go with you. I won't!" This came from Zoe, who now began struggling, trying to free her hand from his grasp. Keegan tightened his fingers.

"Tell him also if he hopes to see her alive to come alone to the Castle MacLeod."

"No, don't tell him that. This monster will kill him. Don't, Miss Phelps! Don't do it!"

"I mean what I say Miss Phelps." Keegan aimed the sword her way to emphasize his point. "Your charming Lady Zoe here will die by my hand. And it will be a long painful death at that. Remember, her life is in your hands."

With that Keegan scooped his captive up, tossing her fighting and screaming over his shoulder, and stepped through the shattered window. He thought he heard something about deadly night vapors from the old woman, but paid it no mind.

Zoe had dropped the candle when he picked her up, so Keegan concentrated what energy wasn't used to keep her squirming body on his shoulder on picking his way through the garden. "Would you hush and be still." Her constant screeching was getting on his nerves.

"Nooo!"

"Then perhaps you'd like me t' drop ye on yur stubborn head." That brought temporary quiet.

"Ouch! Damnation." Keegan felt the tangle of a rosebush just before he caught a whiff of the flower's sweet fragrance. Thorns scraped his arm and he jerked his sword, swiping at the offending bush. There, Lord Foxworth could add a sheared rosebush to the list of charges against Keegan.

Not that Keegan thought he needed anymore than the one he had slung over his shoulder.

At the garden gate Keegan encountered another problem. One he'd temporarily forgotten.

"Monsieur Keegan, what do you have?"

Keegan grimaced, then turned toward the sound of François's voice. "I haven't time t' explain right now." The windows in the house were coming alive with light. The servants would be scurrying about. One would run for the constable. Keegan had to get away from St. James's Square.

"But Monsieur Keegan—"

"For God's sake, François!"

"Help me! If you've an ounce of Christian charity in your blood, help me." Zoe arched to see who the newcomer was. One glance and her heart sank. This little man could do nothing against the mad Scot . . . even if he were so inclined. Which apparently he wasn't, for though he continued to question and argue against the wild man's sanity, he fell in behind as they entered the alley.

There was little light, but still Keegan, followed by François, stayed to the shadows, following the alleys east toward Trafalgar Square. He'd lived in London for near three years, at the time preferring the city's society over the boredom of Castle MacLeod or the dreariness of Edinburgh. So he knew his way around London.

As a laird's son, a wealthy one at that, Keegan had spent his share of time in the houses of the aristocracy. He was well-liked . . . or had been, and visited often at the home of Henry Elliott, the Marquis of Stangmore whose London home they hurried past now.

Fortunately, he'd also familiarized himself with the seedier side of London. For he doubted good old Harry would welcome him with open arms. Even if he was carrying Lord Foxworth's sister over his shoulder.

As if to remind him she was still there, the girl began pounding on his back with her fists. "I can't breathe," she squawked repeatedly.

"I'll put ye down if ye promise to be quiet," he said and she immediately stopped her pummeling.

In the lee of a building, Keegan slid Lady Zoe down till her feet touched ground. "Ye aren't going t' scream now, are ye?"

All Zoe could do was shake her head. And she immediately realized she shouldn't have done that. It pounded. "I . . . I think I'm going to swoon."

He didn't seem the least concerned, though his

hand did tighten on her arm. "Don't," was all her captor said, but it had the ring of a command.

Still, Zoe wasn't sure she could obey. "But I must." She glanced toward the other man who was busy wringing his hands then she leaned against the stone wall behind her. "My head throbs so. I think it shall explode."

"Monsieur Keegan, you must do something."

" 'Tis only because I carried her upside down," Keegan said to his valet, then turned his stare on Zoe. "And unless ye want to be carried thus again you'll hush your mouth and keep up."

"But I . . ."

Her captor's head whipped around and even in the near dark she could feel the intensity of those eyes. Zoe took a deep steadying breath and said nothing else. Somehow she had to escape this madman and get word to her brother. And she must stay alive to do it.

That she was still alive, was a wonder in itself. Her heart was weak. Her humors never quite in balance. And the night air was full of deadly vapors. Miss Phelps said so. Why she hadn't expired as soon as the Scot leaped through her window was a mystery. The fright was enough to stop even a stout constitution. Which, goodness knows, hers wasn't.

But she'd survived this long. And now her purpose was clear. At least it was, until her breathing became labored. Goodness, the man was nearly running through streets and back alleys. He seemed barely winded, but it was all Zoe and the Frenchman could do to keep up.

"Ouch. Oh."

"Now what?" Keegan jerked to a stop. It was either that or drag the girl's limp body behind him. She'd stopped dead in her tracks and was now hopping about on one foot. "What the hell is wrong with ye?"

"My ankle." Zoe tried to be brave but felt large tears plumping over her lashes. "I fear 'tis broken."

She expected a bit of sympathy at least, but got none. Instead the dreadful man stooped in front of her and yanked up her nightrail. Without so much as a by-your-leave his large hand clamped her ankle, pressing here, turning there.

"I don't think 'tis broken," he announced as he stood.

"But it hurts."

"Hell and damnation," Keegan muttered. "Can ye stand on it?"

Tentatively Zoe lowered her foot, careful to put only a little weight on it. "I'm really not sure. Perhaps if I had a cane."

"Which I'm not seeing at the moment."

"Yes, well. Do you suppose I could rest for a while?"

"Yer most august Ladyship," Keegan began, his teeth clinched. "It may have escaped yer notice but we're not out for a leisurely stroll in Coventry Gardens."

By this time his voice was seething with repressed annoyance.

"Now unless you wish to be retossed over me shoulder—"

"That makes my head hurt."

"Aye, well then ye'll step lively, albeit with a limp."

Zoe quickly did as he ordered.

One hand was firmly in his grasp. The other she used to hold up her skirts as she hobbled along. The Frenchman brought up the rear.

"Where are we bound?" And did he plan to walk all night? Zoe never imagined a kidnapping, which of course she'd never really imagined at all, could be this unpleasant. At this pace her heart was sure to give out soon and then her dear brother would be at the mercy of this barbarian.

Zoe wasn't surprised when he didn't answer her inquiry. He'd been ignoring her every moan and complaint, along with the other man's questions, since the ankle mishap. But she was just as shocked as he seemed to be when they turned into a side alley to avoid a coach and were immediately swallowed up by a swarm of humanity. The byway was packed with people, all milling about, spilling from the gin halls lining the street. Some carried torches and the sudden light made Zoe squint.

"Be quiet if ye know what's good for ye," her captor said. Then he worked at turning them about, distancing them from the crowd, who seemed to be having a drunken fine time laughing and singing. But there was such a crush and so much jostling about that he couldn't manage.

As for Zoe, she was simply overwhelmed. Until a miracle happened. One moment the Scot's viselike grip manacled her arm, the next she was yanked away. The face staring down at her was dirty and near toothless, but at least it wasn't the wild man who was after her brother.

"Help me," Zoe begged the wretch whose foul

breath made her want to gag. "Please help me. I'm Lady Zoe Morgan of St. James Square. That man kidnapped me. I'll give you money if—"

Just then the object of her lament pushed himself between her and her savior. "No, no. This is the man who kidnapped me. I'm—"

"A bit touched," Keegan finished for her, pointing a finger to his temple. "But I keep her 'round for obvious reasons." His hand clamped over hers.

"No doubt the same ones I'm thinking of," Zoe heard her *savior* say. His voice was slurred. "What say we share her?"

"Don't believe him. I'm not insane. I *am* Lady Zoe—"

"Sharing sounds right by me. She's becoming a bit of a bore with her strange ways," Keegan said. The man before him was obviously soaked in gin, as were most of the other revelers, some of whom seemed a bit too interested in Zoe's insistence that she was wealthy.

"Sharing?" Zoe felt the blood rush from her head. This was it then. Her moment of passing. She was to die in the midst of a throng of foul-smelling humanity. Somehow she'd never imagined it quite like this.

"Ye know, on second thought, I'll be keeping her for myself," Keegan managed as the mass of people spilled out on a small square. Able to maneuver now, Keegan bolted away from the man and, pulling Zoe after him, darted into the darkness between two buildings. He could only hope that François followed.

Stepping into a recessed doorway, Keegan drew his broadsword.

"No, please don't kill me."

"Hush up." Keegan pushed his captive behind him and waited for the sound of running feet. There was none. "Well, it seems your admirer isn't up to a late-night run." Keegan resheathed his sword. "Not that I blame him much. God, I should have simply let him have ye."

"Let him have me? He would have saved me from the likes of you."

"He'd have had his way with ye, robbed ye blind, then slit your throat for good measure." Keegan could feel her recoil. "And don't ye forget it. You're not in St. James Square anymore."

"Perhaps." Zoe tried to stiffen her spine. "But 'tis not as if you don't plan to do the same thing to me."

"Now that's where ye be wrong, yer Ladyship." Keegan left the relative safety of the doorway. "I've no desire to rob ye. Nor have my way with ye for that matter. As for slitting your throat, I'll only be doing that if ye cause me any more trouble."

"You're a barbarian."

"True enough." Keegan lifted his sword when he heard footfalls, but lowered it again when he recognized the wigged head of his valet. "But 'tis your brother and those like him that helped mold the man ye see today."

"I'll not believe that. My brother is an honorable—"

"Ha!"

"What do you mean 'ha'?" Zoe scurried to keep

pace, for they were off again. "I'll have you know Fox is a gentleman and a fine soldier. He received a commendation from the king's brother for his bravery during the recent insurrection."

"Oh, did he now?" Keegan stopped so quickly his captive bumped into his back. "Well, it be just like the British to reward a man for slaughtering defenseless old men. Women and children too, if the truth be known."

"Fox would never—"

" 'Tis obvious ye don't know your brother as well as ye should. Now come on with ye."

"I can't." Zoe backed away as he dipped down to toss her over his shoulder. "No, please. You might as well kill me now as carry me about like that."

"God, ye're a complaining soul, aren't ye?" Keegan sighed. He'd planned to get as far from the city as he could tonight, but Lord help him, he was tired. And hungry, and in need of some clothes other than the rags he wore. François was giving him that look like he was ready to argue. And goodness knew, his captive was nothing but trouble.

Perhaps a few hours' rest was the wise thing. Keegan glanced about trying to get his bearings. They were close to Pall Mall. A smile brightened his face. "Come on with ye."

"I really can't," Zoe huffed.

"I think a short break is in order too, Monsieur Keegan."

"It won't be far, and then ye can both rest a bit."

At No. 32 Pall Mall Keegan slipped behind the building and pounded at the back entrance.

"Who lives here? Where are we?"

Ignoring her questions, Keegan identified himself, before the giant of a man answering the door could slam it in his face.

"Master Keegan?"

In the oscillating light from the candle the man seemed genuinely perplexed.

"Aye Ripley, 'tis me, and you'll simply have to take my word for it till I can take a razor to my face. Is Mrs. Salinger in?"

"Yes, but she's abed." The giant backed up as Keegan ushered François through the doorway. Keegan followed, dragging Zoe behind. The Ripley looked at her with the same distrust he initially gave Keegan.

"Wake her up," was all Keegan said as he led the way through the back halls toward a sitting room.

From what she could tell, this house was near as well appointed as her brother's at St. James's Square. Hope began to flicker in Zoe's breast. "Who lives here?" If it was a member of the aristocracy, which, of course it must be, she would tell her story and put an end to this living hell. Perhaps back under Miss Phelps's care and with a fortnight of bed rest she might yet survive this ordeal.

In the meantime Zoe half fell, half swooned into the nearest chair. Her captor didn't seem to notice. He was pouring himself a glass of port, which he drank with relish. He repeated this, still not paying Zoe any mind. She considered trying to sneak out of the room while his back was to her but she was so dreadfully tired. Besides, as soon as the owner of the house appeared . . .

Katherine Salinger entered the room in a flourish

of flowing silk. "Keegan?" She rushed toward him, stopping short when he turned to face her. "Oh my God, it is you. Though one would be hard-pressed to know." She laughed, a tinkling sound that reminded Zoe of silver bells. "I was afraid one of my patrons would insist that we attend your hanging today."

Hanging? Zoe sucked in her breath and two pairs of eyes turned her way.

"Ah, what have we here?" Katherine moved gracefully toward the settee. "Did you bring me a new girl?"

Her captor seemed to ignore that question. He simply introduced her to Mrs. Salinger. Zoe supposed she should respond, but she was simply too tired. Besides, she wasn't completely naive. She'd just figured out what type of house this was.

Three

"Do ye suppose there might be a room where Lady Zoe can rest?" Keegan gestured toward Zoe with his wineglass. "A room where she won't be disturbed," he added, his dark brows lifting. Ripley had disappeared toward the back rooms as soon as they'd arrived, taking François with him, and Keegan silently cursed him now for not taking care of this little detail first.

Without a word Kate crossed to the mantel and pulled on the bell rope. "We aren't accustomed to entertaining ladies here, but I'm certain we can find something."

" 'Twould be a boon if the window were high enough off the ground t' avoid temptation." His narrowed gaze shifted toward Zoe. " 'Twould be a shame if she fell t' her death."

"Am I to gather that your . . . guest is not accompanying you voluntarily?" Kate asked as the door opened and Ripley entered.

Enough was enough. Zoe didn't care if she was so tired she could barely move. She didn't like being talked about as if she weren't even in the room. "I was kidnapped from my home by this . . . this barbarian," she said, straightening her spine and forc-

ing her exhausted body to sit upright. "If there is
an ounce of charity in your soul, you must see that
justice is done. Return me to my home."

Zoe took a breath, then changed her tactic. The
expression on the other woman's face seemed to indicate that charity of soul wasn't something that consumed her. "I'll pay you a hundred pounds." Still
no response. "Two hundred." Zoe sprang to her
feet. "Five hundred."

"For God's sake, Kate, either accept the chit's
bribe or tell her t' be done with it."

His tone, the condescending manner with which
he lifted the glass to his lips, told Zoe what she
should have known from the beginning. The brute
wasn't the least worried about her convincing anyone in this household to help her. With a defeated
sigh she plopped back on the settee.

She must have looked comical doing it, for the
woman laughed, a deep musical sound that grated
on Zoe's frayed nerves. But worse, the wild man's
mouth flattened and he shook his head in disgust.

"Now Keegan love, you've stopped her and it was
just becoming interesting. How high do you think
she might have gone?"

"Do ye have a room for her or not?" He didn't
seem interested in any more idle chatter.

Kate merely shrugged and instructed Ripley to
take her to a room on the top floor.

"I won't go." Zoe clutched the arm of the settee
and watched apprehensively as the barbarian took a
deep breath.

"If she gives ye any trouble toss her over yer shoulder."

"No." Zoe dug her fingers deeper into the fabric. "She's a wee bit of a thing, though I'll wager 'tis tough to maneuver the stairs with any baggage. 'Twould be a shame to drop her on her head."

The warning was all too clear. Zoe pushed to her feet before Ripley, who seemed to have every intention of following the Scot's instructions, could carry them . . . and her . . . out. "All right. I'll go," she said with as much dignity as she could muster under the circumstances. As she walked from the room Zoe heard her tormentor remind Ripley not to forget the lock.

Kate waited till the door closed to refill Keegan's glass. "Who is she?"

" 'Tis as she said." Keegan took a drink. "A lass I kidnapped."

"Oh, I believed her. I'm just wondering why."

"These be desperate times."

Kate leaned toward him. "Yes, but I've never seen you *that* desperate."

Keegan chuckled and allowed his finger to stray along Kate's collarbone. "Aye and not everything is about sex."

Kate clasped his hand, lowering it to cover her breast. "Strange words coming from you." When he didn't respond to her invitation, but continued to stare into his wine, Kate moved away. "Would you like to bathe first?"

"Actually I need to talk to ye."

Gracefully lowering herself onto the settee, Kate patted the cushion beside her. When he ignored her gesture she smoothed the silk surface with her palm. "What happened to you, Keegan? One day you were here in London, the bane of every mother with an impressionable daughter, the next I discover you've run off to the Highlands to join that dreadful revolution. Then the trial. Now this . . ." She let her arms open to encompass him. "What on earth were you thinking?"

"I . . ." Keegan took another quick drink. "There isn't much to tell. Or at least ye seem to know the most of it."

"The defeat of the Prince's army is all anyone speaks of. The Duke of Cumberland—" Kate ignored the derisive sound Keegan made, "is considered quite the conquering hero."

"He's a fat butcher."

"Goodness." Kate laughed again. "That's hardly the way to speak of the king's son."

"Ye weren't there, Kate." Keegan paced to the fireplace and rested his arm on the mantel. "It was he who gave the orders for the slaughter after the battle. It must have been."

"That's war, Keegan. The surprising thing is that you became involved. I thought you had no interest in the Jacobites."

"I thought as much myself."

"Then why?"

Keegan couldn't blame Kate her curiosity. He'd sat in this very room and scoffed at men for doing less than he'd done. He'd derided those men who frequented the Cocoa Tree coffeehouse and plotted revolutions. Now he was one of them. Worse, for he'd been part of the revolt . . . the failed revolt. But what was done was done. Though he'd live with the expressions of his dead brothers, with the memory of his father's tortured face for the rest of his life, there were other things to consider. "I'm going back to Scotland. Can ye help me get there?"

"Keegan." Kate stood and came toward him. "Again I ask why."

"Can ye help me or nay?" Keegan turned on her, then softened his expression. "Kate, I know 'tis a lot I'm askin' of ye."

"You have no idea."

"Kate."

"Scotland is no place for you Keegan. Nor is London. Take yourself away someplace. France perhaps." Kate almost added that she could join him there.

"That's what François keeps sayin'. But 'tis Scotland where I must go."

"It isn't safe I tell you. Besides, there's nothing for you there. Your land was confiscated." She allowed the hands that reached toward him to drop to her side. "I've that on very good authority."

"One of yer high placed gentleman friends?"

"Yes. And you'd do well to take heed." Her eyes implored. "You'll be shot if the army finds you there. It doesn't make sense."

"I have t' go back."

"Oh . . ." She whirled away from him in frustration.

"Me father's dead, Kate, and me brothers, too. There's no one else."

"All the more reason for you to listen to me. You've only yourself to think of now." Kate clasped his arms. "Do it."

"There's the clan. What's left of them." Keegan

raised his eyes till they met hers, then turned away from her bewildered stare.

"My God, Keegan. What has happened to you?" It was as if he'd left a charming rake and returned a man with the weight of the world upon his shoulders.

"Can ye help me or not?" Keegan realized his tone was sharper than he wished and scrubbed his hands over his whiskered face. He had no desire to explain himself more than he already had . . . at least not until he himself understood what drove him.

He sucked air into his lungs and began to apologize.

"Don't." She cut off his words. "I know a man . . . Oh, Keegan, I don't wish to be the means of your death."

"What about this man?" Keegan stepped toward her.

"He's Irish." A smile spread across her face. "A true rogue. And a smuggler." Kate settled into a winged chair. "Normally, of course, he secrets things into the country. But I'm sure he can get you to Scotland . . . if you're certain that's where you wish to go."

"Aye. Tell me how to find this rogue."

"Are you sure I can't persuade you to stay a bit longer?"

"Are ye that anxious to see my neck stretched?" Keegan sprawled on the high tester bed in Kate's room where he'd passed the night . . . alone. After she gave him the name of her smuggler, whom Keegan gathered also shared Kate's bed and affections, he'd bathed and gone to sleep. But despite the need to be gone, Keegan was sorely tempted to linger. The sheets were sweet-smelling. He was clean. The bed was soft and Kate with her golden hair curled about her naked shoulders looked inviting enough to weaken any man's resolve, especially a man who'd spent the last few months without a woman's touch.

"As you well know, Keegan MacLeod," Kate said, her voice smooth as honey as she glided toward the bed, "I can think of many things to do to your neck, and not a one includes stretching it."

Chuckling, Keegan rolled to his side as Kate climbed the bed steps and inched onto the mattress. Memory was a strong aphrodisiac. She wore a loose-fitting gown of red silk that Keegan knew from experience covered skin as soft and fragrant as a flower petal. When she leaned toward him, her hair brushing his chest, the decision was made.

Her tinkling laughter rang out as Keegan's arm enveloped her. She pressed her hand down his body, smiling and licking her painted lips when she found his manhood. "That didn't take long, did it?"

"What be that you're saying about my length," Keegan countered with a laugh. " 'Tis always seemed sufficient to satisfy ye, if memory serves."

"Oh Keegan, no one can satisfy me like you." Kate moaned as he brushed the silk down her arms.

Keegan wasn't fool enough to believe every word Kate said, but he had been one of the few the courtesan allowed into her bed without payment. Not that he hadn't given her occasional gifts, but that was because he chose to. As she had chosen him to warm her bed on those rare nights when her patrons were elsewhere.

She moaned again when he buried his face between her breasts; groaned when the knock came at the door.

It was testimony to Keegan's months at New Gaol that he immediately rolled across the bed and reached for his broadsword. Kate simply called for the servant to enter.

"I'm sorry to be bothering you, mistress." The girl kept her eyes averted. "But she insists that she needs a bleeder."

"What the hell?" Keegan grumbled.

"Who are you talking about, Macy?"

Keegan was certain he knew. Rolling from the bed he pulled on the clean breeches Kate had supplied, grimacing as he buttoned the flap over his swollen member. "Is the lass ill?"

"I can't say, sir. She seems right enough except that she is a bit pale."

"Who are we talking about?" Kate sat up. Her breasts peeked through the veil of tumbled golden hair.

"Hell and damnation, that girl will be the death of me yet." Keegan stomped into first one boot, then the other.

"Ah, your little hostage? You never did tell me exactly why you kidnapped her."

" 'Tis a long story. But I can tell ye a more complainin' lass you'll never find." The fine linen shirt muffled his words as he pulled it over his head.

There were more clothes, a waistcoat and jacket of silk, a cravat, but Keegan didn't bother with them as he headed for the door. Before brushing past the servant girl he looked about to ask Kate to wait where she was, but she'd already left the bed. Her billowy robe now covered her discreetly from head to toe.

Keegan unlocked the door on the third floor and entered without so much as a polite tapping. His hostage, as Kate called her, was plumped on a pile of pillows. As the servant said, she looked pale. Other than that, and that she was a bit on the bony side, Keegan thought her fit enough.

"What's this I hear about yer demandin' a surgeon?"

Zoe's mouth opened but no sound emerged. She was shocked by his manner, of course. No one had ever marched into her room unannounced before. But there was more. She could hardly believe this was the same man who'd kidnapped her last night. But it was. There was no mistaking that Scottish brogue. Yet he looked so different. Oh, the hair was still long and unkempt, perhaps lighter than she'd earlier thought. But he was now garbed in the clothes of a gentleman. And his face . . . Now that it was clean shaven she could see . . .

"Did ye hear me lass?"

Zoe swallowed, snapped away from her contemplation of his firm mouth by his words. Somehow he seemed more intimidating today. "Yes," she finally managed.

"Yes, what? Be ye ill?"

"I've rigidity of my vessels," she finally managed to say.

"Yer what?" Keegan's own rigidity was waning, but he'd never heard of a woman suffering from that.

"My vessels," Zoe explained. "They are rigid." He still looked at her as if she were speaking in a foreign tongue. "Thus making it difficult for my blood to flow freely." Zoe's lips thinned in exasperation. His expression seemed to say that she was insane rather than himself. She tried again, wishing Miss Phelps were here. She was ever so much better at explaining these things. "My heart is weak and—"

"How do ye know that?"

"Well . . ." No one had ever questioned it before. It was simply understood . . . and had been for as long as she remembered. "Well, I simply do." Certainly a good enough explanation for the barbarian. Yet he couldn't seem to let it go at that.

"What happens to ye? Do ye get the bloody flux?"

"No." Zoe sat bolt upright. Of all her ailments that was one she'd been spared.

"Spots? Chills? Do yer limbs go stiff? What?"

A more cloddish and unsympathetic creature she'd never seen. "Weak," she said, lifting her chin and staring down her nose at him. "I am very weak."

"Weak." He seemed to ponder the word, finally tilting his head and studying her. "For this ye need to be bled?"

"That's what Dr. Owen recommends, yes."

"What else does the doctor tell ye t' do?"

"Bed rest, of course."

"Of course."

Zoe ignored his sarcastic tone. "And thinned broth to eat."

"And . . . ?"

"And what?"

Keegan expelled his breath in frustration. "What else do ye eat?"

"Occasionally some meat, if it's fine enough, and bread too, at times." She noted his surprised expression and her tone became defensive. "I've very poor digestion."

Keegan strode to the bed and looked down at her, his eyes narrowed. She was a bit older than he'd thought last night. Near twenty he'd wager. Thin. Not unattractive, if you cared for the skinny type, which he assuredly did not. But her eyes were large, dark-lashed and an interesting shade of grey, and her features delicate. Certainly not what he'd call robust, but neither did she appear sickly. Of course he was no doctor. Perhaps she was ill.

Hell and damnation, it would be just his luck to kidnap a damn invalid.

"Get yerself up and dressed," he finally said.

"But—"

"We haven't time for a physic now. Perhaps when we get to Scotland . . ."

"I'll be dead by then," Zoe said with a bit of satisfaction. How dare the brute not care about her health. If only Miss Phelps were here.

Her words did seem to take him back a bit. He looked at her, then at the untouched tray beside her bed. "I suggest ye partake of yer breakfast before we leave."

"It won't settle well on my stomach."

"Just eat it."

"Just eat it," Zoe mimicked as soon as the door shut behind him. A lot he knew. He wouldn't be the one to suffer if she ate the clotted cream and berries, the ham and biscuits. If she drank the chocolate. Zoe could almost see Miss Phelps shudder at the thought of such strong foods entering her charge's delicate system.

Weak tea is what she needed. And a bit of thin broth.

But there was none of that about. And she was hungry. With a resigned sigh Zoe plucked a bright red strawberry from the silver bowl. Experimentally she dipped it in the cream, then nibbled.

A quarter of an hour later, when a maid came to dress her, she'd emptied the platters and drained the chocolate pot.

Since she rarely felt well enough to go out, and her visitors were confined to Dr. Owen and a few solicitous friends, Zoe usually wore only a loose-fitting morning gown. She wore stays, of course, and occasionally small hoops, but for the most part her dress was informal.

Today however she was garbed in a borrowed riding habit of dark green camlet. There was a jacket and waistcoat and petticoat slightly shorter than she normally wore. The servant assured Zoe it was the fashion. And since she'd never owned a riding habit; or been riding either for that matter, Zoe had to take her word for it. Of course the clothing was too large for her, hanging loosely at the shoulders and waist, even after the maid stitched it.

The girl was nice enough, though she wasn't very

interested in how tired Zoe was, nor would she agree to do anything about her predicament. Apparently kidnapping wasn't considered worth mentioning in this place.

The servant had just placed a cocked hat, tilted at a jaunty angle atop Zoe's dressed hair, when the wild man reentered the room. As before he didn't bother to knock. And as before Zoe was taken aback by his appearance.

The transformation from barbarian to gentleman was complete.

He wore nankeen breeches and a frock coat of the fashion that Fox preferred when not in uniform. His hair was brushed and Zoe could only stare as he entered. She'd always thought Fox the most handsome man alive. With his black hair and dark eyes she'd considered him the epitome of manhood. But though the Scot little resembled her brother, except for his height, she had to admit he was not difficult to look upon.

"I see ye're ready to leave, Lady Zoe."

She was *not* ready to leave for Scotland. "This has progressed long enough. I demand you set me free." Zoe had practiced her short speech in front of the cheval glass and thought she did an admirable job of sounding incensed.

However Keegan MacLeod didn't seem impressed. He threw back his head and laughed. He didn't even allow her the satisfaction of a response. "Come along with ye," is all he said.

At least they weren't going to walk the entire way to Scotland.

Zoe followed Keegan MacLeod down a back stairway to the courtyard. He handed her up into a chaise. Before climbing in, the wild man, who didn't really look like a wild man anymore, kissed the woman he'd called Kate.

It was a long kiss, like none Zoe had ever seen before. Certainly not the chaste press of lips she exchanged with her brother. Zoe didn't mean to watch, for it seemed very personal, but she couldn't help herself. There was a great entangling of arms and straining of bodies. The entire process made her very uncomfortable and Zoe found herself squirming in her seat.

When he finally pulled away, Kate's mouth was wet, as were her eyes. "Be careful, Keegan, and God bless."

"Aye, and the same to ye. Thank ye for all ye've given me. I'll send the coach back. And I'll find some way t' repay the coin."

François, noticeably quiet this morning, climbed onto the box, and then the Scot was sitting opposite her as the coach rumbled over the cobblestones. For all she hated the circumstances, Zoe had to admit it was a pleasant enough ride. At least it would have been, had the shades not been rolled down filling the interior with gloom and shadows.

"Do you suppose we might roll up a blind? I can barely breathe." True, Miss Phelps thought the London air bad for her health, and so it most likely was. But since she was bound to die anyway from her mistreatment, it would be pleasant to see some of the sights they passed.

But that was not to be, for the barbarian only shook his head. "Though I doubt ye'd have any more luck with yer tale of woe here than ye did last night, I'd just as soon not be explainin' myself t' someone ye might call out t'." He watched her as the coach slowed. "And I wouldn't be thinkin' of jumpin' either," he added with a meaningful look toward the pistol that lay on the leather seat beside him.

Zoe briefly considered leaping from the coach and running for help. But without the steps lowered there was a good chance she'd fall, or break her ankle.

Which reminded her that she'd twisted it last night. Beneath her skirts Zoe turned her foot one way then the other. It didn't hurt at all. Which surprised and pleased her. It also made her remember the way she'd felt when the wild man touched her. When he'd lifted her skirts and circled her ankle with his fingers.

"What be wrong with ye now?"

Slowly Zoe looked up till their eyes met. Even in the dim light she could tell his were a vivid green. They stared at her intently. Zoe tried not to notice. She tried not to recall the feel of his hands on her. But the more she tried, the more she thought of it. And the warmer she became.

Pressing a palm to her flushed cheek she leaned back against the leather squab. "I think I'm feverish."

Four

He didn't care.

That should hardly come as a shock, Zoe realized. After all, she was only a hostage to him. And he *did* mean to kill her brother. All and all, not the type of man who considered others' infirmities?

Still, Zoe was hard-pressed to accept his lack of response when she declared herself feverish. Just the hint of such always put Miss Phelps into a flurry of activity. She would send one of the servants, usually the footman, to fetch the good doctor, as she called him. Then she'd administer a dose of bark and some diluted tea. By this time Zoe would be nestled in bed, topped by an extra quilt and awaiting the inevitable bleeding.

It was not an all together pleasant regimen, true. However, without Miss Phelps's diligent care Zoe would not have lived to her present age of one and twenty. For according to the beloved nurse, no one expected frail Zoe to pass her third birthday.

Certainly her mother and father had given up on her recovery from the dreaded scarlet fever. They had bundled off their two sons and headed for their country estate in Devon. They returned, of course, after Zoe recovered from the fever. But her health was never good after that.

Which was why her treatment from this barbarian was certain to lead to her demise.

"Ye look well enough to me."

Zoe glanced up, surprised he'd spoken. They'd ridden for what seemed miles without him so much as glancing her way. Now he studied her from beneath hooded lids.

So he thought she was in the bloom of health, did he? It simply showed how little the Scot knew. But when she opened her mouth to enlighten him, his attention was already turned toward raising the blinds. Zoe was so pleased by the sunlight and breeze that entered the coach that she forgot about her complaints.

"We're across the bridge and out of the city," he said by way of explanation.

So he no longer feared detection. Zoe found the knowledge somehow depressing. Not that she'd held out any hope of rescue. But she couldn't remember the last time she left London. "Did you say we've crossed London Bridge?"

"Aye."

"But I thought we were going to Scotland. 'Tis to the north, I believe." A passable knowledge of geography was one thing Zoe prided herself on. Knowledge gleaned from books, of course, but knowledge all the same.

"It is."

"Then why . . . ?" Had he somehow guessed that Fox might be at the family estate in Devon? A cold sweat beaded Zoe's upper lip.

"I've a mind to take a packet north."

"A packet?" Her relief was short-lived. "Do you mean a sailing vessel?"

"Aye."

"Oh, but that won't do at all."

"Why might that be?" Keegan shifted in his seat. He had a strong notion he knew.

"My weak stomach, of course."

He was right. Keegan shut his eyes and counted to ten, slowly. "I imagine you'll be all right. A bit of seasickness never killed anyone."

Zoe's eyes widened. "Not normal people perhaps. But Miss Phelps says—"

"Do ye never grow tired of quoting the venerable Miss Phelps?" Keegan meant the question in the most rhetorical sense, yet his captive seemed to ponder his query, finally shaking her head slowly.

"You simply don't understand. I'm not—"

"A normal person," Keegan finished for her. "Actually, I'm beginnin' t' grasp that concept."

Zoe settled back against the cushion with a satisfied smile. "Good, then you accept that I can't travel to Scotland by boat."

"What I understand is that you'll be spendin' more than a wee bit of time, green around the gills emptyin' yer weak stomach into a pail."

He didn't give her any time to respond. While her mouth was still open in shock he tapped his walking stick on the coach roof. When the driver stopped, the Scot climbed onto the box beside him, leaving Zoe alone in the coach—which was just as well for she was tired of his odious company.

And this way she could look out the window to

her heart's content, surveying the bucolic countryside. And despite the circumstances, enjoying herself. The last time she was in Kent she was three
years old. Hardly an age when she could remember
the green pastures and quaint villages. Yet they all
seemed familiar. Her imagination was quite lively,
and, coupled with the descriptions Fox gave her, the
countryside of her mind's eye held a strong resem-
blance to the real thing.

Even though she would never see him again, it
was comforting to know that Fox might be nearby.
That is, as long as the Scot didn't realize it. When
Fox returned from Scotland he'd wanted Zoe to accompany him to Ashford Hall for a visit before he
returned to his regiment. The wound he'd received
at Culloden, a mere scratch, he'd assured her, was
healing nicely, and he thought some country air
would do them both good.

"And I have it on good authority that the earl is
not in residence," Fox had said with a grin. The
earl was their older brother Dalton, whom Zoe remembered as a prig. Of course she hadn't seen him
since her parents' death some twelve years ago. But
she knew he wasn't one of Fox's favorite people,
which was good enough for her.

Zoe had been tempted to go with Fox. She loved
him and enjoyed his visits immensely. But she'd declined.

Miss Phelps thought it ill-advised for her to travel
so far. Her exact words had been, "The harsh road
will surely kill my dear Zoe." Fox had questioned
that judgement, but though Zoe had wished more
than anything to accompany her brother, she was

forced to agree with Miss Phelps. After all, the sainted woman had taken care of Zoe for all these years, keeping her alive longer than any naysayer thought possible. How ironic that she should end up on a journey where the south of England was simply a starting point.

Zoe's attention was so absorbed by the sights around her, the oak forests and meadows, sights she'd only heard of from Fox, that she forgot for nearly an hour to worry about her breathing, or the state of her heart. She didn't even give her health a thought when the coach swayed to a stop before an inn on the outskirts of a small village.

Church bells pealed through the late afternoon air, vying with the sounds of children playing and chickens squabbling about. Zoe slid from one side of the coach to the other gazing from the windows till the door opened with a jerk. There stood the Scot, hat in hand.

For an instant Zoe forgot to be frightened by him, forgot the circumstances. He stood in the waning light, the sun catching the glints of copper in his dark hair. The shadows tracing the hollows of his cheeks. His eyes looking very green.

Then he grimaced, his slashed brows lowering, and it all came back to Zoe in a rush. The wild Scot. The kidnapping. Her need to save Fox. And her own ill-health.

Zoe moaned as she climbed from the coach. Her limbs ached. Her heart raced. As her feet settled on the dusty lane, her head felt light.

"What be the matter with ye now?"

The Scot offered his arm and Zoe had no recourse but to lean upon him. "I fear . . . oh my, I think I shall swoon." Zoe actually felt her knees buckle and her body begin to sag.

But she didn't fall. Nor did he scoop her into his arms as she thought he might. As Fox had done the few times she'd been foolish enough to venture too far in the gardens with him.

Instead she felt her hand gripped, and a strong arm wrapped round her waist. He was walking her along the dusty dirt road that ran beside the hedgerow away from the inn. Her feet began to move of their own accord, and Zoe looked up at him in surprise.

His strides were long and it was all Zoe could do to keep up as he walked toward a stone bridge. It crossed a brook that babbled its way alongside the road before swerving across to meander through a field of clover. Once they were on the bridge the Scot stopped. His hand loosened on hers and his arm no longer held her upright.

Nor did it need to.

To Zoe's surprise and pleasure her head no longer felt like it was about to take flight toward the bank of mauve-tinged clouds. Nor did her legs wobble. She let her hands rest upon the stone railing and took a deep breath, filling her lungs with the sweet smells of hay and lavender.

"Feeling a bit better are ye now?"

His smile was smug. "Perhaps a bit."

"Lookin' better too, I'd say. The color in yer cheeks is becomin'."

His words flooded more pink to the area he'd described. "No doubt too much blood. It's been awhile since I was bled."

"Aye, the rigid vessels." Keegan scooped a stone off the road and tossed it into the stream. "Ye seem to be gettin' along fine without the blasted bleeder to me."

"Are you a physician now?"

"Nay." Keegan shrugged. "Just wonderin' what causes ye to be so sick, when ye don't seem sick."

"Well, I am." Zoe turned to face him squarely. "Miss Phelps says 'tis a miracle I've lived this long." She lifted her chin. "And I shan't live much longer."

"Ye say it as if ye're proud of the fact. As one who came within hours of meeting his own demise I'd say 'tisn't something to relish."

"I don't. Goodness." Zoe crossed her arms. "Don't you think I'd like to be healthy like other people? To do all the things they do? To see some of the places I've only read about?"

"I don't know. Do ye?"

"Of course I do." Zoe unfolded her arms, then self-consciously brushed out her skirt. "But I can't."

Keegan shrugged again. "Well for the moment ye must be pretendin' ye can."

"What are you talking about?"

"I've sent François in to see about our rooms. The innkeeper is t' think we're man and wife."

"But—"

"Simply act as if we are when he's about and there'll be no problem." Keegan patted the pistol in his pocket knowingly.

"What if I refuse? What if I say simply kill me now?" Her chin tilted at a defiant angle. After all, she was bound to die anyway. True she'd never thought *this* was how she'd succumb, but . . .

"Ye don't do as I say and it will be more than ye I'll be hurtin'."

"Who . . . ?" Realization of who he meant dawned and Zoe's eyes widened. "But surely you wouldn't kill the innkeeper. He's an innocent."

"That be up to ye now." His eyes narrowed. "I'm a desperate man, Lady Zoe." When the color drained from her face, Keegan continued. "Play yer part and no one gets hurt." Keegan's hand clamped under her elbow as he started back toward the village. For the sake of his peace of mind he ignored her mumbled reference to her dear brother. He didn't wish to delve into that tangle of worms. The woman obviously adored her brother, which to Keegan's way of thinking proved her a poor judge of character.

Of course that was hardly her only flaw. He'd never known someone so preoccupied with their health. The woman was obsessed. No doubt that harpy Miss Phelps was to thank for that. Unless there truly was something wrong with her.

Keegan glanced down at the woman by his side. She was a tiny thing, and pale to be sure. Delicate was the word he'd use to describe her, like a rose, soft and pink. But a rose with thorns.

The inn wasn't the worst he'd ever been in; it wasn't the best either. But then he wasn't exactly flushed at the moment. It was only thanks to Kate's generosity that they weren't spending the night under the stars. Keegan could just imagine his little English rose's reaction to that.

Though Keegan had sent François inside earlier to relay his needs, by the look of the innkeeper no preparations had been made. He leaned his ponderous belly over the stained bar, watching an increasingly belligerent squabble between two patrons. Nor was François anywhere to be seen. If Keegan knew his valet, he'd given the orders then retreated to his own room with a bottle of the inn's best wine.

With his hand firmly on his captive's elbow Keegan approached the innkeeper. He reluctantly tore his attention from the argument, which to Keegan's discomfort appeared to concern the recent uprising of the Jacobite Scots. The sympathies of the crowd of yeomen seemed squarely in the corner of the man professing his hatred of the "popish barbarians."

Pride made Keegan's anger flair; reality cooled it.

He smiled at the innkeeper whose bulbous nose bore the purplish hue of a man too used to imbibing his own ale. " 'Tis a heated argument, they've got going," Keegan said, doing his best to soften the edges of his Scottish brogue.

"What? Oh, well, ol Webster's got a right to be angered. Fought against the Scots in '17. Lost his leg to the bastards."

"Too bad," Keegan acknowledged. "Is the room my wife and I require at the ready?"

"Eh?" The innkeeper reluctantly dragged his focus back to Keegan. "Should be soon. I sent my girl to see to it. You can wait over there." He pointed a sausage-like finger toward a bench before yelling his agreement to a sentiment shared by most of the crowd.

Needless to say Keegan disagreed, which was to say he didn't think all Jacobites should be disemboweled. However, by the expression on his captive's face, Keegan guessed he was a minority of one.

Using his body to block her from the room's view, Keegan settled her onto a bench. He didn't think she was about to blurt out who he was. But then he wasn't certain she wasn't. He caught her eye and gave her what he hoped was a menacing look. If she realized how potentially volatile the situation was, how vulnerable he was at the moment, she gave no indication.

Her large grey eyes remained fixed on his, only flaring slightly when someone in the crowd mentioned Keegan's name.

"Escaped in the night he did. Broken out by an entire regiment of them blood-drinking heathens. They're waiting at the ready right now. Gonna sweep over England killing innocent women and children in their sleep." This pronouncement was followed by loud guffaws and chants of "Kill the bloody Scots."

Keegan swallowed and didn't move, though his natural inclination was to race from the inn as fast as he could. There must be twenty men in the taproom, and though most were old, he'd noticed a dozen beefy young men, farm workers most probably. One or two he could possibly handle. Twelve irate yeomen he could not.

Luckily no one appeared to be paying him much heed . . . especially without his regiment of heathens in plain view. But there was Zoe. If she realized how easily one word from her could ignite the crowd she showed no sign. But the apparent ease with which she sat, her head slightly bent to one side, made her all the more dangerous in Keegan's eyes.

He considered leaving. He even reached down to take Zoe's hand. He was certain the coachman had unharnessed the horses. The man himself was most likely well into his third pint by now. But the air in the inn was becoming stifling. Even before the innkeeper called out to him.

"You've come from London town, ain't you now. What be the word on the street?"

"Yeah, tell us."

"Is the duke calling the troops to arms?"

"Is there panic like before?"

Keegan took a deep breath before turning to face the crowd squarely. It gave him the added advantage of blocking Zoe from their view. "I saw no such thing," he said, slowly, before turning back to Zoe. "But I haven't been about much. My wife has been ill."

"But you had heard of the rebel's escape. All London is talking of it. He cheated the hangman. One of the leaders of the revolt he was."

That was news to him, or at least it had been until his trial. Keegan gave a noncommittal snort, then turned to help Zoe to her feet. Unfortunately she chose that moment to jump up and move to his other side.

"I've heard of him," she announced in an unfamiliar bold tone. Keegan very nearly swallowed his tongue.

"Aye . . . yes, but these gentlemen aren't inter-

ested in idle female gossip," Keegan said while draping a seemingly protective arm about her shoulders.

"Well now we're always interested in news from
London. Fellow riding toward Brighton brought us
word of the escape."

"We have nothing t' add to his story. Is that room
ready yet," Keegan said, doing his best to circle Zoe
toward the stairs. She wouldn't budge.

"From what I heard, your informant is greatly exaggerating the circumstances of the Scot's escape
from prison. Talk in London claims him to be
alone . . . or to have kidnapped someone."

"Kidnapped? Now why would he go and do a fool
thing like that?" one of the patrons asked. He appeared to be a country squire with his old-fashioned
bag wig sitting askew on his head.

"Exactly," Keegan agreed. "It makes no sense.
Come along now dear." His arm tightened the circle
about her, managing to turn her about without being too obvious. At least Keegan hoped so. He gave
her a glare meant to say keep your mouth shut. She
looked back, her grey eyes all innocence.

That's when she tossed another comment over her
shoulder. "I heard he has a vendetta against the
brother of the woman he kidnapped."

"You don't say?"

By this time most of the inn's patrons were on
their feet, moving toward Zoe . . . and Keegan *en
masse*. They were like rabid dogs, anxious for any
tidbit of information about the escaped Jacobite.
And Zoe had plenty of firsthand information to tell
them.

Their questions came fast and heavy now.

"Who did he kidnap?"

"What was the feud about?"

"Where was he taking her?"

"Has the poor woman been violated by the dastardly villain?"

"Oh, no, I don't think so," Zoe assured the crowd who now had Keegan and Zoe surrounded with the banister at their backs. "Despite his foul deeds I don't think the man is all bad. But he should be brought to justice," Zoe was quick to add.

By this time Keegan had his hand over the carved handle of his pistol and was calculating how long it would take him to dash to the door. That is if he could make it to the door.

"What does the Jacobite look like? Has anyone seen him?"

"Nay."

"Yes."

Keegan and Zoe answered as one, then turned toward each other, their gazes locking.

" 'Tis time we retire, wife," Keegan said, grinding his words out between tightly clenched teeth.

"But they have a right to know the truth. Don't you agree?" With that Zoe jerked out of his startled embrace. "He's a big man, so the gossips say. Brawny. Not unhandsome. With dark hair, the color of mahogany, glinted through with copper." Every eye in the tavern was glued to Zoe as she spoke. "I hear tell his eyes are green like the sea at eventide. And his voice is deep, with a touch of the Scottish burr that he does his best to hide when traveling incognito."

"That be enough of your stories now my love,"

Keegan said in a falsetto that had even him grimacing. It also turned a speculative eye or two his way.

"Now what way would this vile person be heading, do you think? North?" The innkeeper's already narrow eyes became mere slits.

"No one knows," Zoe said. Then her tone turned conspiratorial. "Some think he's bound for his homeland. The Scottish Highlands. Others think France his destination. Or the New World." She took a step forward, nearly out of Keegan's reach. "Who knows, he might be in this very room."

She leaped forward, but Keegan was quicker. His hand snaked out, grabbing her arms and jerking her back against him as the collective crowd seemed to grasp what she was trying to tell them. Anyone still in doubt knew the truth when they saw the pistol aimed at the poor woman's lovely throat.

"Anyone move and I'll kill her."

"The Scot, by God, it's the Scot."

"Aye and this be my captive, the Lady Zoe Morgan. Unless you wish to have the fair lady's demise on your heads you'll clear a path for us to the door."

"We can't let you leave."

"Oh but ye can, I assure ye. Now move."

At first the group, as if of one mind, stood rooted to the floor. Then with a nudge of the muzzle into Zoe's soft neck and the expected gasp from her, movement began. First one, then another of the tavern's patrons shifted to form a narrow gauntlet for them to pass through. Dangerous, to say the least.

It appeared the best he would get.

And time was not on his side. Already he could sense a reluctance in some of the men to let him go. Naught had been mentioned of a reward, but that possibility existed and Keegan doubted Zoe's life would stand for much compared to a bag of gold.

Truth be known, he had no desire to kill the chit. Despite her obvious desire to see him swing at the end of a rope.

Not trusting the quickness of his hostage's feet, Keegan grasped her about the waist, keeping the gun pressed to her side. Then without another word he strode through the group. At the door he paused, motioning her to open it.

"*Now*, Zoe," he hissed when she faltered. "Or I swear I'll kill ye."

"Stop him!" she yelled, and Keegan was too amazed to do a thing. "I shall die anyway."

That was all the brave men of the inn needed. They surged toward Keegan.

"Damn!"

Jerking the door open he shoved Zoe into the night, then turned and fired the pistol.

Five

He had maybe two minutes. Which was how long it would take this rustic crowd to figure out he'd used his one shot for nothing more than to create havoc.

Ne could only hope the report was affecting them the way it did Zoe who was holding her ears and looking dazed. But then not much affected other people like it did Zoe. He grabbed her hand, ignoring her protests that she was now deaf, and raced behind the tavern. It had started to rain. A heavy drizzle thickened the air and slimed the cobblestones, reminding him of that fateful morn at Culloden.

Keegan forced that thought from his mind. He didn't need a reminder of the dead faces of his brothers, the tortured body of his father. Not now. Now was for finding a way the hell out of here before the enraged surge of drunken humanity burst through yon door. He'd seen the fowling piece behind the bar, and could imagine the innkeeper would love to earn his place in village history by bringing down an infamous Jacobite like Keegan MacLeod.

"Ouch! Oh, my ankle."

"We haven't time for yer complainin'." The ripe
smell of straw and manure assaulted Keegan as he
rushed into the stable, practically dragging a limping, and despite his admonition, complaining, Zoe
behind him.

"I think 'tis broken. Nay! Oh, no, I can't possibly . . ." A sharp intake of breath severed Zoe's protest as she was unceremoniously yanked up onto a
horse behind the Scot. Her first instinct was to fight
her way off . . . that is until she started to slide and
realized how far up she was. Zoe didn't need her
captor to growl, "Hold on," for her arms to clamp
madly about his waist.

Then Zoe squeezed her eyes shut as the huge animal thundered out into the rainy night.

At least she wasn't deaf. For sounds assailed her.
Shouted orders to halt. The clatter of hooves over
stone. The Scot's pounding heartbeat. Or was that
her own? Pressed against him as she was, it was hard
to tell one from the other. Except that what she
heard sounded strong and steady, and hers definitely was not.

Zoe expected hers to expire at any moment. Perhaps her weak heart had managed to continue beating through her abduction and the long coach ride,
but it would never survive this outlandish treatment.

Every bone in her body jammed and jarred as the
horse, its bony back bunched between her legs,
pounded past the screaming men.

A shot exploded through the air. Zoe screamed.
The Scot cursed. Fragments of prayers filled Zoe's
mind, but she was too frightened or numb to say

them aloud. Or perhaps she'd lost the ability to speak.

His hands fisted in the horse's mane, Keegan swerved the heaving animal off the road, into a copse of dripping trees. At least he hoped they were trees. Blanketed beneath the billowy down of clouds and mist, even the sliver of moon was gone. The night was nothing but black and wet.

Keegan ran his palm down his mount's smooth neck and listened. Behind him Zoe made little mewling noises, which he tried to ignore. She was wet and cold and uncomfortable. Well so was he. If not for her grand play at heroics they'd be warm and comfortable curled up together in bed.

Damnation. Where had that thought come from? They might have been safe and dry, but they sure as hell wouldn't have been curled up together. Why he'd as soon bed a . . . Keegan couldn't come up with an appropriate comparison and let the thought slip from his mind.

It was listening that he was after anyway. He held his breath waiting for the telltale plod of horses' hooves on the road behind him. He waited, clicking off the minutes in his head, relief swimming through him as the time passed and no sound echoed through the night.

There had been an attempt to follow at first. At least Keegan thought he'd heard horses, seen flickers of light from torches when he looked back. But apparently the good people of Wickshire put comfort before valor, at least where he was concerned.

He waited a bit longer, then urged the horse back onto the road. They moved slower now, slogging through the mud. No more headlong dashes through the puddles. Still, Keegan ached, imagined the horse did as well. But he kept them heading south. He must have dozed, for the cheerful chatter of birds seemed to rouse him. He hadn't noticed the rain stopping, but it had, though the air still hung heavy.

The pewter sky gave him the first inkling of the countryside he rode through. The land was flat, stretching on seemingly forever. When he spotted a building Keegan thought he was dreaming or at least hallucinating. It sat a good twenty rods off the road, behind a grove of alders. Made of stone, with its roof of thatch it appeared deserted.

Cautiously Keegan turned the tired horse off the muddy road. Zoe still had a death grip around his waist. He could feel her body pressed against his back. It was the one part of him that was dry and warm.

At close range the barn appeared dilapidated and unused. Keegan pried Zoe's fingers loose, and slid from the horse's back. As limp as a rag doll, his captive followed.

"Christ, Zoe." Keegan grabbed her about the waist before she slipped to the ground. "Stand on yer feet."

"I can't. I'm dying."

"Ye're not dyin'." Keegan scooped her into his arms. "Ye're just tired, as am I." Depositing her, sodden and slack beneath an oak, Keegan said, "Be still now," just before she slumped over on her side. With a shake of his head, Keegan drew his broadsword and set to investigating the barn.

Within minutes he was back, pulling on Zoe's arms, forcing her to sit upright.

"Stop," she mumbled. "Just let me die in peace."

"Yer not dying, I tell ye. Though if ye don't get out of those sodden clothes ye may be soon. Now come on with ye."

Zoe opened one eye, then the other. Then she moaned. "Why don't I just die?"

"Well now Lady Zoe, I can't rightly say." Keegan pulled her to her feet. "Perhaps yer stickin' around t' make my life a living hell."

"Your life?" Zoe revived herself enough to slap at the hands clamped to her wrists. "Just who is it that dragged me onto that horse and rode me about all night?"

"Ye could have had yer dry bed, Zoe, if ye hadn't decided to open yer mouth back at the inn. Did ye really think that band of yeomen could save ye?"

"I thought it worth a try," Zoe said with a sigh. She was on her feet now, being dragged toward the barn. Inside it was warmer and dry and musty. Zoe was too tired to do more than stand where he left her when the Scot's rough hands released her.

"Here." He paused when she did nothing. "Well, take it." The "it" was a moth-eaten horse blanket, so dirty Zoe could see dust motes dancing about it in the pewtery light. But she obeyed his command . . . at least the first part of it.

"Now take off yer clothes and dry off. I'll be seeing to the horse."

Keegan wiped the mare down with straw, then backed her into a stall. The only grain he could find was moldy, so he gave the horse some water and the promise of some grazing time later in the day.

Peeling off his jacket Keegan returned to the stall where he left Zoe. "Are ye decently covered, lass?"

No answer.

Hell and damnation. Was the woman so daft that she tried to escape him again? "Zoe?" Anger fueled his tired body as Keegan swung around the wooden divider only to stop short at what he saw. She lay crumpled in the straw, still fully clothed in her sodden gown. So still was she, and so pale in the grainy light filtering into the barn that he feared she might have finally fulfilled her own prophecy. Had her weak heart, as she called it, simply given out? His own gave a little jerk at the thought. Then reason returned and he dropped to his knees beside her.

"Zoe lass, yer goin' t' have t' get out of these wet clothes." He touched her cheek, letting his fingers drift down to the hollow of her neck where her pulse fluttered. She made no response beyond a muffled moan. "Come on now with ye, or I'll be forced to bare ye meself."

Still nothing.

"Damn ye, Zoe Morgan. I'm nigh as spent as ye, and as cold and clammy." He pushed to his feet and tossed his jacket over the stall divider. "I've half a mind t' leave ye as ye are. Then ye'd be knowin' what it is t' really be ailin'." But even as he spoke, Keegan was kneeling by her side, fumbling with the silver buttons of her riding habit. The fabric was wet, his fingers cold, which made the task difficult. "Ye'd think I never disrobed a lass before," he muttered, then grinned. He'd certainly never done anything quite resembling this.

With the jacket unbuttoned, Keegan pulled Zoe up till she was sitting, her head lolling to one side, her neck looking incredibly fragile. "Here ye go now," Keegan said as he pulled first one, then the other arm from the saffron-colored sleeves. She did no more than moan a protest as he unfastened her wet lawn shirt at the jabot and sleeves, then pulled it over her head.

"Ye best revive yerself," Keegan warned as he pulled off her skirt and hoops.

It was testimony to the time they'd spent riding through the rain that her underclothing was as wet as the riding habit itself. With a sigh, Keegan snatched at her corset laces. She was lying now on the horse blanket, her damp hair tumbling across the straw. Her slight frame was spare but not without womanly curves. Keegan found his fingers slowing and his eyes wondering as he removed her shift.

He swallowed, feeling uncomfortably like a voyeur. With a groan he grabbed for the other blanket he'd found, tossing it over her body. There, she was covered. But that didn't erase from his mind's eye the vision of her lying there, naked to his view.

He'd scarcely thought of her as a woman before. Odd, for now that he thought on it she was pretty enough with her grey eyes, calm and misty as a Highland dawn. But she was a vexation to him, had been from the moment he'd kidnapped her. And her annoying habits, the complaining of imaginary illnesses, the defense of her bastard brother, her attempts to escape him, were all he'd allowed himself to notice.

Till now.

Well, any such thoughts about her would have to cease. Keegan jerked his waistcoat off and added it to the line-up of clothing, Zoe's and his own, draped across the wooden divider. His shirt followed, then his breeches. He may have kidnapped the chit, but his purpose was honorable. And he intended to keep it that way.

And damn his traitorous body for responding as if it would be otherwise.

Despite their dampness, Keegan opted to keep his drawers on. With his broadsword and pistol by his side he lay down in the straw, close to, but careful not to touch his captive. But the morning's chill soon had him squirming closer, inching beneath the edge of the blanket, shaping his body to the curves of hers.

"Hell and damnation," he cursed when she turned, then slid her arm across his chest. *"Now* ye move."

In the groggy netherland of half-sleep Zoe dreamed that someone, who she supposed to be Keegan MacLeod, was sticking needles into her skin. Begging him to stop did no good. He simply laughed, his eyes burning into her with a strange demonic light and told her he'd do as he pleased.

Oh, she despised him. Which wasn't altogether easy to do. For in the back of her sleepy mind there were fragments of dreams of another sort. Sensual dreams unlike any she'd ever experienced. The touch of warm skin. The smell of a man's body.

And it wasn't just any man.

Even in slumber Zoe knew it was the barbarian Scot who triggered these feelings in her. "No. No." The sound of her own voice, lifted in protest, stirred Zoe awake. She lay still a moment, listening, before opening her eyes.

She was alone, though she could hear sounds. Her hand closed over something prickly and she lifted the straw only to let it drift from her fingers. She remembered now, vaguely, riding through the rainy night. Finding shelter toward morning. Keegan MacLeod.

With a shiver, Zoe pushed herself to sitting, discovering in the process that she wore no bodice . . . or clothes of any kind. Gasping, she clutched the blanket, pulling it to her chin, baring her feet and lower legs by her action. What she saw made her forget her nudity. "Oh, no," she whispered on a resigned sigh. "Not that."

Keegan crunched a bite of apple, making a face as the tart juice hit his tongue. Not quite ripe. But then he hadn't exactly had much to choose from. And he was damn hungry. He was lucky to find an estate nearby . . . and to meet a dairy maid willing to trade a loaf of bread for a smile and a few flowery phrases. But he always had been a charmer. At least that's what his da and brothers had told him.

He took another bite of apple, then tossed it aside. The sharp taste did nothing to wash away the memory of his brother's lifeless eyes. Or the sting of watching his father die at the hand of the English butchers.

Splashing across a gentle brook, Keegan followed the footpath he took earlier when he first awoke. The sun was high, setting the water asparkle like a serpentine jewel. Pretty country, but it lacked the drama of the Highlands, of home.

Soon. He would be home soon.

Keegan shifted the pouch he'd fashioned from his jacket. It was full of oats and bread, plus a jug of cider. Enough nourishment to get the horse and himself to the coast. Oh, and Zoe, too.

Keegan shook his head as he approached the fieldstone barn. Zoe. God in heaven, what had he been thinking when he kidnapped her? He may as well have fastened a ball and chain about his neck. She had no idea how a captive should behave. Of course he wasn't real certain himself. But he sure as hell didn't think it was continually asking questions. Or complaining about this illness or that. Or looking so damn delectable and virginal lying on a moth-eaten horse blanket.

Looking at her, his mind and other parts of his body had been so filled with lust he'd had a difficult time not acting on it. Lord knows he'd barely slept at all, lying there beside her. He should have taken advantage of the milkmaid's kind offer to meet her behind the stable. True, she wasn't delectable, and hardly virginal, but she would have relieved a lot of the tension he'd been feeling of late.

Not that the thought hadn't crossed his mind to just spend a bit of this energy on Zoe herself. It occurred to him a lot as he stared at the barn rafters while she slept peacefully beside him. Hell, rape was part and parcel of kidnapping. Wasn't it?

"No! Don't come in here."

"Hell and damnation, Zoe. What's gotten into ye now?" Despite his words Keegan paused in the doorway of the barn. Afternoon sunlight rayed in through the window holes, showing a scene much like the one he left earlier. The horse, old and a bit swaybacked, still stood in the stall. Zoe still inhabited the one to the right. She was covered with a grey blanket that she had clutched to her chin, obviously unaware of the exposed swell of her left breast.

Keegan let out a breath and stepped inside.

"No, please, I mean it. You mustn't come near me." She accompanied her words with a scooting motion that put her perhaps another inch further from him.

"Zoe." Squinting, Keegan studied her again . . . her face this time. Her expression showed real fear, and for just a moment Keegan recalled what he'd been thinking right before he entered the barn. So he wouldn't mind making love to her, and she was his captive. That didn't mean he was going to use her to relieve his baser needs. Despite how he felt about her brother. "I'm not going to hurt ye lass."

"I'm telling you for your benefit to stay away. No, don't come any closer."

"It's because of yer clothes I'm guessin'. True, I undressed ye, but it was for yer own good. You'd a caught yer death in those wet clothes. And I didn't so much as peek." Keegan grinned at his lie. "Had me eyes closed the whole time."

"That's not the problem . . ." Zoe began, then stopped, her eyes growing large. "*You* took off my clothes?"

"Aye." Keegan settled the jacket pouch on the straw-littered floor. "Did ye think yer lady's maid happened by?"

"No, of course not. I can't remember. I thought I'd done it myself. Besides it was always Miss Phelps who helped ready me for bed. She said the maids were too rough with my delicate person."

"Ah, well she may have been a wee bit wrong about that." Keegan figured he wasn't entirely gentle with his undressing . . . especially when he was hurrying to get her covered.

Zoe sighed loudly. "It doesn't matter. Not really. For I'll be dead within a few days."

"What the hell!" Keegan stepped closer, despite her protest. "For the love of God, I've said I wouldn't kill ye, and I won't. Despite that little show back at the tavern for which I should have beat ye to within an inch of yer life."

Keegan noticed two fat tears spill over her lashes and roll down her pale cheeks and he felt like the worst kind of demon. Palms up, he took another step closer. "Now there be no reason to go cryin'. I was only speakin' hypothetically, ye understand. There'll be no beatin'."

"I thank you for that, but perhaps it would be better if you'd just kill me and be done with it."

"What, are ye daft?"

"Then I wouldn't have to suffer the black vomit and deliriums." Zoe bit her bottom lip. "Or is that the plague?"

"Ye're talking in circles here lass, and I'm losin' my patience. Now get dressed with ye. I've brought some bread. We'll eat and be on our—"

"You don't understand," Zoe cried indignantly. "I have the pox."

"The pox! For God's sake Zoe, you couldn't possibly have the pox." Could she? Hell no, this was no doxy. And if she'd been so much as touched before he'd be surprised.

"Smallpox," she amended. More tears followed the path of the others before she sniffed and took a deep breath. "But I shall be brave. I just hope you don't . . ." Zoe paused. Why should she hope the Scot didn't have the dread disease? It would certainly keep him from killing Fox. And it would serve him right for kidnapping her. After all, she could have gotten it from him. He *had* been in prison.

Despite all that, Zoe wasn't sure she wished smallpox on the Scot. He was so healthy and virile, Zoe hated to think of him as gaunt and infirm.

She could see herself that way. Propped on a pile of fluffy feather pillows, beneath a counterpane of white. Sipping broth from a silver spoon, Miss Phelps coaxing her along. Except there was no soft bed or silver spoon. Certainly no Miss Phelps to care for her. She was likely to die on this heap of dirty, prickly straw.

Zoe glanced up as the Scot knelt beside her. He really was tempting the Fates.

"What makes you think ye have smallpox?"

His voice was gentle, though Zoe noted a touch of amusement in that deep burr. And he seemed unable to control a twitching of his lip. So he thought her dire straits laughable. She would show him.

"There," she said, as she yanked up the blanket, baring her feet and lower legs. "See for yourself."

Keegan's gaze left hers to travel down the length of her body. When he reached her exposed limbs he rocked back on his heels. "And just what am I supposed to be seein'?" Except slender ankles and well-shaped calves.

Zoe bent forward, loosing a bit more hold on the blanket. Keegan's eyes flicked up, catching a curve of rounded shoulder before moving down to follow the jabbing motion of her finger as she pointed to the smattering of raised pink bumps marring her ivory flesh.

"Aye," Keegan said with a lift of his brows. "Ye have some flea bites to be sure."

"Flea bites." Zoe nearly bent double in an attempt to study the swelling more closely. "Flea bites?"

"I've me fair share of them too. The blanket is more than likely infested with the vermin." Her first reaction was to toss aside the offending wool. Keegan could see it in her eyes. But to his chagrin she remembered what she wore beneath, and caught herself in time.

With a resigned shrug Keegan pushed to his feet and grabbed up the grain. "There's some bread and ale over there ye can have once ye've dressed yerself." Keegan scooped the grain into a bucket and offered it to the mare.

Zoe in the meantime didn't move. She just continued to stare at her legs, mumbling something about smallpox.

"Ye'd think ye weren't pleased that yer not goin' t' die. Are ye that anxious to be rid of my company?"

She glanced up and her lips thinned. "Of course I'm anxious to be free of you . . . you lout. And don't laugh. You are a lout and much worse. But I do not wish to die," she added quickly. "It's just that I thought . . . well, you know what I thought."

"Aye." Despite her warning there was laughter in his voice. "Ye thought ye had smallpox."

"Well, I've never slept with fleas before."

"I have." The laughter was gone. "Ye get used t' it."

"I don't wish to." Zoe scratched at her leg. "They itch." When that complaint brought no response, Zoe wrapped the blanket about herself and rose. Her clothes, looking sadly the worse for wear, were draped over the stall divider. Keeping a wary eye on the Scot who seemed engrossed with feeding the horse, Zoe pulled her shift over her head. It tangled with her hair. The corset was next. It was a complicated garment, one she'd never managed alone and she almost asked her captor for assistance. But somehow she managed. By the time she was fastening the bodice, hunger was hurrying her fingers.

The bread was coarse, probably wouldn't settle well on her delicate stomach, but Zoe ate it anyway. She actually nearly finished it and the ale before she thought to question the Scot. "Is this to be shared?"

"Nay, I've eaten already. Have yer fill." Keegan was busy fashioning a halter of sorts out of pieces of leather he found in the tack room. When he finished he led the horse outside, threw the blankets over her back and offered Zoe a leg up. As soon as her legs spread to wrap around the horse, her muscles screamed in pain. Still embarrassed by the smallpox fiasco, Zoe kept her counsel. Instead she asked, "Where are we going now?"

"T' Harmouth on the coast. I've a man t' see about passage north t' Scotland." Keegan mounted the horse behind her, his arms circling her, grasping the makeshift reins. When Keegan clicked the mare into motion she slid back, nestling in the wedge of his thighs. His groan had her twisting about.

" 'Tis painful, isn't it? But I'm not complaining as you can see."

Perhaps she wasn't, but Keegan felt like it. It was bad enough having Lady Zoe Morgan as his captive. But he didn't like the idea of being captivated by her charms, however limited. His mind was made up. First chance he had, he was leaving Lady Zoe behind. He'd find another way to avenge his father.

Six

They reached Harmouth by midafternoon the next day, after what Zoe considered a grueling ride. She imagined the Scot felt the same, for he was quite uncommunicative. When he did speak, it was to bark a one word response, accompanied by a few grumbling remarks about her penchant for complaining. The savage. Certainly Zoe had no desire to carry on a conversation with the barbarian, but he didn't seem to understand how truly uncomfortable she was.

Her bottom was sore, her legs rubbery, and her flea bites itched. Only the memory of her captor's face when he told her she didn't have smallpox stopped her from letting him know how she felt. So she kept quiet, even when she was so tired she felt her next breath would be her last.

But somehow or another she continued to breathe, and her heart kept beating and she was still alive when the Scot reached up to help her from the horse.

The village itself was small, clinging to a stormswept perch of granite. Crooked narrow streets wound through the whitewashed stone buildings that huddled, nearly on top of one another as if protecting themselves from the salt wind. Like the land surrounding it, the village was sparse and un-inviting.

And of the lot, the Hungry Rook seemed the most uninviting of its buildings. The broken-hinged shingle—depicting a fierce and incredibly ugly bird, its beak open—slapped and creaked with each fresh gust of wind off the channel.

The door slammed open and a grizzled old man, as hunched and bent as the dense furze dotting the slopes, teetered onto the street. One eye was covered by a dirty black patch. The other, a washed-out blue, studied Keegan and Zoe.

"I'm lookin' for one Padraic Rafferty," Keegan began. "I've heard he favors these parts."

"Have ye now?"

"Aye, and I'd be appreciatin' it if ye'd tell me if he's here."

"Was," the old man said before spitting. He backhanded his mouth, then aimed his good eye toward Zoe. "Who's this fair bit o' female?"

Zoe found herself being hauled behind the Scot as he answered. " 'Tis none of yer concern, old man. If ye won't be answerin' me about Captain Rafferty, I'll be findin' someone who will."

The one-eyed man simply shrugged his narrow shoulders and started off down the hill. Keegan watched him go, then twisted about, catching Zoe's gaze.

"Do I need to be tellin' ye to keep yer comments to yerself inside. These men aren't known for their gentlemanly manners. 'Twould be best if ye just stay at my side and keep your mouth shut."

"Better for whom?"

Keegan's eyes narrowed. "Now what ye be meanin' by that?"

"Well, I assume it's your own skin you're watching out for, not mine. You are after all, an outlaw. Surely these men, rough as they seem, would—"

Zoe's words were interrupted by a bark of laughter as Keegan threw back his head. "So ye think they would do the right thing, do ye? Save yer pretty neck, I imagine yer hopin'." He shook his head when her expression showed that was exactly what she was thinking. "These men are as much afoul of the law as me . . . maybe more so. Ye're in the midst of a village of smugglers and pirates Lady Zoe."

Keegan wasn't sure she believed him, but he hoped for her sake she did. He'd just as soon not have her with him but at the moment there wasn't much he could do about it. So with a last warning look, Keegan led the way into the tavern.

Inside, the air was thick with smoke and the acrid smell of sweat. The noise, quite loud when they entered, soon dissipated to a muffled whisper as all eyes turned on Keegan and Zoe.

"Mind yerself," is all Keegan said as he motioned for her to seat herself on a bench against the dingy wall. Acting more confident than he felt, Keegan settled down on the chair beside her, leaning it onto its back two legs. It wasn't long before a barmaid approached. She smiled, showing teeth the color of tobacco, and offered Keegan a view of her pendulous breasts.

"What can I get for ya, goven'r?"

"Rum."

The doxy's marble eyes darted toward Zoe, who stared at her with unabashed curiosity. "And for the lady?"

"She'll have the same." Keegan's hand snatched the barmaid's arm before she could turn away.

Her smile turned knowing. "And be there something else I can do for ya? A big bruiser like yerself must get pretty tired of sticking it in that poor excuse for a woman."

"Now lass, she's not that bad. A bit on the thin side perhaps but nothing a good sea voyage wouldn't cure."

"Is that what you're planning to do? Take her on a trip?"

"It might be. That is, if I can find a certain captain by the name of Rafferty. Might ye know the lad?"

"Oh, I know Paddy all right." The barmaid leaned her hip against the table. "He's got a real strong ache for me, if ya get my meaning."

"I think I do." Keegan leaned forward, the chair legs slamming to the floor. He let his hand drape the generous curve of her rump. "So where might I find yer friend Paddy?"

Twisting about, the doxy stretched across the scarred table toward Keegan. "I think ya should spend a bit of time with me first then I'll tell—"

The loud slap of a hand across her buttocks had the woman squealing and slithering off the table. Entranced by her brazen ways, Zoe too, was caught off guard. She let out a startled squeal, then looked up at the man who'd interrupted the barmaid's shameless flirtation with the Scot.

He pulled the woman to her feet, then gave her a shove in the direction of the bar. "These gentle folk aren't interested in the likes of you, Limmy. Now be off with you."

"Ya don't scare me none, Keefer Holt," the girl said defiantly, yet Zoe noted that she scrambled away, all the time gingerly rubbing her bottom.

"You'll have to excuse Limmy," the man said, with a formal bow toward Zoe. "She hasn't the manners of a sow." This brought a disgruntled noise from Limmy, very similar to the sound a sow might make. But the man ignored it as he lifted Zoe's hand to his lips. "A lady as fair as you shouldn't have to be exposed to such as she."

"Well, I . . ." Zoe swallowed, stumbling over her words. She'd never had her hand kissed before. And the man doing it now was clearly proficient at it. He stared into her eyes, his being a brown, so deep as to be nearly black. His lips were firm, and slightly moist, and though not nearly as well-defined and attractive as the Scot's, Zoe felt heat rise to softly color her cheeks. That is, until the Scot snatched her hand away. Then her face turned a darker shade of red.

"I apologize, sir," the man said to Keegan. "I didn't mean any offense. I only wished to pay my deepest respects to your wife." His gaze shifted toward Zoe as she opened her mouth to correct his misconception, but a grunt from the Scot made her close it again.

" 'Tis nothing," Keegan said with a slight nod.

"I am Captain Keefer Holt, of the good schooner *Sea Maiden*. Perhaps you saw her in the harbor?"

"Nay." Keegan folded his arms across his chest and leaned back. " 'Tis Padraic Rafferty whom I seek."

"Alas, you must seek him in heaven . . . or perhaps hell."

"He's dead?"

"I fear so. Though it could hardly come as a shock if you knew Padraic." Keefer paused to shine a brilliant smile toward Zoe.

"Which I didn't," Keegan said, managing to regain the man's attention.

"In that case I assume you wished to make his acquaintance for one of several reasons. Either you were in need of some contraband . . ." He paused again to study Zoe. "And I doubt that's the case. Or you wish to take a sea voyage." When Keegan said nothing, Keefer continued. "My own vessel, *Sea Maiden* is at your disposal."

"Thank ye, but I'm not lookin' to take a trip."

"Really?"

Zoe watched Keefer lean back in his chair, his pose mimicking the Scot's. The men seemed to study each other.

"That surprises me," Keefer said. "For with that Scottish burr broadening your speech I would have thought you might feel an escape to the Continent should be in the offing."

He knew.

Zoe's heart pounded and she tried to send the sea captain a subconscious message. Anything to let him know that she was held hostage and who the

Scot was. But before she could gain the captain's
gaze, she glanced around and found herself caught
in Keegan's. He looked down to where his hand cradled his pistol. It was beneath the table, obscured
from all but her view, and aimed toward Zoe. She
felt her breath catch and decided against any more
foolish actions.

At least for the moment.

She even nodded her agreement when Keegan
gave some inane explanation of why they were seeking Padraic Rafferty. He held her close to his side
as they exited the tavern.

Outside, the air's bite was tangy with salt, refresh-
ing after the confines of the tavern. Keegan took a
deep breath and pulled Zoe away from the entrance
before letting loose his frustration.

"Damnation," he growled. "What in the hell am
I t' do now?"

The question was obviously rhetorical, for he
didn't look to Zoe for an answer but she gave one
anyway.

"You could give yourself up. Return to London
and—"

"Let them hang me? 'Tis that yer suggestion?"

He stared at her dumbfounded and Zoe had to
admit he had a point. "I could speak out for you.
Assure the authorities that no harm came to me by
your hand."

"That's a comfort t' be sure. But the truth of the
matter is that I'd be hanged with or without ye."

"Then why not take Captain Holt's offer? It seems
to me that he is as good as that other man to take
you where you wish to go." Probably not something

she should suggest, seeing that he planned to take her with him, but it was out of Zoe's mouth before she could stop it. And it hardly was more unreasonable than his response.

"I did not like the man."

"That's ridiculous. He seemed nice enough to me."

"And why shouldn't he with all his hand-kissing and long soulful glances."

"What?"

"But mark me words lass, he's not a man t' be trusted."

"Ah." Zoe raised her chin. "And I should take the word of the man who kidnapped me, and threatened to kill me for that?"

"Hush with ye." Keegan grabbed hold of her arm, yanking her along down the steep slope that led to a small protected harbor. "I've said ye won't be hurt."

"Which is a bit difficult for me to believe when you've a pistol pointed at me. I've known since I can remember that I'm bound to die young, but I never thought it would be at the hand of a brigand such as you. I should have been in my bed, with Miss Phelps at my side, and the doctor."

Keegan just rolled his eyes heavenward as he hurried them both toward the cove. He wasn't interested in hearing again a catalogue of her ailments, real or imagined. And he was beginning to think they were mostly imagined.

Glancing at her now, scurrying along beside him she seemed healthy enough. Her skin had picked up a bit of color, either from the autumn sun, or from the exertion of keeping up with him. Whichever, the shade was most becoming. He could almost believe that Captain Holt had been taken enough with her to risk a husband's wrath. Except that he knew the bastard's type—had run into his share at the gaming tables.

But it was no longer the loss of a few pounds that rested on his ability to read people. His life depended upon it. And in an odd way, Zoe's life. Which he shouldn't take the time to worry about, but which he did all the same.

All the more reason to abandon his original plan and get rid of her as soon as he could. But one look at Harmouth was enough to make him realize this wasn't the place to leave her. She may have been flattered by Holt's attentions but men like that would eat her alive.

Unbidden and unwelcome came another thought. Men like himself would too.

An afternoon spent conversing, or trying to, with the locals offered no more information than he already had. Most everyone seemed to agree that Padraic Rafferty was dead, the victim of a shipwreck. No one seemed willing to take a trip north to Scotland, at least not for the money Keegan had to offer.

As dark settled over the small hamlet Keegan rented a room in Harmouth's most respectable and only inn. Somehow or another, perhaps because she was tired, Zoe managed to keep from making any comments that could jeopardize his well-being.

The room was cramped, the sloped ceilings made for a man much shorter than himself, but at least it was decently clean. Not that Zoe seemed to mind.

She took one look at the room, walked to the bed, and fell across it, almost instantly asleep.

He'd told her tonight she would be tied up in case she had any ideas of escaping. But she looked so sweet, so innocent, Keegan hadn't the heart to do it. Besides, she wasn't likely to awaken. He'd probably have his hands full in the morning getting her out of bed. Especially when he told her they were going to start north across land toward Scotland.

So Keegan positioned his pistol beneath the thin pillow, his broadsword at his side, and lay down beside her. Tired as he was, sleep did not come quickly. Especially when he started wondering whether, for her own comfort, of course, he should loosen Zoe's gown. He finally decided he was a damn rake for even thinking on it.

But the image from the morning in the barn was hard to escape.

She dreamed she was strong and healthy, her hair streaming down her back as a magnificent horse galloped across the fields. She could smell the wildflowers, hear the birds singing, and feel the wondrous sun on her face. It was a lovely dream, made all the more so by the man who rode by her side. He made her happy, made her heart sing. And when she looked over at him Zoe saw it was the Scot.

Her startled gasp woke Zoe up.

For a moment she lay still, waiting for the remnants of the dream to fade, letting her eyes adjust to the darkness. She was lying on a bed that she barely remembered seeing before, beside the man from her dream. No. The man who kidnapped her.

Slowly, barely able to believe her good fortune, Zoe lifted her arms. He hadn't tied them as he'd threatened to do. She could just barely make out his silhouette in the darkness, but his low snores were proof enough that he was asleep.

He was asleep and she was free. Well, not quite yet, but soon.

With as much stealth as she could muster, Zoe inched across the mattress. Thin and decidedly not down-filled, the ticking gave little as she moved. For which she was profoundly grateful.

Unfortunately the flooring was as thin as the bedding, making a loud creak as she lowered one foot to the boards. Her breathing stopped, as did his. Heartbeats passed, and Zoe expected to feel his hand clasp about her arm at any moment. But it didn't. When the snores resumed, Zoe sucked in a welcome gulp of air.

She slid. She slithered. She managed somehow to go from prone to standing without waking him. Now to get out of the room. Pausing, Zoe glanced back at the Scot's sleeping form. At the broadsword beside him. It would be so easy.

In disgust she turned toward the door. She couldn't kill him. Not even with his threats against Fox ringing in her ears. She would save Fox by warning him. And the first step in that was finding him.

On tiptoes Zoe approached the door. A quarter moon provided the light she needed to find the latch. But not enough to find the key.

"Blast it," Zoe mumbled as she squinted her eyes,

trying to pick out a glimmer of brass in the room. Nothing. The barbarian probably had it beneath his pillow.

Zoe's gaze locked on the broadsword again, then shifted to the window. Open, letting in the briny smell of the sea, the window seemed the perfect escape. Perhaps a bit less than perfect when Zoe actually looked down toward the street. Still, how far could it be, especially if she hung from the sill and dropped down slowly.

And truthfully, what choice did she have?

Gathering her courage as well as her skirts, Zoe climbed through the opening. Hanging onto the rough sill, her feet dangling far above the dirt road, Zoe had a fleeting wish that the Scot would awaken. She even considered screaming for him, but instead shut her eyes, held her breath and let loose her grip.

She landed on her feet, then fell back onto her bottom.

"Oh, no," she whimpered. "I've broken my ankles." She sat in the dirt, almost expecting Miss Phelps to come bustling out of the shadows with a helping hand. But of course that was foolish. There was no one to help her but herself. So after several moments and two attempts to rise, Zoe managed to stand. Her ankles were sore but they did support her weight and after a few steps, truly weren't that painful.

Not that she wouldn't have preferred resting them on a soft pillow to limping down the deserted street toward the Hungry Rook, but these were desperate times.

Despite the late hour, the tavern was teeming with

life, most of it quite disreputable. But Zoe held her head high as she entered the establishment. The din of noise subsided as first one, then another, patron nudged his companion and nodded toward Zoe. She had another, irrational, but none the less real, desire to race back to the Scot for protection.

That thought vanished as she saw Captain Holt making his way toward her across the crowded room. She smiled and he returned the gesture, though his seemed a bit wobbly. From drink she imagined. Oh well, she wasn't after a saint, only someone to return her to Fox.

"Mistress Zoe, I must say I'm surprised to see you here. Surprised but pleased." He accompanied his words with a lift of her hand to his lips. Zoe caught the unmistakable odor of rum on his breath.

"Actually," she began, then glanced about at the myriad faces turned her way, "do you suppose there is somewhere we might speak in private?"

Nodding, he led her toward a table in the corner. Three men, one with only a stump for his right leg, grumbled their objections but clattered out of their seats when the captain gave the order.

With a bow he offered a chair to Zoe. The captain was shorter than she had earlier thought, a bit coarser, but his dark eyes were friendly and she really had nowhere else to turn. When they'd both settled into seats, Zoe began again.

"First of all I think you should know, I'm Lady Zoe Morgan." She watched as his brows lifted. "I know you must think it strange that I've come here, but let me assure you it was not by choice."

"I don't understand. Your husband . . ."

"He's not my husband but my kidnapper. Please!" Zoe covered his hand with her own. "You must take me to my brother. He will reward you handsomely."

The captain's eyes lit up. "Yes, I imagine he will."

He came awake with an abruptness begun during his months at New Gaol. As on so many of those mornings, it took Keegan a moment to realize where he was. Free was the first thought that came to mind. Alone was the second.

"Damnation!" Keegan jumped to his feet, stomping on his boots in almost the same motion. Where in the hell could she be? He grabbed up the broadsword and pistol before striding toward the door. Finding it locked was a surprise, but then how would she have gotten the key without waking him? How in the hell did she get away without waking him? Keegan cursed the softhearted impulse that had kept him from tying her the night before as he strode to the window.

He didn't know how she did it, but she must have used the window to escape. He half expected to see her broken body lying in the dirt when he looked down. Instead he found nothing but dusty road.

So she was gone. Keegan took a deep breath and leaned against the window's sash. He didn't know whether to be angry or relieved. The more he thought on it, the more relief won out. Without her he could travel faster. And if Fox Morgan was in Scotland, he'd find him—with or without his sister.

Yes, Keegan decided as he fished the key from his pocket, this was all for the best. He'd get something to eat, and then be on his way. Keegan was still trying to count his blessings when he went belowstairs. But there were a few things that bothered him. Like where did she go? And with whom? Keegan had an idea he might know the answer to that one. What would she do for money? And how in the hell was she going to stay alive?

The innkeeper greeted him with a smile that quickly vanished when Keegan grabbed the man's tunic and hauled him closer.

"What do ye know of a Captain Holt?"

"Why sir, I don't understand your question. If you'd just let me down."

"Tell me man, is he a smuggler? A pirate?"

"Oh that and more," the innkeeper's wife said coming up behind her husband. "But you've no need to worry on him. He's sailing off this day. Heading to Scotland I hear."

"Hell and damnation!" Keegan growled before letting the innkeeper loose.

Seven

Keegan agreed with the gulls laughing at him as they swooped and glided on currents of air. He was a fool. There was no denying it in his mind. Zoe Morgan was out of his life. No more listening to her complain. To her questions. To her constant stream of illnesses. He should be thanking the Fates. Hell, he should be riding off across the downs toward Scotland.

Instead he picked his way along a crooked path that led to the foam-covered black rocks below. This wasn't the main road from the village to the sea. But then Keegan didn't feel he should announce his arrival at the harbor. Not for what he had planned.

Which was not to say he actually had a plan. More like a general idea. Which was to rescue Zoe . . . whether she wished it or not.

The *Sea Maiden* was still docked and it didn't appear it would be sailing anytime soon. Keegan couldn't see anyone on deck. Keegan grabbed onto a bunch of pale broom grass as his feet slipped on the lichen-covered rocks. Damnation. One would think for a Highlander he'd be better able to traverse this type of terrain. This was what living in London had done to him.

He could feel the spray now, salt-tinged and shooting up from the boulders below. He paused, surveying the harbor. No one seemed to have noticed him yet. And he wished to keep it that way—which eliminated walking up the gangplank. The only other way aboard was the rope ladder—which of course meant a swim he wasn't anxious to take.

With a disgruntled curse, Keegan slipped the pistol from his pocket, hid it behind an outcrop of rocks and walked into the buffeting surf.

The sea was choppy, churned by the underwater rocks, and hard as hell to swim. By the time Keegan reached the *Sea Maiden* most of his energy was spent. But he managed to cling to the rope ladder until he caught his breath. Then slowly he began to climb.

He wished he could unsheath his broadsword, but decided the weapon would do him little good against a boatload of pirates, which is what he might find at the top. Instead he found the deck still empty. Deciding not to question his good fortune, Keegan leaped over the rail. He made it to the hatch without being detected, and hurried down the ladder.

From the inquiries he had made in the village, he figured Zoë was on board. Which meant she could be anywhere. Keegan let his eyes adjust to the feeble flickers of light thrown off by a taper dripping wax over its wrought-iron holder. If he was holding someone hostage he'd either put them in the hold, or lock them in a cabin.

Keegan just couldn't imagine Zoë amid the bilgewater and rats of the hold so he made his way aft, toward Captain Holt's cabin. Despite his attempts to be quiet, his sea-soaked boots squished with each step. Outside the closed door, Keegan unsheathed his broadsword, then tapped on the door with the hilt.

There was no response. He tapped again. "Zoe."

This was met by a muffled noise he couldn't decipher through the rough-planed boards. His attempt to lift the latch met with no success. The damn thing was locked. Keegan sucked in air and glanced around. Then with as much strength as he had he slammed his shoulder into the door. Once, twice. Till his body ached and the wood splintered. The third time he went sailing into the cabin.

"Zoe?"

She was alone in the room, sitting in a chair. Actually tied to a chair, her hands twisted behind her back, her eyes as big as saucers above the scarf gagging her.

"What the hell?"

Keegan strode toward her, not liking the way she shifted herself as far away as she could. She let out a muffled squeal when he lifted his sword, but sank back in relief when he used it to slice through the ropes. Her wrists were red and welted, and Keegan noticed her staring at them with concern as he jerked off the gag. She swallowed, then worked her jaw from side to side.

"Are ye all right? He did not hurt ye any did he?"

"No." Her voice was rusty with disuse. "Well yes. Look at my arms."

"They'll heal."

"Yes, but . . ." Zoe stifled a sob. "Oh Keegan, you

were so right about him. He's a monster. He took me hostage and . . ." Zoe let her hands slip off the Scot's wet arms where she'd grasped him. "What am I telling you this for? *You* kidnapped me first. *You* threatened to tie me up." She jerked away from him. "What are you doing here anyway?"

"Rescuing you," hardly seemed the appropriate thing to say in light of her accusations . . . her true accusations. Keegan opened his mouth, then shut it, finally blurting out a mixture of fact and fiction. "Ye were my hostage first, and I keep what is mine. Now come on with ye." He paused, cupping her cheek with his hand. "What is it? Ye're as white as the ghosts hauntin' Castle MacLeod."

"I imagine it's because she sees me."

Keegan didn't have to turn to know who that voice belonged to. He took a deep breath, set Zoe aside, and whirled about, broadsword raised. He'd cut the bastard to shreds. However, much of his bravado evaporated when he saw the pistol in Holt's hand. Not to mention the ones held by two other crew members. They were all pointed his way. Hazarding a glance over his shoulder toward Zoe, Keegan let the broadsword clatter to the deck.

It was immediately scooped up by one of the smugglers, an odd-looking little man with ears that stuck out like mushrooms and hair the color of carrots. He spit on the blade, rubbed the spot clean with the arm of his jacket and grinned so wide his cheeks protruded.

"Nice weapon, this."

"Pleased I am that ye approve," Keegan said, his

voice laced with sarcasm. "Now if ye'll be givin' it back to me, my wife and I'll be on our way."

"Your wife, eh?" Holt chortled. "Now that's strange. Lady Zoe gave a completely different tale, didn't you my dear?"

Lady Zoe? The look she gave him was contrite, when his gaze met hers.

"Yes, she was very talkative." The captain strode into the cabin, after first shaking his head at the splintered door. "And the person she spoke of most was you."

"She's a bit touched." Keegan started to lift his finger to his temple, stopping when a pistol was cocked.

"She said you'd say that, didn't you, sweetness?"

"I am not your sweetness."

"That's right. You're Lady Zoe Morgan, sister of Lord Foxworth Morgan, and worth a pretty ransom unless I miss my guess." Holt's teeth gleamed in his swarthy face.

"She's worth nothing to you. Let her go."

"Ah, such chivalrous words, and from one who's worth a tidy sum himself. Isn't that right Lady Zoe?" When Zoe said nothing the captain continued. "As it is, Keegan MacLeod, you've saved me and my men a bit of trouble. We were coming to get you before we sailed. Weren't we, men?"

"Aye, we were at that," answered the tar holding Keegan's broadsword. The other sailor seemed content to let their captain do the talking.

"We thought it only fitting that we return such a savage Jacobite as yourself to the proper authorities in Scotland."

"The truth of it is," the sailor said as he jabbed at Keegan with his own sword, "they don't much care if you're dead or alive."

"My brother wants him alive." Zoe stepped forward, positioning herself between Keegan and his tormentor, ignoring the blade suddenly pointed her way. "There's a feud between the two, and not one that Lord Foxworth wants settled by some pirate . . . or the courts."

"What you're saying Lady Zoe is—"

"Is that your best chance of receiving the most money is to take us both to my brother. Unharmed." Zoe stood as straight and tall as she could, ignoring the crick in her back and shoulders from being subjected to such barbaric treatment as being tied to a chair. Her wrists hurt too, and her jaw was sore. Yes, she certainly had her share of complaints . . . quite legitimate complaints. But they seemed to pale in comparison to the idea of the pirates killing the Scot.

Which was not exactly rational on her part. The man had kidnapped her, threatened her brother, made her life miserable. Still, she couldn't erase from her mind the moment he came exploding through the door, nor the expression on his face when he saw her.

Zoe counted the seconds by the pounding of her pulse as Captain Holt stared, first at her, then Keegan. She could almost hear his mind calculating, weighing his desire to kill Keegan against his lust for money. Greed won . . . at least for the moment.

"Lock them both in the hold while I give this more thought."

* * *

"Would you please stop pacing? You're making my head hurt."

Keegan didn't miss a step, though he did shoot a look over his shoulder toward the woman perched on a coil of rope. A look meant to quell any further comment. He should have known it wouldn't work.

"I should think we're better off now than we were before. Though goodness knows, it is damp in here. And the noxious fumes in this air . . ." Zoe gave a delicate sniff, "can't be good for one's health."

"But then these friends of yours aren't concerned about our *health,* are they?"

"You needn't be so sarcastic. They aren't my—"

At that moment the Scot acquiesced to her wish. He stopped pacing. Right in front of her. With an intensity that made Zoe lean back against the oozing bulkhead, Keegan stared at her.

"*I* should be on me way to Scotland." Keegan plowed fingers through his wet hair, then repeated the words, his voice lower, almost as if he were talking to himself.

"Well, *I* should be ensconced in bed, plumped by goose-down pillows, snuggled beneath a comforter."

" 'Tis not night," Keegan commented absently. He was now, single stubbed candle in hand, examining the boundaries of their prison.

"I know that. My health as it was . . . is . . . I spent a good deal of time in bed."

"Alone? Nay, forget that, of course ye were alone," Keegan said with a wave of his hand. Keegan stopped studying the lock and straightened. "Did not ye get bored with being abed all the time."

"Well yes, I suppose." Zoe drew her knees up, circling them with her arms. "But Miss Phelps said it was for my own good."

"Ah, Miss Phelps."

"Don't say her name that way."

"What way?" Keegan gave the door a hearty kick, regretting it as pain shot through his toes.

"You know what way. Miss Phelps is a dear woman who did her very best to keep me well. You simply don't understand how sick I was . . . am."

"And that's a wonder, since ye've been tellin' me from the moment we met."

"You mean the moment you dragged me from my home." Zoe's hands dropped to grasp the coiled rope, her feet hit the planked deck.

"Aye." Keegan sucked in a deep breath, then let it out slowly. "That probably wasn't the most rational thing I've ever done . . . or the kindest."

Or the kindest? The very idea that he would consider that, surprised Zoe. Taken aback, she was at a loss for words.

Which meant Keegan went back to testing each board in relative quiet, with only the swish slap of the water against the hull for company. He'd about given up, the area certainly seemed to be secure, when the toe of his boot found a soft spot in the wood.

"Come here, Zoe." When she did, Keegan handed her the candle, positioning her so he had the full benefit of its light. He glanced about, his gaze catching on the iron hoop of a broken keg.

"What is it?" Zoe leaned closer.

"I'm not sure yet, but the wood's a wee bit rotted, and I think . . . Aye." Keegan scraped through the board. "We can make ourselves a hole."

"But where does it lead? Do you think we can get off this ship? Hurry, dig faster."

"Hold the light steady, for God's sake. And I don't know where it leads. Most likely another section of the hold."

"So what good will it do us to get there?" Zoe leaned down to better see, then jerked back suddenly. "Ouch!"

"What in the hell is troublin' ye now?"

"Nothing. I'm all right," Zoe said, her voice tight.

"Then move the candle so I can see. And it may help us t' break out of this hold because the next one may not be locked, Lady— All right, tell me what's wrong with ye." Keegan hadn't missed the soft whimpering sound. Elbows on knees he twisted toward her on the balls of his feet. But though he tried to appear concerned about her well-being— she was obviously in some sort of pain—she just kept shaking her head and insisting she was fine.

Finally with a shrug of his shoulders Keegan decided to take her at her word. He angled the pointed end of the barrel hoop toward the bulkhead and shoved forward. Just as she let out a wounded cry.

"Ach, ye're drivin' me mad is what ye're doin'." Keegan pushed to his feet, covering the two paces between them quickly. "Now tell me what's troublin' ye? Did Holt hurt ye, the bastard?"

"No." Zoe tried to take a backward step but his

hand shot out, grabbing her arm. The candle flame flickered.

"Then what?"

"I've . . . I've a sliver in my eye."

"A sliver?"

"Yes." Zoe blinked, wincing at the pain. "A splinter of wood flew up."

"And landed in yer eye."

Zoe nodded, then swiped at the tears that rolled from her left eye.

"Let me take a look."

"No." She cringed back. "It will be fine, really."

"I'll get it out for ye."

"It's—"

"For God's sake, Zoe, give me the candle."

"Nothing," Zoe whispered as Keegan took the light from her hand and set it on a barrel. Then he pulled her close to it, positioning her so that he could peer down into her eye.

"Is it this one?"

"Yes." Zoe's voice was little more than a breath of air. He touched her cheekbone, pressing the skin down, then pulled away to wipe his hands down the side of his damp breeches. When his fingers grazed her face again he leaned closer, so close that she could see the prisms of green and gold that colored his eyes.

Zoe swallowed. "Can you see anything?"

How could he possibly concentrate on some tiny speck in her eye when her fragrance perfumed the air? Even in this dank boat hull, with tar and bilge-water seeping through every beam, the gentle smell of roses filled his senses.

And her skin. He had no idea it was so incredibly soft. He closed the distance between them, making no more pretense at looking at her eye. It was her mouth that drew him. Soft. Pink. Inviting.

She tilted her head up, her gaze catching his before he dropped it again to her mouth. Then her lips parted and Keegan was lost.

The kiss was tentative at first, a mere mingling of breath, a petal-soft touch. Then Keegan grasped her head, curving his fingers through her hair, pulling her more tightly against him. Zoe gasped when his tongue slid over hers. But it was such a warm, wonderful feeling she forgot to protest.

She'd never been kissed before. Not like this. Fox kissed her on the cheek, of course, and sometimes if he was being solicitous on the forehead. But that was nothing . . . nothing like this. Zoe could drown in this. She could float about light-headed, her body nothing but warm mush. She could swell, and swoon . . . and ache.

"What is it lass?" Keegan's voice was gruff as he gazed at her through a sensual fog. She pushed at his arms. He'd been aware enough to notice that, but not much more.

Now she looked up at him, her eyes misty and unfocused . . . as if she might be ill.

"I . . . think I may faint." Now that his arms no longer held her upright, Zoe thought it a distinct possibility. "And . . ." She folded her arms low over her abdomen. "There's this dreadful pain."

"Pain?" Keegan took her elbow and guided her toward her barrel seat.

"Yes, it's like—" Zoe clamped her mouth shut.

She almost told him of the pains she experienced during her monthly cycle. "I've had them before." She waved her hand hoping he would turn away. What if it was time for her cramps? How could she endure them without Miss Phelps?

"Well, I best get back to me hole." Keegan gave her one last look before retrieving the candle and makeshift tool. Lord, she was a strange one. Not that he wasn't in some pain himself. That kiss had sent a surge of energy to his groin that still kept it stiff. But that kind of ache was to be expected, even anticipated, if there was some relief to be had. Which of course in this case there was not.

Keegan hacked away at the opening, then using his hands, tore away a piece of the rotted wood. One more hunk and it was large enough for him to crawl through. He was so excited Keegan didn't notice at first that Zoe was back, holding the candle and craning her neck to see.

Keegan glanced back at her. "What of yer eye?"

"My eye? Oh, 'tis much better." Actually, Zoe hadn't given it a thought since he kissed her. She blinked several times to make certain there was no pain. Then with a half smile she shrugged her shoulders, bobbing the light from the candle.

"What are we going to do?" She hoped he thought to include her in whatever he was planning. Despite her fear of him—Zoe paused, did she actually fear him—she couldn't help think herself better off with the Scot than the pirates. At least he never gagged her.

"Here ye go, hand me the candle."

Reluctantly Zoe held the foul-smelling, sputtering

wax toward him. Was he going to leave her here in the dark then? But before she could ask, he motioned for her to follow, then crouched down to squeeze through the hole, into the darkness.

"I've a thought we should hurry before they—"

Keegan's words were cut off as the sloop listed to one side then jerked back.

"Before they what?" Zoe grabbed hold of a barrel. "What's happening?"

Keegan let out a curse before standing upright. "Before we sail, goddamn it. Which is exactly what's goin' on now."

"What shall we do?"

"Hurry. We'll go on deck and jump overboard and swim for— What in the hell are you yankin' on my arm for?"

"Hush." Zoe cocked her head to the side. "I think I hear someone coming."

"Blast it all to hell." Keegan heard it, too. Two, maybe three men were approaching the hold's door. He could hear voices now, and one of them was Holt. "Here, help me move the keg over to cover this hole."

"Shouldn't we climb through and run?"

"They'd catch us before we got to the hatch." The keg slid across the deck with a scraping noise. "Cry."

"What?" Zoe huffed out her breath. She wasn't used to moving heavy objects.

"Cry. Make noise. Whine." Keegan no sooner got the last word out than she was flopped on the coil of hemp seemingly weeping her eyes out. She sniffed. She whimpered. She made enough racket to cover any noise Keegan made with the keg. He'd just covered his tracks by swiping the dirt about on the deck when captain Holt shoved open the door.

He held a pistol, as did his companion. They were both pointed at Keegan.

"Christ. Doesn't that woman ever shut up? I should have given you a gag for her."

Zoe sucked in her breath, made a show of mopping her eyes, and quieted her sobbing. She didn't want that filthy rag stuffed in her mouth again.

"Just thought you might like to know we've set sail for Scotland," Holt said leaning against the door and looking quite pleased with himself. "In less than a sennight we'll be collecting a tidy ransom for handing you both over to Lord Foxworth." He paused, chuckling. "We might even stay around a bit to see you hang from the nearest gibbet."

"I think I'd like ta see that, Cap'n," the other man said, rubbing his jaw.

"In the meanwhile you two just make yourselves as comfortable as you can." Both pirates were laughing as they shut the door. The unmistakable grating of a key in the lock followed.

When the last echo of their bootfalls disappeared, Zoe leaped up from her perch. "Shouldn't we hurry?"

" 'Tis too late."

"Too late? But what of our escape? Jumping from the boat?" Zoe stood hands upon hips wondering what was keeping him from reacting.

"We be too far from land by now to do aught but drownd ourselves." Which wasn't exactly true. Keegan imagined he could manage the rough swim.

But Zoe never would. He was surprised she'd accomplished the walk across the gangplank without spraining her foot.

Whether he liked it or not, Keegan felt responsible for her. He should never have kidnapped her in the first place. That was evident almost from the beginning. But as much as he loathed her brother . . . hated him for the death his father endured . . . Zoe wasn't to blame.

Perhaps he should be glad for the turn events had taken. Captain Holt didn't know it but he was giving Keegan what he wanted at the moment, a fast trip to Scotland. The accommodations were somewhat lacking, of course, but with the hole in the bulwark, Keegan might be able to augment whatever the good captain felt compelled to give them in way of food.

Of course once they arrived in Scotland, Keegan would have to manage to escape before being handed over to Foxworth. But that shouldn't be too difficult . . . as long as no one discovered he wasn't really a prisoner.

Aye, things had worked out fairly well . . . except that he was bound to spend the next seven days with a woman who was slowly driving him insane . . . not to mention wild. But he'd control his lust. Keegan glanced over at her . . . somehow.

She was staring at him, her eyes wide, her lips parted. "I don't understand how you can be so complacent," she said with a huff.

"And I don't know why ye're so worried. Yer brother will pay the ransom." And then he'd be rid of her and she'd be safe. Keegan's eyes narrowed.

She was a bothersome woman. What if Foxworth was as callous toward her as he was with his word? "Won't he?"

"Yes. Yes, of course he would."

"Would? Ye mean will, don't ye?"

"Will."

She was biting at her bottom lip in that way that Keegan had come to realize meant there was something amiss. He approached to within inches of her. "Zoe? What is it yer not tellin' me?"

"Well . . ." She let the word expand while the hair on the back of Keegan's neck stood on end. "You know when I told you Fox was in Scotland?"

"Aye."

"I told Captain Holt the same thing."

"So?"

"I told him that after I realized he wasn't to be trusted."

"And?"

"I don't know for certain where Fox is."

Eight

As imprisonment went, Keegan had endured worse.

Actually, there were times he found this particular confinement rather enjoyable. Of course it helped that he wasn't truly confined at all.

The first night, after he and Zoe had been rationed a half trencher of pease and hardtack, Keegan crept through the hole, listening as he went to Zoe's warnings to be careful. Security on the *Sea Maiden* was, to say the least, lax. With a minimum of stealth Keegan managed to pilfer extra food and candles from what served as the sloop's galley.

Once back inside the hold, after the barrel had been rolled back to conceal the escape hole, Keegan unwrapped his prize. Though she oohed and aahed over his bravery, Zoe assured Keegan the greasy mutton would make her ill. She wouldn't do more than nibble a few bites till hunger got the best of her. Keegan watched as she tucked away a joint of meat.

"What is it?" Zoe glanced toward the Scot and swallowed. He watched her, an amused expression on his face.

"Not a thing." Having nothing else, Keegan used the back of his hand to wipe his mouth . . . and hide the smile. " 'Tis only surprised I am that a slip of a thing like ye can pack away food like a foot-soldier."

Embarrassment pinkened Zoe's cheeks. "I was hungry."

"Which is not a bad thing."

"Perhaps." Zoe wiped her fingers down the seam of her skirt. "But I shall pay for eating such rough fare. Miss Phelps was quite adamant about my diet." Leaning her head against the bulkhead, Zoe sighed. "I dare say I feel a bit indisposed even now."

But though she tried to conjure up a distress of the stomach, Zoe could not. She admitted, to herself at least, that she felt very well.

The second night out to sea Keegan grew bolder. He raided the galley, but then he crept along the passageway and entered captain Holt's cabin. With only a sliver of moonlight to guide him, Keegan found his broadsword and two pistols. Grinning, feeling like one of the ghosts of Castle MacLeod, Keegan took his booty back to the hold.

Zoe was impressed when he showed her, but wary. "Won't Captain Holt notice them gone?"

"Aye," Keegan chuckled. " 'Tis more than likely."

"But what if he suspects—"

"Us?" Keegan lifted a dark brow. "I imagine we'd be the last on this vessel he'd think would be stealin' from him. We're prisoners or have ye forgotten?"

Which Zoe had to admit made sense in a way. So she watched as Keegan secreted his weapons in an empty keg, and ate the boiled fish and biscuits. Despite her laments to the contrary, it settled quite well on her stomach.

As a matter of fact, despite not seeing the sun for several days, Zoe felt better than she had for years. Even the swaying of the sloop didn't make her nauseous as she thought it would. Nor did the lack of being bled cause her any discomfort with her rigid vessels.

She felt so well that on the third night as Keegan was sliding the barrel away from his exit hole, she cleared her throat. "I'd like to go, too."

"Are ye daft? 'Tis no place for a woman. There be dangers at every turn."

"You said it was easy as fooling a Sassenach."

"Did I now?" Keegan had to grin as she stood before him so seriously nodding her head.

"Yes. And I am so tired of being locked up in this place, despite the extra food and blankets you've secured."

"Being locked up is no fun, I'll admit."

"How long were you . . . imprisoned, I mean?" Zoe didn't know what made her ask. After all it was a point rather left undiscussed.

"Long enough to not wish it on me worst enemy." He took her hand. "Come on with ye then. But mind, ye must be quiet and stay close."

Zoe nodded, not trusting herself to speak as she bent over and maneuvered through the hole. The hold into which she stepped was dark and foul-smelling. Her fingers clutched the Scot's hand, as she shuffled along behind him.

"Where are we going?"

"Hush with ye."

"But I can't see. Can you?"

"Nay." Keegan paused and felt her bump into his

back. "But I've managed t' find me way before, so if ye'll kindly be quiet . . ."

"Yes, of course." Zoe resisted the urge to speak again as they crept into the passageway and up the ladder. The occasional lantern, oscillating with the sway of the vessel made it possible to see now.

On deck Keegan motioned for her to follow, so Zoe lifted her skirts and darted toward the mast. Several pirates lay about, flat on their backs, snoring. None appeared to notice Zoe or her companion.

Zoe flattened herself against the mast. "Shouldn't we tie them up? . . . or shoot them?" she whispered.

"Shoot them? My, my, but we're a bloodthirsty little thing."

Zoe felt her face flush. "Well, they did kidnap us."

Keegan lifted his brows. "Remind me t' sleep with one eye open from now on."

"You know what I mean. Who knows what they might do to us?"

"For the moment nothing. Not as long as Holt thinks there be coin t' be had. Besides, I don't think we could sail this vessel by ourselves. And we do have an advantage or two the crew does not know about." Keegan patted the pistol stuck in his waistband.

That said, he led the way toward the small area used by the crew to cook their meals.

Tonight the pirates had feasted on a stew of sorts, salty, but, Zoe had to admit, tasty. She squatted in the shadows and ate while the Scot looked about for something to drink. He found a jug, took a swig, then offered it to Zoe.

"Mmmm, no," she said around a mouthful of stew. "It wouldn't agree with me, I'm sure."

Keegan's grin was sly. "Now, that's where ye be wrong, lass. I've a feelin' it would help yer digestion quite a bit."

"Do you think so?"

"I've no doubt in the matter."

The hand that reached up was tentative. "I suppose a little drink won't hurt." But the swallow she took was more like a gulp.

Keegan stooped, pulling her against his chest to muffle the sound of her sputtering coughs.

"That's . . . awful," she finally managed. "I feel as if I'm on fire."

"Well now, it does have a bite. Nothin' so smooth as good Scotch whiskey. But it's a mite better the more ye drink."

"That hardly seems possible," Zoe said. As if to prove her point she took another drink. This time she only coughed once and blinked back tears. The third swig was only followed by a grin.

"That be enough for ye, I'll warrant," Keegan said as he pried the jug from her fingers. "We need to be gettin' below before one of these bloody pirates is awakened by the call of nature."

"What about Holt?"

"What about him?" Keegan pulled Zoe to her feet, wondering if he should just toss her over his shoulder. Her speech was slurred enough to wonder if her balance was in jeopardy.

"I thought we were going to sneak into his cabin." This was followed by a giggle.

"Well, lass, ye thought wrong. Come on with ye."

"But you did." Zoe resisted the tug of his hand on her wrist. "I want to tie him up. And gag him."

"Not tonight."

"Then when?" Zoe jerked her hand away and folded her arms. Her chin shot up stubbornly.

"For God's sake Zoe! We can't take over the ship now. We're too far from land."

Obviously that was the wrong thing to say to her, for before Keegan knew what she was about, Zoe darted across the deck. She was leaning over the rail, searching the darkness when he wrapped his arm about her waist.

"Bloody hell, are ye tryin' to give me heart failure?" Keegan turned her in his arms, studying her upturned face in the slice of moonlight. Her eyes sparkled with excitement. Her mouth, that mouth he couldn't seem to eradicate from his thoughts, curved upward at the corners. She seemed alive and desirable and he worked to retain his annoyance.

"I knew this was a bad idea," he mumbled, not certain whether he meant allowing her to accompany him on deck, or kidnapping her in the first place. Or any of the multitude of inclinations he'd had in the interim. Just the memory of what he'd endured because of her made his scowl deepen.

Zoe didn't notice. "Would it really give you heart failure?" Her smile never faltered though her large innocent eyes widened.

"What are ye prattlin' on about lass?" Keegan tried to pull away but somehow her arms had worked their way about his neck.

"If I fell over the side? Would you be heartbroken?"

The question was asked without guile, and for a moment Keegan considered answering it in kind. Of course he'd be heartbroken. Despite her annoying habits, of which there were many, he'd come to like Zoe—like and desire.

But he had to remember his purpose in kidnapping her in the first place. No matter how fond he might be of her, it was avenging his father that mattered most.

Keegan tried to ignore the collapse of her smile as he muttered something about needing her to flush out her brother. "Come on with ye." It wasn't necessary to disengage her arms. They now hung limply at her side. Keegan grabbed her hand, dragging her back toward the galley. She stood quietly still while he quickly wrapped the jug and foodstuff in his jacket and tossed it over his shoulder.

What was wrong with her?

Zoe blinked, trying to focus her mind, but found nothing but blurred images. Had she just wrapped her arms around the Scot? It didn't seem possible, yet her hands seemed to tingle, and the feel of his tousled hair seemed real.

Zoe pushed that disquieting thought aside and tried to concentrate on what she was doing. Basically, she was placing one foot in front of the other as the Scot led her across the deck. Why was she following him? He'd kidnapped her from her home. But then he did seem the lesser of two evils, she remembered as the prone form of a snoring pirate caught her eye.

Actually it was the tar's knife that truly snagged her interest. It was broad, tapering to an evil-looking point. It was just the type of weapon she needed if she ever hoped to gain her freedom from *both* her kidnappers.

Yes, she would secret it beneath her skirts. Save it for a time when she could use it. On the Scot? Biting her lip Zoe stared at the broad back of Keegan MacLeod. Could she ever plunge a blade into his flesh? She'd just begun turning the question over in her groggy head when his fingers let loose of her hand.

Zoe lunged to the side, nearly tripping over the sleeping pirate's legs. Ignoring his stench she grabbed for the carved knife handle just as his eyes opened.

He looked at her, and she at him. Then they both let out a yell.

Zoe's was cut short as she was unceremoniously tossed over a shoulder. Blood rushed to her head, confusing her already rum-soaked mind. But she managed to hang onto the knife as she was bounced and jostled down the ladder. Darkness overpowered her as Keegan rushed through the outer hold. Then she was being pushed and shoved into the small compartment being used as their gaol.

She was none too gently flattened onto the straw and ordered to stay put, in a gruff whisper. Too afraid to do anything but, Zoe watched wide-eyed as the Scot pried open a barrel, tossed his booty inside and slammed the lid back on. Then he covered the escape hole, kicked straw about, blew out the sputtering nub of a candle and plopped down on the floor beside her.

It wasn't until she felt his weight pressing into her side that Zoe remembered to bury the knife beneath the straw. Any sound she made was drowned out by the grating of the key in the lock.

"Don't utter a word," Keegan hissed into her ear as his fingers worked on the buttons of her bodice. He heard her sharp intake of breath when his hand clamped over her breast, the soft moan when his lips covered hers.

Then the door slammed open and light filled the hold.

"What the hell?" Keegan did his best to sound disgruntled. His hand lifted to shade his eyes and he counted two pirates plus their captain.

"There she is, Cap'n, just like I told ya."

"Actually you said she was on deck." Holt's gaze traveled over Zoe. "Which she obviously is not."

"I'm tellin' ye, Cap'n, she was there. Stole me knife she did."

"What's this all about?" Keegan pushed to his feet, wishing now he hadn't opened Zoe's bodice. Captain Holt couldn't keep his eyes off the V of the shift that covered her breasts.

"Reggis here claims he saw Lady Zoe on deck."

Keegan snorted. "Takin' the night air, was she?"

"She was stealing me knife and scarin' me half out of me wits. When I woke—"

"Ye were asleep? On watch?" Keegan arched a brow as the tar turned crimson beneath his weather darkened skin.

"Just restin' me eyes if truth be known."

"I'd say 'tis more like dreamin' of beautiful ladies."

The third pirate, the one named Stancil, snickered, then laughed aloud, earning himself a punch in the side from Reggis.

"I weren't dreamin' I tell ya, she was there."

"Aw, come on Reggis, ya can see she's here havin' herself a little rough and tumble with the Scotsman."

"I'm tellin' ya she was—"

"Enough!" The captain's voice thundered off the beams. "Search the hold."

"You're wasting your time." Zoe rose, brushing straw from her skirt. She ignored her gaping bodice as she faced Captain Holt. "I can tell you all you need to know."

"Zoe." Keegan reached toward her but she stepped out of his grasp. A cold wash of impending doom flowed over him.

"Can you now?"

"Yes." Zoe straightened her back. "If I'd been on deck with a knife you'd be dead, your throat slit from ear to ear." She shifted her gaze. "And that goes for every one of you."

Keegan suppressed a grin as he watched the captain's face go pale, then scarlet. His eyes narrowed, then with a sweep of his arm he ordered the other two to follow him from the hold. "It's too dark tonight, but in the morning I'm sending someone down here to go over every inch of this hold."

Keegan waited for the door to slam and the lock to rattle before letting out his breath. After lighting the candle he pried open the barrel and reached for the jug. He took a swig before he passed it to Zoe, who still stood facing the door.

"What are we going to do?" she asked. Without

turning around she accepted the jug and took a deep drink. "They'll find the hole if they really look."

"That they will."

"Well then?" Zoe faced him. "What are we to do?"

Keegan took another drink before passing the jug. "It seems t' me *we* should have thought of that before wakin' one of the pirates."

"I . . . I tripped over his legs."

His expression registered doubt. "Where's the knife, Zoe?"

"What knife?"

"The one that fish bait Reggis was squealin' about. The one ye stole from him."

"There's no knife. You heard the captain. He most likely dreamed the whole thing."

"That was me sayin' that and ye and I know he didn't dream any of it." In two strides he was beside her. "Have ye got it hidden in yer skirts?"

"No. Stop it. What are you doing?"

"Searchin' ye like those bloody pirates should have done." Keegan sifted through layers of petticoats with one hand while the other warded off her flailing hands. "What were ye plannin'? To stick a knife in my ribs while I lay sleepin'?"

"No." Zoe tried pulling away. His palms were curved around her thigh, following it down to the top of her stockings and back. "Will you stop! It isn't there."

Keegan let his fingers linger. "Well now, I can't tell that." He shifted his palm to the warmth between her legs. "Where is it?"

"I don't have a knife."

His thumb inched up. "Zoe?"

"I don't . . ." Zoe sucked in her breath as he moved ever closer to the spot where heat speared painfully. "It's in the straw," she blurted out. Her breathing was shallow, but no more so than his.

There was a moment when Zoe thought neither of them cared about the knife anymore. He looked at her and she looked at him and the heat between her legs seemed to warm the air between them. Zoe remembered how on deck she'd wanted him to kiss her and her lips parted.

Then he stepped back. Her petticoats fell to curtain her legs.

"Where in the straw?" he asked, but he was already kicking about. When he heard the scrape of the blade on wood, he smiled, then bent over to retrieve the knife. "Now Zoe, I think I'll keep this, if ye don't mind."

"But I do." Which was a silly thing to say, for it was obvious he didn't really care what she thought or wanted. In disgust Zoe picked up the jug and took a big swallow. Then another. "I still don't know what you plan to do in the morn when they come searching."

"Nor do I." Keegan stuck the knife in his boot. "Perhaps we shall have to slit all their throats tonight. It was a jest, Zoe," Keegan added when she went pale. "Though goodness knows, ye be the one who suggested it."

"I don't think I really could. Despite what I said to Captain Holt." She took another swig. "What is it like to kill a man?"

Keegan slid down the bulkhead till he sat in the straw. He looked away. "Not something I would recommend."

"But you want to kill my brother."

His stare found hers. "Aye. For as hard as it is to kill 'tis harder still to watch those ye love suffer."

She was treading on dangerous ground. Zoe knew that. Yet she wanted to know. After all this time she wanted to hear what Keegan thought her brother had done. She took another fortifying swig. "Tell me," was all she said and passed the jug to him.

Keegan swirled the liquor around then took a swallow. "They were dying all around me. My brothers. All three of them died that morning." He shook his head. "Why I lived t' tell of it is beyond my ken. But it was only me left to protect our da, and me that failed him.

"It was a battle."

When he looked up, Zoe continued. "I've read of it in the newspaper. You couldn't have saved your father." She took another drink. "So many men died."

"Aye, honorable deaths. That I could have accepted . . . for him . . . for me. But I listened t' yer brother and handed over my sword. And watched as they tortured my da. Watched while they stripped him naked and sliced through his flesh. And all the while I tried to get loose and kill them."

Zoe watched his hands clench, then took another swallow. "I don't believe . . . Fox wouldn't do that. He wouldn't torture an old man. He just wouldn't."

Keegan leaned his head against the bulkhead and shut his eyes. "Believe what ye like."

"I will." Zoe pushed onto her knees. "You don't know Fox. You don't—"

"That's the funny thing." He looked at her from under heavy lids. "I thought I did." He shook his head. "When I first saw him it was as if he and I . . ." With a self-disgusted shake of his head Keegan continued. "As if I had known him before. 'Tis why I trusted him. 'Tis why I must have my revenge."

His words vibrated through her and for the first time she felt niggling fissures of doubt. Could Fox have done something so heinous? Again Zoe reached for the jug.

"He was the only one who ever cared about me," she said after lifting a corner of her skirt to blot at the rum dripping from her chin. "Except Miss Phelps, of course."

"Of course."

His tone made Zoe look up. Her eyes were narrowed . . . and slightly unfocused. "I can't understand what you have against Miss Phelps. She was . . . is a saint. She took care of me night and day, seeing that I never had to so much as lift a finger . . . for as long as I can remember."

"She also fed ye nothin' but broth, and saw ye were bled regularly. Don't forget that."

"It was for my own good," Zoe said, but with less conviction than previously. To blur her own doubts Zoe took another gulp.

"What of yer mother and father?" Keegan asked, then added. "Ye might wish t' be careful with the rum. 'Tis fairly strong."

"I'm fine. Never better." Zoe shrugged. "My parents died when I was nine. But even before that I didn't see them much. I really was ill most of the time." When he didn't argue with her, Zoe took another drink and continued. "My brother became the Earl of Werwick then."

"Foxworth?"

"No," Zoe giggled. "My brother Dalton. He's a prig." Her lashes drifted down as her head lolled back against the bulkhead. "Not like Fox at all." She didn't say anything for a long time and then her eyes opened and her gaze met Keegan's. "I am sorry about your father . . . and your brothers."

Zoe watched him take a deep breath and nod. He looked so sad she wished she could console him somehow. But she was afraid that wasn't possible.

"Keegan."

"Aye."

"I know you think I . . . I exaggerate about being sick." Zoe struggled to her feet. "But I think . . . I think this time I really am." She just managed to make it to the corner before heaving up all the food and rum she'd consumed.

Nine

"Zoe."

"Ohhh. Please, let me die in peace."

"Zoe, for God's sake get up with ye."

"I can't." With a moan Zoe slitted open her eyes. Her tormentor squatted beside her, shaking her shoulder, making the nausea worse. "I know you think this is my imagination . . . but it isn't. I'm really going to die this time."

Keegan braced himself against the ship's roll, cursing under his breath when he lost his balance, falling against Zoe. "There's a storm. From the feel of it the *Sea Maiden* isn't faring well."

"I'm dying I tell you." Zoe gave him a feeble shove, then groaned. "I think I shall be sick again."

"Here." Dragging her up, bending her across his stabilizing arm, Keegan held Zoe. But she only gagged a few times, then fluttered her hand to indicate she was finished. "Do ye feel any better?" Keegan pulled her against his body.

"No." The room tilted and Zoe grabbed her head. "I'm dying I tell you."

"I've no doubt ye feel like it. Perhaps even wish ye were. But 'tis just the price ye pay for drinkin' strong spirits."

"But I didn't—"

"Ach, but ye did."

Zoe blinked. She vaguely remembered bringing the jug's mouth to her own . . . often. But surely she hadn't been drunk. "I have to lie down."

"Ye can't. We need to get above deck."

"But—"

"Zoe, for the love of God, look at me." He swung her round to face him just as the timbers groaned and the deck heaved. They both flew against the bulkhead in a tumble of petticoats and legs. Keegan quickly sat up, bracing himself and Zoe for the violent lurch as the *Sea Maiden* righted itself in the roiling surf.

It never came.

"What is it? What's wrong?" Zoe scrambled to her feet, her queasy head and stomach momentarily forgotten.

"I'm not sure." Keegan clawed at the barrel top. The two pistols, he jammed in his waistband—the broadsword, he strapped about his middle. "Come on with ye," he yelled as he rolled the barrel away from the escape hole.

"Won't they see us?" Zoe hesitated for a moment. "It's daylight." She doubled over to push through the hole. "I'm so sick," she muttered, but by this time she realized the Scot was paying her no mind. As she stepped into the main hold she realized why.

Briny water lapped around her knees, soaking her skirts. And it seemed to be rising as she stared down at it.

"Come on." The Scot grabbed her hand, nearly pulling her arm from its socket. She had no choice but to follow as he sloshed through the chilly water, fighting past the floating debris.

In the eerie light streaming in from above, the ladder speared out of the water at an awkward angle. Zoe wasn't sure how they reached it, for the water seemed to rise faster than they could move. She tripped once, going under the water before the Scot could pull her up. Soaked, hair plastered to her head, Zoe trudged through water, waist-deep now.

"Can ye swim?"

"What?" Zoe spit out salty water, then coughed, finally realizing what he said. "No! No."

Water splashed down the hatch in waves. The Scot pushed her in front of him, latching her fingers around the rung. "Hold on," he yelled, his face close to hers. Still, she could barely hear his words. Above her the sea roared, and the wind screamed.

And the ship groaned.

Then just as her toe caught hold of a ladder rung, a deafening cracking noise sounded. It was followed by a violent lurch that pried Zoe's fingers from the splintery wood and sent her sailing through the air. She landed with a splash, having no time to do more than gasp a startled breath before sinking beneath the dark water.

"Damnation!" Keegan grabbed for Zoe with one hand, managing somehow to hang onto the ladder with the other. The damn ship was breaking to pieces, seawater pouring through tears in the hull. He'd lived on the rock-strewn Scottish coast long enough to know it wouldn't take long before they sank. His only chance was to get above deck . . . immediately.

With a curse he jumped into the swell of water filling the hold. It was too deep to stand, too murky to see. Keegan dove beneath the surface where he'd seen Zoe sink, feeling his way to the tilted deck, pushing off the bottom when his lungs screamed for air. He jackknifed under again, and this time his fingers tangled with something long and silky.

Zoe's hair.

With all his strength Keegan kicked, surging toward the surface, pulling Zoe with him. His mouth broke clear and Keegan gulped air as he shoved Zoe out of the briny water. An empty keg floated by and Keegan managed to curve her arms under his about the rounded sides.

She was pale in the watery light and Keegan tried not to believe the worst as he scissor-kicked toward the ladder.

The sloop was in constant motion, jerking this way and that, with explosive noises that sounded like the felling of giant trees. Keegan had seen the rocks work their destruction before. With the white-tipped waves crashing over them the hard granite outcrops near the shore were deadly. And quick.

Time was of the essence if they were to have any chance of survival. Keegan blinked water from his eyes and glanced toward Zoe as he maneuvered her, floating atop the barrel toward the ladder.

Had he been foolish to jump in the water after her? Undoubtedly. Keegan reached for a splintery rung. But then no more so than he'd been with everything else he'd done since first laying eyes on her.

Pulling himself onto the ladder with one hand,

Keegan managed to yank Zoe free of the barrel. As he did she coughed, a sound that lifted his spirits a bit. "Come on with ye now, lass," he muttered between his teeth as he strained to lift her toward him. Despite her slender size she was heavy, her clothes waterlogged and her limbs little more than dead weight.

He finally managed to rest her, leaning against the ladder, then heave her over his shoulder. She coughed again, a gurgling sound, that grew more intense as he shifted her body. Then as quickly as he could, Keegan scrambled up the ladder. With each step the wobbly structure groaned. When he was but two steps from the waterlashed deck, the sloop jerked violently.

Pain rattled through his body as he slapped against the ladder, clinging with fingers and toes to the splintery wood. Zoe's body shifted, and Keegan lifted his shoulder, trying to keep her perched, swearing he would not go after her again if she slipped down into the water.

His muscles straining, Keegan pulled her up through the hatch. The deck was slick, awash in saltwater, and tilted at near a forty-five-degree angle. Getting off the sloop had to be his first priority. He slid Zoe down, wedging them both in the lee formed by the side of the quarterdeck.

"Zoe!" Keegan yelled her name above the fury of the storm. "Wake up, damn ye." Squatting down he cradled her head, turning it to the side when she started coughing again. Her body shook with spasms as she retched out seawater.

"Can ye hear me, lass?" Keegan gave her a moment—all he could spare—to rest before pulling her to sitting. "Zoe? Are ye well enough to move?"

Well enough to move? She was well enough to do nothing but die. Zoe didn't think she'd ever been so ill in her short sickly life. Her throat burned. Her chest felt as if a knife had plunged inside to cut out her weak heart. And her head felt as if it might explode.

This was it then. She was going to die. Somehow she'd never pictured her demise in quite this fashion, with water pelting her face and the wind roaring in her ears. But here it was. Zoe opened her mouth to tell the Scot of her impending death but nothing came out of her tortured throat but an inaudible croak

Which apparently the Scot took as her agreement that she could move, for with one jerk he had her standing. Or actually leaning, for the *Sea Maiden* was tilted at such an angle that Zoe couldn't understand why it didn't sink. That is, until Keegan dragged her toward the side and she saw the rocks. They seemed to be all that kept the battered vessel afloat.

"Croak. Squeak." Zoe lifted her arm, pointing toward the spot where the jagged rocks tore into the hull.

"I don't see any lifeboats. We'll have t' swim for the shore."

Swim? Was he mad? First of all Zoe couldn't see a shore. Nothing but rocks and wild surf that were grinding the boat to firewood. Secondly, as she'd already proven, she couldn't swim. "Croak. Croak. Squeak!" Zoe shook her head wildly, and tried again to speak, but the Scot wasn't looking at her.

Wiping hair and water from her eyes, Zoe followed his stare and saw the ghostly figure of Captain Holt standing not two rods away. One arm hugged the mast, still standing, though perched at an angle as if aiming toward the horizon. In his other hand he held a sword.

"Get back below. You're my prisoners," he yelled.

"Are ye daft? We need to get off this sloop before there be nothing left of her."

Zoe tried to swallow but couldn't, as the Scot started inching her along toward the raised sword.

"The *Sea Maiden*'s a fine vessel. She'll weather this storm. See if she doesn't."

Zoe's scream was a strangled squeak as Captain Holt let go of the mast and lurched toward them. He fell just as a giant wave crashed over the hull, washing him toward the edge.

The schooner groaned. A loud cracking sound erupted. The deck vibrated and split open. Zoe looked at Keegan. He looked at her. Before she could utter a sound to stop him, he ran, pulling her toward the spot where Captain Holt was swept away. Hand clasped with hers, he jumped over the side into the dark oblivion of the churning sea.

He disliked nearly everything about Colonel Upton—had since the first time their paths crossed, nearly two years before. The colonel postured now, leaning back in the carved chair and stared at Fox over the rim of his glass of claret.

"I'm surprised to see you return. I'd have sworn

your departure had all the earmarks of finality stamped to it."

Fox shifted his weight, refusing to ask permission to sit, from this puffed-up prig. He had his reasons for returning; as he'd had them for leaving. "I assume you've read my orders." Fox nodded toward the parchment recently removed from its leather case.

"Oh, I've read them. But frankly, Major Morgan, I'm baffled."

Fox resisted the urge to say he wasn't surprised. "I'd be glad to clear up any mystery."

"Would you now?" The colonel's lips toyed with the goblet rim before sipping. "Perhaps we should begin with why you find it necessary to rejoin your regiment. You were quite adamant, if I recall, about leaving His Majesty's service."

Not His Majesty's service. Simply Colonel Upton's. Unfortunately at Fort William in the Scottish Highland they were one and the same. Fox stiffened his spine. He'd known this would be unpleasant. It was a price he was willing to pay. And in the end he knew Upton had no choice but to accept him. "I've been assigned to command a small company to track down the Jacobite rebel, Keegan MacLeod." The order was signed by the Duke of Cumberland, the king's son.

"Ah, yes, I heard he'd escaped the noose. Crafty fellow, that. But what makes you think he'd come anywhere near here? If he had an ounce of sense he'd be long gone across the channel to join his prince in exile."

"The Highlands are his home." And Miss Phelps

had told him, once he'd calmed the woman down enough to make any sense of her. But Fox didn't feel it necessary to tell Upton of Zoe and her abduction. "Castle MacLeod is his family seat."

"No longer. All property belonging to the rebels was confiscated. He has nothing here. Nothing but a date with the hangman."

"I don't think MacLeod will see it that way."

Upton emptied his glass, wiping his mouth with a lace edged handkerchief. "You speak as if you know the man."

"We've met."

The colonel's forehead wrinkled in inquiry.

"Immediately following the battle at Culloden. MacLeod surrendered himself and his father to me."

"Ah yes, I do recall something of that. I believe you mentioned the episode during your . . . rather lengthy recital of reasons for resigning your commission."

"I never resigned."

"No, of course not. You simply rushed home to the family estate to lick your wounds. Did you ever reconcile yourself to the fact that battles involve killing, Major?"

Fox's jaw ached from the strain of keeping it clenched. He longed to give the colonel a similar pain, one caused by slamming his fist into the man's ruddy face. But he'd already burned bridges that he was now forced to repair. "Yes sir," he said through his teeth. "I've reconciled myself to what happened at Culloden." To the unnecessary killing after the battle. To the rape and slaughter he'd been unable to stop. That Colonel Upton had watched with an amused eye.

Candlelight from the chandelier overhead gleamed on the colonel's gorget as he leaned forward. "Are you certain you're up to finding this renegade if he is in Scotland?"

"I'm sure." Fox had been a soldier for twelve years and his honor and bravery had never been questioned before. It galled him now.

"You seemed to show signs of sympathy for the rebel, if I recall."

"I'd pity any man forced to watch the slaughter of his father . . . sir."

"His father was a rebel leader."

"And as such deserved to be tried, not disemboweled for the entertainment of the troops."

"You forget yourself, Major."

Fox tried to calm the anger surging through him. Antagonizing Upton was not to his benefit. "I apologize sir. If there's nothing else, I've had a long journey."

"Of course." Upton flitted his fingers. "You will keep me informed as you hunt down the renegade?"

"Yes sir." Fox turned on his heel and left the room. He didn't stop walking until he reached the gates of Fort William. He faced north toward the base of Ben Nevis, toward the Highlands. Where Keegan MacLeod was, or would be soon. He'd lay his life on it.

Closing his eyes, Fox rubbed a hand down over his face. Goddamn the man. Colonel Upton had been right about one thing. There was a time when

Fox sympathized with Keegan MacLeod . . . empathized, at least. But no longer.

The Scot made himself one tenacious enemy when he broke into Fox's house at St. James's Square. When he kidnapped Zoe. Fox discovered what had happened when he stopped in London, on his way to Scotland, after a brief visit to Ashford Hall. He'd gone there to recuperate from a wound in his leg. But it was minor, hardly more than a scratch.

Colonel Upton was more correct than he knew when he chided Fox about the battle. He simply hadn't been able to come to terms with the slaughter that followed. So he'd hastened to Ashford Hall, preferring the calm of the Devon countryside to London.

Damn, if he'd only stayed with Zoe . . . Or if he'd tried harder to convince her to accompany him to Devon . . . Fox took a deep breath. He couldn't think of that, not now. Now all his strength, all his energy must go toward capturing the renegade. Making him pay for what he did to Zoe.

Poor, fragile Zoe. She could barely walk into the garden without swooning. There was no way she could survive what the rebel put her through.

But he would pay for hurting Zoe. Fox would see to that if it were the last thing he did on this earth.

Ten

She came awake by degrees. First hearing a roaring in her ears, then slowly noticing the chilled dampness beneath her cheek. It wasn't until the whisper of salt-laden breeze stirred the curls on her forehead that Zoe pried open her eyes.

At first she couldn't remember where she was or how she'd gotten here. She did know that every inch of her body hurt. Moaning, Zoe pushed up on her elbows and glanced around.

She was on a rocky beach, her clothes and skin encrusted with sand, her shoes lapped by the frothy surf.

What had happened?

Zoe sat a little straighter as memories faded in and out of her mind. There was the sloop, *Sea Maiden.* And the storm. Zoe recalled the flooding below deck and their attempt to climb the ladder, hers and the Scot's. He'd carried her up and together they leaped over the side into the sea.

"Oh my." She remembered it all now, with a clarity that made her shiver. They'd jumped and gone under, the water churning and bubbling as if they'd suddenly fallen into a boiling caldron.

But Keegan had held onto her and pushed her

to the surface. They'd struggled, fighting their way toward the shore.

And then . . .

Zoe couldn't remember anything else.

"Keegan," she said softly. Then pushing to her feet, she called his name again. Her gown was stiff with salt and uncomfortably damp, but Zoe ignored that as well as the ache in her head and her sore muscles as she scrambled down the beach.

"Keegan, where are you?" Zoe jerked up her skirts after tripping over a torn petticoat. "Scot!" The beach, a small, semicircular cove surrounded by rocks was empty except for herself and a pair of noisy black rooks. Where could he be?

Zoe's eyes strayed toward the rocks offshore. They seemed so much closer in the light of day and with the storm blown off to some other place. But the sloop was still there, or what was left of it, looking like a broken toy, abandoned and forgotten by a spoiled child. The water between rock and shore was quieter now, a clear green that reminded Zoe of the Scot's eyes.

He couldn't be there, sunk to the bottom, drowned. Tears burned her sore eyes. What if he was? What if he'd given her one last mighty push toward land only to flounder and sink beneath the sea.

"No." Zoe wiped at the tears that ran rivulets down her salt-stained cheeks. She couldn't bear the thought of him, so strong and masculine, dead. "Damn you, Scot," Zoe mumbled as she slogged through the surf, ignoring her soaked shoes and hem. She might hate the fact that he was dead but she also realized she shouldn't. He was her kidnapper. Her darling brother's sworn enemy. Why should she care that she'd survived the storm and he hadn't?

Wasn't this the answer to her prayers? She'd find out where she was and get word to Fox . . . Zoe glanced about at her desolate, windblown surroundings. Somehow. And then she'd go back to London and forget any of this ever happened.

Except that she was crying in earnest now and thinking of such foolish things as the way the Scot's lips turned up and his eyes crinkled when he smiled. And that the sun could make his dark hair shine with burnished highlights as bright as any copper penny. And that when he held her she felt warm and safe despite the fact that he was a renegade outlaw.

"Oh Keegan, please don't be dead," she sobbed, then jerked to attention as she heard a strange noise. It was somewhat like the keening of the wind, but deeper. And it came from behind a large rock jutting out into the surf. Cautiously she stepped into the waves and peered around the glistening limestone.

Then she was trudging through the cold water as quickly as she could. "Keegan. Keegan, are you all right?" He lay face up, his eyes closed, a nasty purplish-red welt peeking from beneath the tangled hair on his forehead.

Zoe dropped to her knees beside him, touching his shoulder. He made no sound now, nor did he move, even when she called his name. Rocking back on her heels Zoe let her eyes travel down his body.

She couldn't see anything wrong with him other than the bruise, and his chest moved up and down. He was breathing.

What was she to do? With all the times Miss Phelps had nursed her, Zoe felt she should have some idea what was to be done. But she didn't. Gingerly her fingers traced the outline of his wound, careful not to put pressure on it. Then her fingers strayed down his cheek, brushing across the rough whiskers to find the sensual line of his lips. They moved ever so slightly when Zoe's thumb skimmed across them.

She'd admired his lips even from the first when he frightened her the most. They were strong and firm and resolute. Zoe smiled despite the circumstances. Odd to describe someone's mouth as resolute. But the Scot's was. And it intrigued her.

As feathery as mist, Zoe slid her fingertips along the seam of his lips, slipping along the moisture. His breath warmed her flesh, a deep even rhythm that soothed her worried mind. One couldn't breathe so well and not be all right. Could one?

Zoe's gaze slipped back to the nasty wound on his head. Zoe sighed. She really should do something. Perhaps if she could find some help. But as her fingers reluctantly trailed off his mouth, he moaned. It wasn't a loud sound, but it was there, as plaintive as the wind.

It was almost as if he didn't want her to leave him. Foolish as it was, she felt the same. Without thinking of the consequences Zoe leaned forward. Now her lips caressed his. Lightly. Carefully so as not to hurt him she learned the texture. Tasted the salt. And him.

Something inside her ignited with the same odd joyous ache that was no stranger to her now. His lips were smooth, a delicious contrast to the whiskers that tickled the delicate skin of her chin. She longed to rub her hands over him, to feel the wide shoulders and brawny arms visible beneath the torn fabric of his shirt. She longed to be drawn into him in a way she could only imagine.

But she did none of that. She held herself stiffly, her eyes closed, letting only the subtle movement of her mouth breathe life into him.

So absorbed was she in the way her body reacted to the slight contact, Zoe didn't realize at first when his own lips came to life. The pressure, so deliciously light, wove slow, heated spirals of desire through her. Then his lips opened and his tongue, so wet and aggressive startled her. Zoe's eyes flew open.

And she stared directly into the bottomless green depths of his.

"Oh." Embarrassed into motion, Zoe tried to jerk away, only to discover that he'd managed to cup the back of her head with his palm. He held her motionless a mere whisper's breath from him, staring at her intensely.

" 'Tis alive ye are?" he said, his voice rising in question.

Zoe swallowed, then nodded. "It would seem so."

"Would it now?" The fine lines beside his eyes deepened as he smiled. "I'd've sworn 'twas a heavenly angel greetin' me with a kiss."

Heat flooded Zoe's cheeks. She tried to pull away again only to have his arm tighten. For a man newly waking from an unconscious state, he was amazingly strong. "I . . . I wasn't sure you were alive. You've a nasty bruise on your head."

"Aye." Keegan wrinkled his brow but did not loosen his hold on Zoe. "It feels as if a giant claymore crashed down over me."

"I think it more likely a brush with the rocks offshore."

"Is that what ye think?" His tone was low . . . seductive.

"Yes." Zoe wetted her suddenly dry lips.

"Why?" The single-word question seemed to weave invisible threads about Zoe.

"Why what?" Zoe shut her eyes so he couldn't see what a coward she was, for she knew exactly what he meant. He must have known as well for he said nothing else, simply pulled her closer, filling her senses with him. Unable to continue in the dark, Zoe opened her eyes. "It was just a kiss," she said.

"Was it now?" His eyes narrowed. "It seemed like more t' me."

"I feared you were dead, and then I found you and you were hurt . . . obviously." Zoe blinked. "I didn't know what to do so—"

"So ye kissed me."

Embarrassment flustered her senses . . . at least those that weren't overwhelmed by him. Zoe tried to pull away again. "You needn't concern yourself," Zoe said in a haughty tone that she hardly recognized as her own. "It shan't happen again."

"Ach, Lady Zoe, but that be where ye're wrong." With one final tug Keegan closed the space between them. He captured her gasp of protest, molding his mouth to hers and turning it to a sigh.

All manner of thoughts ricocheted through her mind. That she shouldn't be allowing this, was certainly one of them and Zoe did her best to capture it long enough to act upon it. But she couldn't. Not with his teeth taking seductive little nibbles of her lips. His tongue doing a sensual slide across hers.

He was taking her breath away. Making her dizzy. And starting that awful ache again. The one deep in the pit of her being. The one she could never truly rid herself of. It was a pain like none she'd ever known until the Scot came into her life. A bittersweet anguish that grew at times like these, near unbearable.

She felt as if she might burst.

Yet the way to relief, shoving him aside and waiting for the easement, seemed equally unendurable.

So Zoe let the kiss continue, let it deepen and grow, until she sprawled across him, her body pressing his. Her breasts swelled, the nipples grew hard, and it seemed the only relief came from flattening them against the hard wall of his chest.

And as for the excruciating ache between her legs . . . it seemed everything he did made it worse. His hands clutched at her back, then lower, pulling her ever closer.

"I can't stand it." Zoe pried her mouth away from his, shoving at his shoulders and rolling away so quickly the Scot couldn't stop her. Drawing herself up, her knees toward her chest, her arms wrapped about them, Zoe took several deep breaths, trying to control the feeling of loss.

"What is it lass?" Keegan was struggling with his

own breathing, that was now coming in shallow gasps. "What's wrong with ye?"

At first Keegan thought she didn't hear him . . . or was refusing to answer. She simply rocked back and forth, her face hidden, her body trembling. He pushed to his elbows, then after flexing his shoulders, scooted toward her.

"No, don't touch me."

Keegan hesitated, then let his hand fall to his side. "I wouldn't force ye." Despite everything, he almost added, "Ye needn't fear that."

"I don't." Which considering the circumstances was unusual. "It's just . . ." Her voice was small as she peeked over her knees. "There's something wrong with me. Something terrible."

Keegan resisted the urge to laugh. There were quite a few things wrong with her as far as he could tell. But then she had some amazingly good qualities as well. Which were what he'd been dwelling on.

" 'Tis not the most comfortable of places t' . . . Well t' do what we were about. I'd cuddle ye in a down-filled bed if I could."

"It isn't that." Though Zoe had to admit the damp gown *was* chafing her skin. "I have terrible pains." The last word was muffled as she hid her face again in the lee of her knees.

"Pains? What kind of pains? Was I too rough? I'll admit t' gettin' a bit carried away. Did I bite ye?"

"No," Zoe admitted. "It isn't that. 'Tis lower."

"Lower?" Keegan lifted her chin with his thumb. "I don't understand."

"Oh, what does it matter?" Zoe felt tears straining to swim to the surface and blinked. She'd resigned herself years ago to dying young. Her illnesses and Miss Phelps's care were the only constants in her life. So why was she upset now by the prospect? Why now, kidnapped and in a strange land, held by a man who, though he intrigued her, was a sworn enemy, did she mourn the loss of her health?

Melancholy overcame embarrassment.

"Here." Zoe straightened enough to press a trembling hand to her bosom. "And here." Her fingers drifted down to her lap. "There's an ache."

Despite her tendency to exaggerate every little pain, and her constant wailing that she was ill, Keegan wondered if this time there might be something wrong. She certainly seemed sincere about her discomfort. Her bottom lip trembled and two fat tears lost their battle and trailed slowly down her cheeks. Keegan took her hand. Perhaps she hurt herself during their struggle to shore. He'd certainly felt a hell of a lot better before as well.

"Are ye bruised . . . or cut?" True, he couldn't see any indication of a wound but she was covered by her gown.

"No. No." Zoe sighed, wishing she had never brought the subject up. " 'Tis inside. And it only becomes unbearable at times."

"I don't understand."

"When . . ." Zoe felt warm despite the chill breeze. "When we kiss it gets worse," she said in a rush, hoping that would be the end of the discussion. For a moment he sat silently staring at her, then to her mortification, the Scot let out a howl of laughter. Then another. Before her wide eyes he rocked back, his handsome face filled with mirth, his chuckles scaring the gulls away.

Zoe stiffened her spine, her posture in sharp contrast to his doubled over frame. "I fail to see what is so humorous about my disability." She barely got the last word out through her trembling lips. Zoe swallowed. "I know you don't care about me but I'd at least hoped to be in my home . . . my own bed when the end came. Not here on this desolate . . . desolate beach." The tears came in earnest now, accompanied by a low sobbing sound that pierced through Keegan's laughter.

"Now, Lady Zoe, don't go on so," Keegan said around another guffaw. " 'Tis not so bad. And I'd wager ye're not going t' die. At least not from this particular malady."

"How can you be so sure?" Zoe made an effort to control her crying. "You aren't a physician."

"Aye, and 'tis a good thing I'm not." Keegan's temperament sobered. "For that old bastard would probably have ye on a bleedin' cup for something that be as natural as breathin'."

Zoe's head tilted. "How could pain be a natural thing?" In her, it was, of course—but she was different. Miss Phelps had drilled that into her from early on.

"This pain ye speak of, does it make ye feel excited . . . anticipatin' ye know not what?"

Zoe crossed her arms. "That's an odd way to describe pain, but yes, there is that. But we really don't need to discuss it now." She didn't trust the expression on his face. There was still remnants of amusement, yet there was a hint of arrogance as well. As if he was quite pleased with himself for some reason Zoe couldn't fathom. "I'm fine now," she added hoping to put an end to further speculation on his part.

"What of now?" He moved closer, draping his arm about her shoulders.

"Yes . . . fine," Zoe insisted, though truthfully his nearness made her restless.

"And what if I were to kiss ye? What then?" Keegan asked but did not give her time to answer before pressing his lips to hers. He'd meant the gesture as an experiment, nothing more. But before he knew it Keegan was forgetting all but the sweet taste of her.

"Oh my." Zoe leaned away from him. "That's it. The ache is back."

"In me too."

"You?" Her voice rose in surprise.

"Aye. We've the same ache, more or less, my pretty hostage. And though at the moment it feels as if it might, it won't kill ye."

"It won't?" A tentative smile curved her lips. "But it feels so dreadful."

"That's because we haven't managed t' find relief yet." The words vibrated against her neck as he pressed his mouth to her. The tingling brought new quivers of sweet ache spiraling through her body.

Zoe's breathing quickened. She felt dizzy again. "Can we? Find relief that is?"

Now it was Keegan's turn to pull back. He studied her face, brushing a sprinkling of sand from her cheek. She stared at him wide-eyed and innocent, her lips parted. A man would be a bastard to take advantage of her, even if she'd been driving that man near wild with lust for some time.

"Nothin' would please me more, lass. But I don't think this be the time nor place to give in to our desires."

"Well, I didn't mean . . ." Zoe bit her lip and turned away. What must this man think of her? What desires was he speaking of?

"Zoe." His voice was soft and seductive. "Look at me."

Zoe took in a shaky breath and slowly raised her head. He stared at her, his eyes all smoky green and she knew exactly what he meant by desire. The ache was upon her again, stronger and more overwhelming than before. But she knew now that it was no disease but something more consuming by far.

She noticed so much about him, without even trying. The broad curve of his shoulder. The slash of his collarbone. The way his muscles bunched when he moved, and the tapered shape of his hands. It didn't matter that he was grimy and wet. That his hair was tangled and his chin covered with whiskers. Want of him pulsed through her. Shamed her.

She turned away, scrambling to her feet as quickly as her sodden gown would allow.

"Zoe." He followed, his legs a bit wobbly at first. "Stop. I'm not goin' t' attack ye. Listen, I don't know what it is between us, but don't think ye're the only one feelin' it. I want—"

Keegan stopped abruptly when a new sound floated to him, mingling with the sea and wind and the squawk of the gulls. Zoe heard it too for she halted her headlong march down the beach and whirled about to face him. With a finger to his lips he quelled any question she might have. Then he motioned her back, clutching her arm and pulling her down behind the rocks.

"Who is it?" she whispered. "Holt?"

"I don't know. It was my fervent wish that he and his crew perished in the storm."

Hers too, though she didn't want to admit it. But there was someone not far away. She could hear talking and laughing. "I can't understand them," she said, twisting her head to hear better. When she did, Zoe saw a grin spread across the Scot's face.

" 'Tis because they're not speakin' bloody English. 'Tis Gaelic," he said with glee as he stood and called out in the same tongue. Then he grabbed her hand and bounded around the rocks.

Eleven

She was going to be sick. Zoe hunched beneath a rough woolen plaid, her body trembling. Though she was cold, sweat glistened her upper lip and dampened her forehead. Each breath she took made the feeling worse.

Smells hung on the smoke-laden air inside the tiny turf house. Smells that made the ache in her stomach worse. There was the ripe odor of the cattle, penned at the far end of the cabin, the foul smell drifting in the open door from the dung heap and the strong odor of the dye being used to color the wound woolen thread.

But Zoe knew that her discomfort came more from the fact that the Scot had left her here. He'd gone off with the husband of the woman who occasionally glanced up from her work to give Zoe a disgusted look.

They'd come here this morning following the two young boys Keegan found near the rocks. The boys had been bound for the cove to check if the night's storm had tossed any prizes ashore. Presumably that's where the lads were now, pilfering what they could from the *Sea Maiden*'s wreckage. In that regard Zoe wished them well. She also hoped they took care not to encounter any of the crew. What had become of them was a mystery. Presumably they'd abandoned both their ship and their captain.

Zoe glanced back toward the woman as she gave the cradle near her foot a gentle kick. Sleeping on her stomach was an infant. The family's surname was MacNair. The Scot had recognized it immediately, as they had his. Though they'd never met before they had a common bond. They'd both supported the rebellion.

So the two men had gone off together, the Scot leaving Zoe with hardly more than a word. That was hours ago. She should be glad. Now she didn't have to listen to him or look at him. She could even leave the rickety stool and walk outside if she chose. Walk away from this hut. The woman wouldn't stop her. Zoe was fairly certain of that. She wouldn't be surprised if the woman wanted her gone from her home anyway. Hatred hung as thick and foul as the smoke that blackened the walls inside the small hut.

Perhaps that's what she should do . . . escape. Her gown hung on a peg near the small peat fire in the center of the hut. Smoke curled up, some of it escaping through the hole in the thatch roof. The riding habit was most likely still damp, but that wouldn't matter. She'd pull it on and leave. Before the Scot returned. He probably wouldn't even mind if he came back to find her gone. She was a burden to him.

The only problem was, *she* would mind.

Which was so foolish, Zoe could barely comprehend it. She should despise him. She should do anything in her power to be away from him. There was still her brother to warn. Or the authorities. Someone.

But the fact remained. The anxiety that tightened her stomach was because he wasn't here. She'd grown used to him.

"Best t' eat that." The woman gave her one of her acid stares, but her hands, dyed green by the liquid in the heavy iron pot never stopped squeezing the skeins of wool. "He said I was t' feed ye."

Zoe took a bite of the cold oatmeal.

"Ain't no fancy Sassenach food, but ye're lucky we can spare that."

"It's fine." Zoe took another bite. "I thank you."

"Don't want yer thanks."

The words, spoken with such venom, made Zoe pause, the spoon partway to her mouth. "Why do you dislike me so?"

"Dislike 'tis not what I feel for ye." The woman splashed wool into the vile-smelling dye. " 'Tis hate, pure and simple."

The spoon clattered to the rough tabletop. "But I . . . I never did anything to you."

" 'Tis yur kind. Ach, and I knew before the MacLeod said a word, that ye were a Sassenach. I could smell ye comin' up the path from the sea."

Which Zoe found difficult to believe considering the odors she had to compete with. "I really don't think—"

"Which is good, for I haven't a care as t' what ye think."

"But I—"

"What's this now, woman? Where be yer hospitality?"

Zoe pushed to her feet as the woman's husband entered the hut. He was followed by Keegan who lowered his head to enter the dwelling. It was all Zoe could do not to dash across the damp earthen floor to him.

His expression was closed, near as unpleasant as the woman's, as he ordered her to get dressed. "Why? Where are we going?" The questions popped from Zoe's mouth before she could stop them. But she wasn't surprised when he didn't answer. He did say a few words to the woman when she offered him a bowl of oatmeal. He ate standing, and in silence. Only once glancing up, and that to motion for her to put on her gown.

Zoe dressed behind a blanket that served as a room divider between the kitchen and bedroom. The gown was still damp and smelled of the sea, but at least the sand was brushed away. With her fingers Zoe combed through her hair, then braided and twisted the curls atop her head. But there were no pins to secure it, so the hair tumbled down her back.

The Scot had finished breaking his fast when she stepped from behind the curtain. He bade his host farewell in the strange language Zoe heard earlier and ushered her out the door.

"We've a cart waitin' for us down the road a bit," he said as he scrambled over a pile of rocks. The land around it was blackened.

"A cart? Where are we going? For that matter, where are we?"

"Scotland," Keegan answered succinctly. "And we're bound for Castle MacLeod."

Which was where they'd been headed all along,

so it should come as no surprise to her. But somehow it was. Especially when Zoe learned they were only a few days' ride from their destination. That is if the roads were passable, which after the storm yesterday was not a certainty.

The cart was crude, with two wooden wheels and a thick-necked pony to pull it. The bed, filled with straw and sacks of oatmeal was separated from the front by only a roughly hewn wooden seat. Zoe had no doubt they could walk faster than the cart could crawl along the path. But she didn't want to walk, and the Scot didn't suggest it.

He didn't say much of anything after greeting Shamus, the owner of the cart. He was a MacNair as well, an old man who looked as gnarled and twisted as the fir trees near the cliff overlooking the sea.

Despite his being kin to the woman, Shamus was talkative, and if he realized Zoe was English, he didn't seem to care. Zoe was grateful. She found it difficult being treated as if she had the plague . . . the one malady she never did have.

Actually it seemed that Shamus was most interested in conversing with Keegan. But the latter confined his responses to grunts and the occasional curse as the cart flopped into a pothole, so it fell on Zoe to ask the questions that kept Shamus talking as they rumbled along the mud-rutted road.

" 'Tis the truth ye'll be havin' t' watch out for the soldiers from Fort William. They're coverin' the countryside like a giant plaid. 'Tis more than a hunch they'll be searchin' for ye, lad. That's not t' say anyone will tell them ye've returned t' the Highlands. 'Tis just that they seem t' have a sense about things."

He slapped at the pony's rump with a green twig. "I've seen them raid a hut on the only night in a fortnight that a husband crept home to see his family. Tore him away from his wife's lovin' arms and strung him up in the yard, they did, with his young ones cryin' and his wife wailin'."

"That's dreadful." Zoe squirmed around in the itchy straw. "What had the poor man done?"

"The *poor man* was a Jacobite, Zoe," Keegan said, turning his head and seeming to look at her for the first time since they climbed into the cart.

"Is that true?" Zoe addressed her question to Shamus, though she knew before he answered what he'd say.

"The army's bound t' see nothin' like this rebellion happens again, even if they have t' kill everyone who so much as tipped his bonnet at the Prince."

"The MacNairs are fine," Zoe pointed out. "I had the impression they fought in the rebellion."

"Aye, and lost a son," Shamus said. "And their house was burned t' the ground, their sheep slaughtered."

" 'Tis worse than I thought," Keegan said more to himself than for anyone else's benefit.

"Ye could not have known, lad, being dragged off t' London like they done. But as ye say times are rough for those of us who followed the Prince." With a grunt Shamus reined in the small pony. They'd come upon a stream. Clear water sloshed over smooth moss-covered rocks, following the fretful channel toward the sea. There was no bridge, which left fording their only option.

There'd been a time when Zoe would have balked, certain the frigid water would be her death. But now she merely sighed, resigned to being cold and wet . . . and somehow having her heart survive.

As it turned out, Zoe was told to stay in the cart while Shamus held the reins and Keegan climbed down to lead the pony into the swirling water. "Watch yerself MacLeod, the current's a mite rougher than ye think," Shamus said with a laugh before the cart splashed into the water.

"I always find meself a point to fix on." The old man raised his voice to be heard over the stream's torrent. "Like that rock yonder. Then I aim the pony's ears on a straight course. Keeps us from goin' too far downstream with the current."

Which was what Keegan was doing now. He seemed to have equal difficulty with the current and the pony. When he finally guided the pony ashore, Keegan announced he would walk for a bit. Zoe rested her head upon a sack of oats and drifted off to sleep, the chatter of Shamus fluttering in her ear, the vision of sunny blue sky above her.

She woke with a start. The singsong tone of the old man's voice was gone. In its place were terse commands. Commands that Keegan obeyed. He leaped onto the cart, burrowing down into the straw and ordering her to do the same.

"What . . . ? What is it?" Zoe batted at the straw and sneezed.

"My God. Don't tell me ye're goin' t' start that?"

"I can't help it." Zoe sneezed again.

In the meantime Shamus was twisted around telling them to hurry. The sharp edge of fear honed his words. "Soldiers are comin'."

For a heartbeat Keegan stopped burying her legs beneath bags of oats. He looked up and their eyes met. They both knew how close he was to hanging from the nearest tree. Even if she didn't call out to the soldiers.

In that moment she wanted to reassure him.

But it was too ridiculous to even comprehend it. So she said nothing, as did he. Then he was pushing her down, covering her head and his with a length of plaid, making a little nest for them beneath the straw. And all the time the cart rumbled along the rutted path.

The sun was blocked beneath the wool, but she could still see Keegan in the dusty light. He lay beside her, his face turned toward hers. One hand rested beside her cheek as if he didn't know whether to place it over her mouth or not.

He did, the moment he heard a yelled command to halt.

The accent was decidedly English, military in tone.

"State your name and business."

The old man took his time responding. "I'm Shamus MacNair, and I be on me way to pay me rent t' the new landlord."

"Who might that be?"

"Angus MacDonald. 'Tis him that lives in the castle now down by Firth Glenmorgan."

Zoe heard the hooves of horses as they pranced

and when the soldier's words came again they were even closer. "What have you here?"

The cart jolted, obviously rocked by the Englishman. Zoe's eyes widened, staring at Keegan over his hand. Her senses were flooded by him. She could feel the tension in his body, hear the pounding of his heart . . . or was it hers, as the minutes seemed to pile one upon the other.

In the background she could hear Shamus listing the contents of the cart. "Oats, and beer, straw for bedding."

Zoe had no idea if the soldier believed that was all the cart held. She wished she could see his face. Wished he would give the order for the old man to move on. If he didn't . . . if he decided to search the cart for himself, Keegan was trapped. A dead man.

And then the tickle started. Deep in her nose. Zoe tried breathing through her mouth, but the Scot's hand pressed firmly. Her eyes watered with the force of trying to avert the sneeze but she could feel it coming nonetheless.

Frantically Zoe lifted her hand and clawed at his. Surprise, then anger darkened his eyes. But he was so taken off guard that his hand slipped a fraction. He expected her to scream. She could read it in the set of his features. But she didn't. After taking a deep breath she pinched her nostrils, just before the sneeze trembled through her.

There was a noise, a slight snuffling sound that the plaid and straw muffled even more. Apparently the English soldiers didn't hear it. Within minutes

Zoe heard the pounding of hooves as the soldiers rode away. And then the cart started moving.

Zoe turned her head toward him. His hand no longer covered her lower face. He'd moved it as soon as he realized what she did. He looked at her now as if she were some strange being he'd never seen before. She knew he wondered why. Why, when her release was at hand, when she could have had her revenge against the man who'd kidnapped her, did she choose to protect him instead.

Zoe wanted to explain it to him. But she'd have to understand it herself first.

And at the moment she didn't.

The road no longer ran along the water. It now twisted and turned, climbing ever higher into the hills. Keegan was walking again, keeping a lookout for other details of soldiers from Fort William. Shamus had warned they were everywhere, a remark he repeated after their encounter.

"I don't know if I'd stay here, if I were ye," he said now. "They must be lookin' for ye lad. Word came that ye escaped before I clapped eyes on ye."

"Perhaps you should listen to him." Zoe twisted on her knees in the cart. Keegan hadn't even bothered to answer the old man, simply trudging on as if he hadn't heard him. "You could go to France." Shamus had told them that many of the chieftains whose land was confiscated had escaped across the channel. Many of the tenants, including Shamus, now paid two rents. One to the new English-appointed landlord, another voluntary rent to the laird across the sea.

Keegan glanced over his shoulder. "Ye'd like that, wouldn't ye? Anything t' save yer brother." Their gazes met but his expression turned sheepish and he went back to looking at the road before him.

"I wasn't thinking of Fox and you know it."

"Aye," he mumbled. "Well, I can't leave. Not without seeing how things are anyway."

And killing Fox, Zoe wondered. But she didn't ask.

Dusk settled quickly over the Highlands veiling them in tones of grey, softening the tumble of craggy mountains. Adding mystery to them.

The air was clear and cold now that the sun hung low over the Atlantic, and Zoe was grateful for the wool plaid. She wrapped it more tightly about her shoulders wondering how much farther they were going to climb this day.

As if in answer to her unspoken question Shamus reined in the pony. " 'Tis as far as our paths are the same." He climbed down from the rickety seat and stretched. "Ye know where we be, don't ye lad?"

"Aye. Castle MacLeod is t' the northwest."

"Right ye are. I'd take ye the rest of the way meself but—"

"You've done plenty." Keegan clasped the old man's shoulders. "I thank ye for it."

"There's an inn down in the glen. If ye hurry ye should make the door before night overtakes ye. Knock on the back door and tell them ye wish t' raise a glass to the king across the sea. Ye'll have no problem."

Keegan nodded. "If there be anything I can do for ye . . ."

"Ye needn't finish it lad." Shamus climbed back

onto the cart. "These be trying times. Now be off with ye. And take care of the lass."

Zoe watched the cart roll away, then turned and scurried to catch up with Keegan. He had already started down the path. He surprised her by pausing till she caught up, then taking her arm. Mist rose in patches at times obscuring the hem of Zoe's skirts.

They walked along a ridge, following a footpath that the cart could never have traveled. Zoe squinted into the ever-deepening night, trying to see some sign of an inn. But there was nothing. The wind rustled, and far off in the distance she could hear the roar of water, whether the sea or a river, she wasn't certain.

But for that, all was quiet with a silence and solitude like she'd never known. It was as if they were the only two people left in the world. The idea made her giddy—and started that odd ache inside her. But she knew better than to mention her discomfort. She knew better than to do anything but trudge along beside him.

The inn was little better than the crude hovel they left this morn. Made of turf with a thatched roof, the whole was but slightly larger. However it did offer shelter from the misty rain that had begun to fall.

Zoe stood behind Keegan, the plaid covering her head, as he pounded on the door. Several people were inside. Zoe could hear them singing as the portal opened a crack.

"What be ye wantin'?" the landlord asked in a most inhospitable tone.

"T' tip a glass to the king across the sea," Keegan countered and immediately the door opened wider.

"Come in outa the weather, lad. Oh, what have we here?" The landlord's gaze fell on Zoe.

"We're but weary travelers lookin' for a place to lay our heads."

"I've a room. Galen Frasier's me name." His pursed lips seemed to disappear in his wide face.

"Galen." Keegan nodded his way. "If ye'll be showin' us—"

" 'Tis customary in the Highlands t' give a name."

Keegan lifted a wet brow. "And here I thought a Highland custom was t' respect a traveler's privacy."

Several of the patrons seated round the white ash of a peat fire guffawed. Then one stood. Tankard in hand he approached Keegan, squinting in the poor light of a fir branch.

"Ye be the MacLeod's son. Keegan, that's the one. Went off to London, ye did."

"And returned to fight at Culloden," Keegan countered.

"Aye he did at that. Got himself caught and sentenced to hang too." The man lifted his mug and took a healthy drink.

"Well, as ye can see I've escaped, and come home."

"Not much to come home to," another of the patrons, a wiry man with pockmarked face, added. "They've confiscated yer land."

"So I've heard."

Zoe lifted her eyes enough to look at Keegan. She'd wondered if Castle MacLeod was no longer his. How long had he known? And if they weren't bound there, then where?

"Do ye have a room for us or nay? 'Tis been a long day and I'm in dire need of a pillow t' lay my head."

Apparently deciding they'd get no gossip from this MacLeod, the proprietor motioned with his pudgy fingers. "There be a hut out back. Inside is a sleepin' box for ye and the lady. Are ye hungry?"

They ate a supper of greasy mutton and hard-boiled eggs, then took a burning branch to the sleeping quarters. The rain fell harder now, blown into Zoe's face like icy daggers. But the small hut was relatively dry and after Keegan used the branch to light the peat fire, it warmed quickly.

Zoe stood near the fire wondering if it were possible to die of exhaustion. Her feet hurt. Her body ached and her head throbbed. But she knew Keegan suffered as much as she. Not that he complained. He simply stood, staring at her. The same expression on his handsome face that she'd seen often since the soldiers came upon their cart.

Zoe unwrapped the plaid, shaking the beads of water from the wool. When she finished he hadn't moved at all. Embarrassed, Zoe tried to walk past him. He reached out, hooking her arm, stopping her.

He stared down into her eyes and "Why?" was all he said.

Twelve

She could pretend not to understand, but it seemed foolish. More foolish than her actions. Around the hut the wind churned the landscape, but inside it was quiet with only the occasional crack of the fire to break the silence. He was waiting for her answer, and for the life of her Zoe couldn't give him one.

"Have you never done something impulsively? Something you look back upon and wonder what possessed you?"

"Aye."

He answered her so quickly and with such assurance, that Zoe's lips thinned. "Saving me from Captain Holt, no doubt."

"Actually, I was thinkin' more along the lines of kidnappin' ye in the first place."

Zoe smiled despite herself. "That was rather foolish, wasn't it?"

Keegan sat on the side of the box bed and pried off one boot. "I've made smarter moves t' be sure."

"Well, I'd be glad to remedy that situation for you."

Keegan glanced up. "Can ye now?" She was angry. He could tell by her stance, feet spread beneath her tattered skirts and arms crossed. And by the delightful color that ripened her cheeks like fine peaches. She was bedraggled, and dirty, her fall of curly hair tumbling down her narrow back, but she was an appealing woman. The eyes, large and grey, reminded him of the girl he'd taken from her home by force, but the rest of her had changed.

"I can," she said, as she paced to the far edge of the hut, a mere rod or so. "As a matter of fact I think we'd all be better off if you'd simply let me go."

The other boot plopped to the soft dirt. "And how do ye figure that?"

"As you said, the entire kidnapping idea was mad."

Keegan leaned back on his elbows. "I don't recall saying that."

"But you must admit it was." She wished he wouldn't recline like that. The position made his chest seem even wider than it already was. And she could see the outline of the bulging muscles in his arms. Zoe took a deep breath. That uncomfortable ache was starting again. "So you see, if you let me go, everything will be as it should." He didn't say anything—which Zoe took as a good sign. "I shall go home to London and you can . . ."

One dark brow arched.

Zoe sighed. He didn't seem to have a lot of choices. "Go to France," she finally said.

"And have the crofters send me a voluntary rent on top of the one they owe the factor so I can live the life of a dilettante in exile?"

No, Zoe admitted to herself, he didn't really seem

like the kind of man to do that. "Then what of the New World?"

"What of it?"

"You could go there. Start a new life."

"I like Scotland."

Zoe crossed her arms. He was being stubborn. "It seems to me you should look to the future." She lifted her hands in a shrug. "But there's nothing I can do for you."

"Are ye forgetting yer brother?" His tone was mild, but Zoe noted the gleam in his narrowed eyes. "Besides," he said, pushing to his feet, "I'm not sure ye actually wish t' be free of me." Keegan followed his announcement with a lift of her chin with his thumb. She really did have the most incredible eyes, wide and serious one moment. Stormy the next. They were definitely stormy now.

"That's ridiculous."

"Then why didn't ye call out to the soldiers?"

That question again. Zoe took a step back. "I fully appreciate the things you've done to save my life. Perhaps I was only returning the favor." Her insides were in turmoil and her head dizzy.

His breath wafted against her cheek. "So do ye consider us even now?"

"Yes . . . no . . . I don't know." Zoe took a deep breath. "I'm not feeling very well."

"Ill again?" Keegan shifted her face to the left, then the right, studying the bright eyes, the shallowness of her breath. "What think ye the problem this time? Fever?"

Zoe nodded. She definitely felt hot with him so close.

"Nausea? Unbalance of humors?"

Yes, yes, all that and more. Zoe swayed toward him.

"And what of yer problem with rigid veins?" His own rigidity pressed against her as Keegan pulled her closer.

"Oh, yes," Zoe agreed. "I definitely think I need a surgeon." But the truth was, Zoe thought she needed something else more. His mouth, those strong, firm lips were only a breath away from her own. And she was sure she would swoon if he didn't kiss her soon. It was all she could do not to beg, not to gasp, when the pressure finally came.

Zoe's arms hung loose, then seemed to take on a life of their own as they wound about his neck. And she was kissing him back as hard as she could. Trying to ignore the ache growing in her nether regions. Finding it impossible.

The only relief she seemed to find was a certain way she wriggled about, pressing herself against Keegan's thigh. He appeared to find the arrangement advantageous as well, for he lifted her higher, molding his hands over her bottom.

His tongue brushed her lips, then inched its way inside her mouth. Bells seemed to ring in her head. One of his hands lifted, his finger tracing the outline of her bodice. Her breasts swelled.

It was happening again. Her entire body felt light, so light she could float away. Her legs nearly buckled and if not for his support she would have fallen to the earthen floor. And her heart, it beat so fast, pounding in her chest that Zoe feared she might expire.

But dying was the last thing she wanted to do. Because she never wanted this feeling to stop. She never wanted to be separated from the Scot. As if in an epiphany Zoe knew why she hadn't called to the English soldiers. And the answer was too frightening to accept.

"No, please." Zoe twisted until her mouth was free from his. "This can't be."

"Hell, Zoe." His voice rasped in her ear, hardly more than a groan.

"I'm sorry." Her own breathing was thready. "This just can't be."

"Now lass, I'm thinkin' it can. We've a warm bed, and I've checked, there isn't a bedbug or flea to be found."

What he had in mind came blindingly into focus. Which is not to say it wasn't the same thing that had been on her mind. "I can't." Zoe shook her head and wriggled free of his knee. With a grunt and a curse he let her go.

"There, be ye happy?"

"I'm sick." Zoe pressed a palm to her forehead.

"Nay." His stare was dark and intense. "Ye're not sick. But ye are a coward."

"No." Zoe shook her head so frantically it did begin to ache.

"We both know what's got hold of us. And we both know it's not goin' away."

"You're wrong." Zoe wrapped her arms tightly about herself. "I really don't feel so well."

"Well neither do I lass, neither do I."

* * *

She didn't think he was really ill, or she wouldn't leave him. Zoe glanced back at his prostrate form sprawled on the box bed. He'd been right. Surprising after the condition of the inn and sleeping hut, the linens were fresh. Not a bug on them. At least that helped *his* sleep.

Zoe hadn't been so fortunate.

After the kissing incident he'd stripped down to his breeches, staring at her the entire time, then crawled beneath the blanket. "There be room for ye here, if ye want it," he'd said before turning on his side away from her.

"I'm fine," she countered which of course was about as far from the truth as it could be. Just looking at him, thinking about lying beside him was stirring her insides up again and turning her feverish.

But he seemed to accept her words. With a shrug of his broad shoulders he muttered an almost inaudible, "Suit yerself."

Almost immediately he'd started to snore.

Which at least let her know he was asleep. As carefully as she could Zoe had inched onto the bed, careful not to let any part of her body touch him. She needed to think and she'd always done her best thinking lying down.

She was falling in love with him.

As often as Zoe tried to put a logical explanation on her actions with the soldiers, with the way she wanted to be with him, she kept coming round to that awful truth. If she didn't escape from him immediately, there was no telling what would happen.

So just as the first faint paling of dawn shone through the smoke hole in the thatched roof, Zoe wrapped the borrowed plaid about her shoulders and crept through the door. Cold rain greeted her, dampening her face, weakening her resolve. Zoe bunched the wool beneath her chin and searched the area. Grey mist rose in wispy threads, concealing the path they used the night before. In the darkness the land seemed haunted and haunting, like something out of a nightmare.

Zoe swallowed and took a tentative step, then another. She looked toward the sky and blinked. Certainly the way would become clear once the day lightened. All she needed to do was find her way back to the main path then walk south. Fort William was south. Fox was south. Possibly. With a resolute set to her mouth Zoe moved through the drifting fog.

"Damn it all to hell!" Keegan exploded through the door of the hut. When he caught the chit he planned to tie her up . . . and gag her. That was it, he'd been too damn lenient with her. Not treating her like a proper hostage at all, but like some . . . some . . . God, he'd almost thought . . . lover. But *that* sure as hell wasn't the case.

Tramping through the mud, Keegan searched about. The rain had stopped and the sun was high, but there were clouds out over the Atlantic that prophesied another storm. And where in the hell was she?

The inn's landlord didn't know. Though he had a difficult time being pulled from slumber, he grinned when he recognized Keegan. "Haven't seen yer woman since ye left with her last night, though I don't mind tellin' ye she is a pretty thing," he mumbled, while rubbing his bloodshot eyes. "Be ye needin' a break for yer fast, young MacLeod?"

"Nay, but I thank ye." Keegan flipped a coin onto the rough table despite the landlord's protests. "Tip a bottle for me this night," he said before grabbing up an oatcake and leaving.

She couldn't have gotten far, Keegan told himself, though he hadn't a clue how long ago she left. He hoped to God she'd waited till morning for the Highlands were beset by dangers in the dark, especially for someone new to them. What appeared a safe step, could be, hidden by the woolly mist, the edge of a giddy precipice.

But he couldn't think of that. Keegan tried instead to think rationally . . . or at least the way Zoe would. She'd want to find the English soldiers. To find her brother. And he needed to stop her before she did. His face grim, Keegan started back toward Fort William.

Zoe paused and stretched, pressing her hands to her lower back. Had she ever walked so long and far in her life? The answer to that was simple enough. No. Before she met the Scot she barely managed to stumble, from her bedroom to the parlor.

She did feel stronger now. That was for certain. And better. Despite the fact that her feet hurt and her legs ached from walking. No dizziness, except of course when she glanced up at the towering peeks, their summits hidden in the clouds. Zoe took a deep breath of clear, cool air and turned her face to the sun.

Then she sighed and stepped to the side of the path. Dejectedly she sat on a flattened boulder. She was lost. Or if not that, at least she didn't know where she was going. Yesterday, riding in the cart, she hadn't noticed the road split quite so often. But today the web of twisted paths was too confusing.

As confusing as the thoughts running through her head. Last night when she decided and this morning when she left, her course seemed to be true and sure. But now . . . Zoe's head sank into her hands and she tried to erase the vision of Keegan last night when he accused her of cowardice. His eyes, thick-lashed and greener than the sea at dawn, still stared at her. Dared her to be honest with him.

Pushing to her feet Zoe studied the two roads forking before her. One seemed to wind higher into the mountains, the other took a lower turn. For a moment she twisted about, surveying the way she'd come. Wishing she could return.

Then with a firm step she chose the low road.

By midafternoon the sun was hot enough to have her sweating beneath the plaid. Zoe took it off, flinging it about her waist and tying it. She stopped by a stream that slipped over smooth pebbles and ate the last of her oatcakes from yesterday, rinsing them down with water. She kept in sight of the road in case any mounted soldiers happened by, which Zoe decided would be a bit of pure luck.

She even went so far as to imagine Fox riding with them. How wonderful it would be to see him. To have him wrap his arms about her and kiss her cheek and take care of her. To remove her from the intense looks and secret desires of the Scot.

But of course Fox didn't come galloping by, nor did any soldiers. Instead she was left to walk farther into the hills. To her left she could hear the ocean and occasionally she caught glimpses of it, a shadowed strip of silver. For clouds were rolling in, dark and ominous.

By the time it started raining again Zoe was nearly running down the rutted road. All around her the hills stretched, heath-covered and bare of shelter. " 'Tis only rain," Zoe told herself, but the wind made a liar of her, tearing at her skirts and hair.

It was then that she heard it, above the howl of the storm. Someone was shouting her name, loud and angrily. Zoe didn't need to turn to know who called her but she did anyway before racing away, off the path through the bracken.

He'd been far enough behind to give her a good start, but Zoe could soon hear his pounding footfalls above the beat of her heart. She never thought he'd follow her. Foolish of her not to consider that possibility, but she thought the wiser course for him was to take flight. What if she had encountered soldiers? What if she'd told them of Keegan MacLeod?

All those jumbled thoughts tangled through her head as she ran, her breath coming in shallow pants. He was almost upon her now. It cost Zoe a precious moment to look around. When she did, she saw his face, wet and angry. He called out to her again, yelling for her to stop, but she ignored him, plunging ahead, feeling one foot, then the other sink into mush. A mush that tried to suck her down.

"For God's sake keep yerself still." Keegan's lips were set in a grim line as he sank to his knees on the wet ground. "Do ye hear me Zoe, ye're only makin' it worse."

"Help me." Zoe frantically shifted her feet, trying to find some foothold and found none. Sinking deeper appeared to be the only result of her flouncing about.

"Zoe!"

The tone of his deep voice, at once commanding and soothing, drew her attention. Zoe sucked in her breath and blinked the tears and rain from her eyes.

"You've fallen into a mountain bog."

"Oh, no," she wailed into the storm, though her predicament was hardly news. "Will it suck me under?" Of all the ways she could end her life *this* was one she'd never considered.

"Zoe, ye're not going t' go under. Now listen and do as I say."

She didn't have much choice, though Zoe wondered if it crossed the Scot's mind to just leave her.

"Give me yer hands. Just one at a time. And try to move as little as possible."

Which was difficult while lifting her hands free of the muck. But Zoe did her best to do as he said. She couldn't wait to feel the solid strength of his fingers around hers. But he didn't reach for her hands, instead he snatched the plaid from the bog. Before she could wonder why the Scot reached down, wrapping it under her arms.

His hands were slippery, but he managed to tie off the plaid. "Now, lass, I'm goin' t' pull ye free." Using the tartan, then his hands, Keegan managed to roll her out of the bog and onto solid ground. She slipped into his arms, wrapping hers around him and laid her head on his chest. He bent over her, using his body to shield her from the wind and rain. Keegan rubbed his palm over her hair and back. He whispered soothing words in Gaelic as she sucked in air and tried to catch her breath.

When she was calm, Keegan tilted her round chin up with one finger. "Are ye better now?"

"Yes." She hiccupped. "I think so."

"Good." Instantly his protective demeanor faded. "Then will ye kindly tell me what the devil ye thought ye were doing? Have ye no sense girl?"

"I've sense enough to try and be rid of you," Zoe countered as she struggled to her feet. Her skirts clung to her legs, thick with mud. "Oh." She was sobbing again and disgusted with herself for doing it. In frustration she wiped her hands down the side of her skirts. When he yelled at her again for being a dolt, lucky to be alive, she slung some of the muck at him.

The last thing she saw before turning to flee was the shock on his face as the slimy mud struck him in the eye.

She hadn't gone three steps before he caught her, swinging her around by the arm. "Are ye mad? Do ye wish t' go stumblin' into another bog? Or perhaps over a cliff this time? That's it, isn't it," he yelled above the howling wind. "Ye're insane and ye're makin' me the same."

"I am not!" Zoe spit sodden hair from her mouth. " 'Tis you. All this is your fault. If you hadn't burst into my library like a . . . like a wild man, I wouldn't be here. I'd be safe and warm and . . . cared for."

"By that old crone, Miss Phelps."

Zoe sucked in her breath. "Don't you dare make disparaging remarks about Miss Phelps. She's kind and considerate, loyal—"

"And she made a damn invalid out of ye."

"What are you talking about?" Zoe's eyes grew wide. "I'm sickly. Everyone knows that . . ." Her voice trailed off as the words filtered through to her brain. Of course everyone knew how delicate she was, how frail and poor of health. But she didn't feel sickly just now. And Zoe imagined she didn't look it either, standing as she was in the pouring rain, shouting at the top of her lungs to be heard over the storm. She probably did look insane.

Taking him by surprise, Zoe turned on the heel of her mud-encrusted shoe. "I shan't listen to you anymore."

"Just where in the hell do ye think ye're off t' now?" This time when he grabbed her arm he whirled her around so hard she bumped into his hard, wet chest.

"Let me go." Zoe took a tentative swipe at his arm, found it felt good and did it again.

"Ach, what are ye doin'?" With his free hand Keegan tried to grab her arms.

The wind whipped her hair and skirts. The plaid still tied under her arms flew out like a banner. The rain poured and the sky darkened and Zoe kept hitting at Keegan till he jerked her tighter against his chest.

"I don't like you. You kidnapped me."

"Aye, 'tis true."

"And you hate my brother."

"True again."

He was taunting her. Zoe lifted her hand to slap his cheek, but the force of her motion dissipated like mist in the sun. Her palm cupped his jaw. Their eyes met. And everything else in the world disappeared. The kiss was open mouthed and hard, sizzling with pent-up desire.

Keegan's fingers tore through her hair, holding her head still for his assault on her mouth. His tongue speared and explored, meeting hers in a devilish dance that sent his blood racing.

Together they fell to their knees, still bound— mouth to mouth, breast to chest. He wanted her more than he'd ever wanted another woman. And he'd have her. Here. Now.

It took a gust of wind hard enough to slap the plaid across his face for Keegan to remember the storm.

Thirteen

"Zoe."

"Mmmm?" Her face strained up toward him, eyes closed when Keegan pulled away.

"Sweetheart, the storm."

"What? Oh . . ." Zoe blinked, then coughed as water streamed into her mouth. What was she thinking? Zoe stared at him in disbelief. His hair was wet, plastered to his skull, but the fire still burned in the depths of his green eyes as he looked back at her.

She was cold, soaked to the skin and windblown, yet all she wanted was to continue kissing him. To somehow ease the ache that settled in the region far below her stomach.

"We need t' find shelter," he said after giving her a quick kiss and grabbing her hand.

"But there isn't any." The watery landscape looked as wild and barren as ever. But the Scot didn't seem to hear her as he pulled her along. The rain, slanting down in blurry sheets made it difficult to see, and after her experience in the bog, Zoe was leery of tramping about. But he was right, of course, they simply couldn't stand out in this weather.

The Scot seemed fairly sure of himself as he led the way toward the edge of a wide abyss. Below them, through the mist, the Atlantic, churned by the storm, slapped against the rocky shore.

"We can't go down there," she yelled, pulling back on the hand he held in his iron grip. She thought he said something about a path but she couldn't hear him well. And he'd already started climbing down the slope of craggy rocks.

They zigged and zagged fighting their way through the crevices, slowly working down the precipice. The rain came in gusts now, carried by the wind that moaned and whipped its way about the face of the mountain, as if trying to dislodge the two trespassers. But occasionally there was a moment of relief from the storm provided by an overhang of rock above them. Even at those times, Zoe was acutely aware of the pounding surf below, waiting to embrace them if they made a false step. Zoe tried very hard to keep her footing.

When Zoe heard Keegan's yelp she didn't know whether to think he'd slipped and they were both moments from eternity, or that the ghostly howl of the wind had finally gotten to him. What she didn't expect was to be hauled into a hole in the side of the mountain.

Zoe swallowed and looked around in awe, her mouth agape. "What . . . ? How did you know it was here?" They were in a cave protected from the driving rain, and though she could still hear the wind's fury, it no longer snatched at her hair and skirts.

"I didn't, not for sure." Keegan was obviously pleased with himself. "But these cliffs are riddled with caves. And if we're really lucky . . ."

"What? If we're really lucky what?" He'd broken

off his commentary to move away from the opening, batting away cobwebs with a windmill motion. Zoe followed in his wake, jumping back when he yelped again.

"It's been used before. By some drovers maybe, takin' their cattle t' market. Or perhaps a Jacobite hiding from the English." He turned, grinning at her, then shook out one dusty plaid, then another, he found in a heap on the floor. "And look," he said, sifting through a pile of burned branches nearby. "Enough of a fir branch for light."

"I don't suppose there's anything to eat?" Zoe tried to peek over his shoulder. Since her appetite had improved Zoe often found herself hungry.

"Sadly nay, but we won't be here forever. The storm will blow itself out soon. In the meanwhile, 'tis better in here than bein' out there."

She couldn't argue with that. Zoe glanced toward the entrance. The inside of the cave, no matter that it was damp, was preferable to the elements outside. When she turned to agree with him Zoe was surprised to find him so close.

"So are ye goin' t' tell me now why ye ran away?"

He stared down at her the way he had on the moor. The kind of stare that got her aching again. Longing for his kiss.

But he didn't kiss her. Instead his hands molded the tops of her shoulders. "Ye could have died out there."

Zoe swallowed. It was so hard to resist the pull of those smoky green eyes. "What do you expect me to do? I'm a captive. 'Tis my right to try and escape."

"And mine t' capture ye again."

"Why won't you just let me go? I won't tell anyone where you are."

His fingers tightened. "Ye expect me t' believe that?"

"Yes!" Zoe's voice calmed. "Yes, I do." Her lashes lowered. When she looked at him again her expression was stripped of all artifice. "Despite what you've done to me, I've no desire to see you hang."

"What of yer brother? Ye'd watch me step up t' the gallows t' save his life."

"I don't think you'll kill him."

"Ach, ye think I've forgotten what he did t' my da?"

"I think you've come to realize it wasn't Fox, but circumstances that killed your father."

His hands left her, and he jerked about, agitation quickening his step. With the wild beauty of the storm behind him he turned to face her. "That's where ye be wrong Zoe. I've not given up on my quest of yer brother and ye've but t' try runnin' from me one more time to see the truth of my words."

Zoe simply stared at him, her eyes defiant.

"Ye think I won't get word t' him that I have ye?"

"It will do you no good."

"I disagree, Zoe. He'd come for ye. We both know that."

"And you'd kill him."

"I'd kill him," Keegan agreed, more to frighten her than because he thought he would. There was a bit of truth in what she said about knowing that it was the evils of war responsible for his father's death. But he couldn't let go of his anger. Not yet.

"You're a beast." Zoe crossed her arms.

"Aye, and that's the truth of it ye speak. But I've told ye before, desperate times make for desperate men." He paused, then stalked purposefully closer to Zoe. "And desperate woman, I'm thinkin'."

"What are you jabbering about?" He was directly in front of her again, close enough for Zoe to smell the wildness of him.

"We both know why ye ran when ye did. Why ye kissed me in the rain."

"You kissed me."

"T' my recollection 'twas a mutual act, that near t' sent the rain about us sizzlin'."

"You mustn't talk like that."

"And ye mustn't be such a hypocrite, Zoe." The back of his fingers skimmed across her neck. "Do ye think I can't see the way yer eyes turn t' silver when I kiss ye." He stepped closer. "Or when ye think I might."

"You mistake my illness for passion." Her breath was coming very slowly.

"Are ye tellin' me ye're sick again?"

"Yes." His mouth was only a whisper from hers. "I ache."

Zoe didn't wait for him to close the distance between them. With abandon her hands reached up, grabbing fistfuls of thick, wet hair and pulling his mouth to hers.

It was no gentle kiss. His open mouth hungrily devoured hers as Zoe's fingers tangled deeper into his hair. And he was right. The moisture on her body seemed to sizzle. Then his lips trailed down her chin to nuzzle the side of her neck. His voice vibrated through her. " 'Tis not a good thing to wear such sodden clothin'. Ye might catch a chill." Which seemed impossible as warm as she was, but Zoe had to admit she liked the feel of his fingers loosening the top button of her bodice. Each inch of skin he exposed received the hot pressure of his lips till he yanked the jacket from her arms.

The ache inside her was growing to explosive proportions. Zoe held her breath and waited for that moment when her poor heart would burst . . . deciding that if this was the cause of her demise, she'd finally found one that suited her.

He undressed her as quickly as he could, considering the damp state of her clothing. The petticoat tabs knotted. The corset tangled. And her stockings were coated with muck. But none of that seemed to matter to either of them.

Zoe tore at his shirt, wanting to feel the firm texture of his skin. By the time he spread out the plaid and pulled her atop him, Zoe was near out of her mind with an aching want.

Keegan ran his hands down her back, curving them over her bottom, spreading her legs. She jerked as he feathered his fingers down the moist crevice.

"I . . . I can't stand it," Zoe whispered against the skin of his neck. She lay sprawled on top him, her breasts which seemed to have swollen to the point of pain, flattened against his chest. She'd been unable to tear off his shirt. But it did gape open, so that some of her flesh abraded the cool, wet cotton, some his fevered flesh. She preferred the flesh.

But though she was naked as the day she was

born, he still wore his damp breeches. He seemed at odds as to what to do. His hands molded her buttocks and back, then fumbled beneath her to jerk down his pants. Both actions had the effect of spinning Zoe further off her center. She'd never felt so light-headed and achy, so feverish and afire.

"Please, oh, please," Zoe begged, though for the life of her she didn't know for what. To say she wished relief from her sweet agony was true, but she didn't want him to stop. Not when his hands had the ability to drive her to such distraction.

And then he shifted and grunted, lifting her up and sliding her back down on his naked flesh. He grabbed her buttocks, spreading her, positioning her. The hard, hot maleness between her legs seemed to taunt her, dare her to find relief. Zoe wriggled down, feeling plump and ripe and wet, ready for whatever he might do to bring an end to her sweet torture.

But he spanned her waist with his hands, stopping her movements. His voice was thick, his breathing hard, and fast. " 'Twill hurt some, Zoe. I'm sorry, but it will."

Hurt? How could anything ache more than the pressure churning inside her? With an instinct as old as time, Zoe arched her body, sliding down till the tip of his hardness, swelled into her body.

"Oh." Relief seemed at hand. Relief in the form of his thick, throbbing, manhood. With a sudden motion, Zoe impaled herself. If there was pain she didn't feel it. Her whole body quivered. Her head filled with a roaring sound, that blocked out even the storm.

She was dying, she knew that. For no one could feel such pure ecstasy and live to tell of it. Zoe wasn't sure what happened next. It was impossible to concentrate. His hands touched her everywhere, finding secret places that turned her legs to jelly and sent her heart pounding.

And then his mouth was on her breast, sucking and nibbling and Zoe couldn't catch her breath. The pressure where their bodies joined surged, built to such a pitch that when the explosion came, Zoe felt as if she'd tumbled off the side of the mountain, hurling through space.

"Mmmm. Am I still alive?"

Beneath her cheek she heard a deep chuckle and opened her eyes. Dark, curly hair tickled her nose. She felt replete and satisfied and the ache was gone. Slowly, for she couldn't move any other way, Zoe lifted her head. Across a wide expanse of chest she saw the outline of Keegan's strong chin. He tilted his head, moving as slowly as she, and stared down at her, his eyes still smoky green.

"What *was* that?"

"Well now, 'tis called a variety of things." Keegan shifted them both till she was nestled half lying on him, half on her side. "But I prefer t' think of it as a little bit of heaven."

"Mmmm," Zoe repeated, for saying much else seemed too difficult to accomplish.

When she woke again it was dark inside the cave and the ache had returned. Zoe moaned, nuzzling with her chin the fingers toying with the curve of her ear. Keegan's other hand rested possessively between her legs.

"More heaven," she mumbled just before his lips covered hers.

When morning came, casting an eery shaft of light into the cave, Zoe yawned and stretched like a cat. Her body was stiff and sticky and still sporting some of the slime from the bog. And she'd never felt better in her life.

"Good morn t' ye."

A smile curved her lips at the sound of his deep voice. Zoe sighed, pushing up on her elbows. The plaid he'd folded over them last night drifted down to her waist. Keegan stood facing her, backlit by the still stormy sky. Hair, tangled and windblown, strong, brawny shoulders and chest, slim hips and long legs. His body, limned by the light, appeared savage, the wild man she'd once thought him to be. Shadows hid his expression, urged her to rise and see him more clearly.

Wrapping the plaid about her shoulders, Zoe stood and padded toward him through the soft sand. Foaming surf and wind-driven rain misted the cave entrance, and Keegan stepped out of the spray as she approached.

"You're wet." Her hand lifted to skim moisture from his shoulder and lingered. He was naked, gloriously unaffected by the fact. Beautiful in a rugged, untamed way that made Zoe want to let the plaid she gripped beneath her chin slither to the cave floor. Yet she hesitated.

"I played the laundress." Keegan pointed to their clothing draped on an outcrop of rocks in the cave. Petticoats, stockings, breeches, they'd all been washed, and hung to dry.

"Lazy me." Zoe yawned again. "I slept through it all."

"Aye, and ye deserved yer rest."

The tone of his voice, the smoky green of his eyes did magical things to the ache already in full blossom. Zoe thought again about dropping the plaid. But before she could, his hand covered her clutching fingers, and he freed the wool himself.

The plaid slid down her body, exposing all of her to the heat of his stare. "I'm thinkin' I know what ye need."

Yes. Thanks to last night Zoe knew exactly what she needed. She stepped forward, but though he bent down and kissed her, Keegan kept a wee bit of distance between them.

"I've ne'er played the lady's maid before I met ye," he said with a grin. "But I'm beginnin' t' see the advantages."

Keegan stepped toward the opening, and returned with a rock, scooped out by eons of time and filled with rainwater. " 'Tis a bit chilly, and we've no soap, but this should wash the worst of the dirt away." And with Zoe standing before him, Keegan tore off a bit of petticoat, dipped it in the water and began to slowly bathe her.

He began with her face, finger-combing back strands of curly hair, lightened by the sun, then wiping the cloth over her cheeks and forehead. His thumb skimmed over her mouth, pausing when she opened her lips and dampened it with her tongue. He ran the fabric over her jaw, her neck, following each stroke with a press of his lips.

Zoe's head fell back, exposing more of her flesh and he feasted, seeming to forget his original goal. "Ye have such incredible skin," he said against her collarbone. "Smooth and smellin' of roses."

"Roses?" Zoe murmured.

"Aye roses." He nibbled then soothed with his tongue. "Sweet smellin' and pink. Ye're like a bud just comin' into full bloom."

Keegan cupped her breasts, testing their weight, enjoying the change in her since they'd met. She was still slight of build, with delicate bones, but now there was some flesh on those bones. With a self-deprecating smile he rinsed the scrap of cloth in the clear cold water.

Her nipples were already pebbly hard, but the touch of the wet fabric made her shiver toward him. Keegan couldn't resist just one tempting taste. But his willpower, never one of his strengths, was fast disappearing. With a groan, he pulled away, leaving the tips of both breasts wet from his mouth.

With gentle strokes he washed her back, then the curve of her waist. Here and there were streaks of mud from the bog, and he rinsed them away, aware of what could have happened to her if he hadn't found her. The Highlands were a part of him, and he found his love of them growing stronger with each passing day. But he knew them to be a ruthless foe for someone like Zoe. Someone who didn't know how dangerous it could be.

"What is it?" He'd stopped his glorious torture

and stood a hand on each of her hips, his eyes as cloudy as the turbulent sky behind him.

Keegan shook his head. "I was just thinking of what the Highlands could do to a delicate rose." But before she could respond to his musings, Keegan dropped to his knees before her. She gasped when he sloshed the cloth through water and pressed it to the delta of hair between her legs.

"I'm sorry the water is cold," he said, but Zoe barely heard him above the pounding in her ears. Besides, she didn't notice the temperature. He'd found the core of her aching and with every subtle move of his hand beneath the cloth made it spiral higher.

Her thighs spread with a gentle nudge and he washed them, spending perhaps more time than necessary where they met her body. Then he reached through and behind, spreading the cloth. And all the while his thick wrist pressed against that part of her that cried out and wept for him.

Dizzy but not caring, Zoe looked down at him. All she could see was the bent top of his head, where his wild hair curled and gleamed with threads of burnished copper in the hauntingly scarce light, and the broad span of his shoulders. Her hands settled there, kneading the strong muscles, giving herself stability.

When he finished, Keegan leaned forward, blowing the soft curls dry. Sending Zoe's world off kilter. She tried to keep some control, but when his mouth touched her she arched forward and groaned, a sound that seemed not to come from her.

He sent the ache soaring to new heights, but by

this time Zoe knew that it was the most wondrous kind of ache and that relief was pure ecstasy. Her fingers knotted and flexed, riding the crest of his shoulders as he plundered and thrust. Waves like those crests spawned by the storm grew stronger, more intense.

Then came the shattering release, that weakened her knees and stole her breath. When Zoe opened her eyes she was flat on her back, Keegan kneeling between her bent knees.

He thrust into her savagely, pushing to the hilt, loving the sensual way she accepted all of him. Loving the soft, sexy sounds she made when he thrust. Loving the way her hands scored his buttocks, urging him back when he pulled away.

Loving her.

It was much later when he finished playing the lady's maid, washing the splendid curve of her calf and discovering how ticklish her feet were. They sat, wrapped in the plaid, leaning against the rock wall, watching the shattering demise of the storm.

"The sun seems all the brighter for the effort it takes to fight the clouds," Zoe said as she nestled her head beneath his chin.

"Aye, there's nothing t' match a good day in the Highlands."

"Do you call this a good day?" Zoe slanted him a look through her lashes.

"I call this a very bonny day," he countered, stealing a kiss before resuming his relaxed position. "Though I wouldn't balk at a bit to eat."

"Nor I." Zoe sighed. "Some clotted cream and strawberries would be nice."

"Clotted cream? Strawberries?" Keegan shifted again. "What of yer weak stomach? What of the thinned broth and tea?"

He watched Zoe's face turn a lovely shade of rose. "I think I do better eating less thinned broth and more clotted cream."

"And so ye shall." Keegan lifted her aside and pushed to his feet. With rapid motions he pleated one of the plaids about his waist and tucked it around his naked shoulder.

"What are you doing?"

"Goin' to find yer Ladyship a bite t' eat."

"But I didn't mean—"

"Ach, but I do." He checked the powder in his pistol, scowling when he found it wet, and chose his broadsword instead. Then he touched the tip of her nose. "We must both be fed if we're t' keep up our energy." His grin was wicked. "And I'm all in favor of that."

"But where—"

"Don't ye worry now." Keegan headed for the entrance, turning before he reached it. "And don't ye be goin' anywhere. I'll be back directly."

He disappeared through the opening just as a shaft of sunlight penetrated the gloom. By the time Zoe stood, and made her way to the door, she could find no sign of him. But then that was not surprising considering the twists and turns they'd taken to find the cave.

With a sigh she glanced toward her damp clothes, unable to help the thought of escape that flitted across her mind. But it was soon replaced by memories of his lips on hers, of their bodies joined, and the way he could shatter the ache of longing.

But now she had a new problem to add to all the others. There was a new ache. And though it settled in the region of her heart, Zoe knew it was not caused by any weakness, or infirmity on her part. It was love for him, pure and simple.

Yet not simple at all.

Fourteen

Four more days passed before Zoe set eyes upon Castle MacLeod. The weather thankfully had cleared, turning the sky a perfect robin's egg blue and the clouds looked like drifts of fine snow. Mist still clung to the hollows, and crowned the mountains. But the air was clean and crisp and the sun a glorious golden orb.

They'd left the cave, their clothes dry and bellies full thanks to the moor fowl Keegan managed to snare. Nothing was mentioned as they walked north, about the night they'd spent cocooned in each other's arms, protected from the storm. Nor did the Scot make further reference to her attempted escape, or his threat to contact her brother.

But Zoe could tell the Scot's mind wasn't on revenge, as they made their way deeper into the Highlands. It was as if the closer they drew to their destination, the stronger the pull. Zoe couldn't understand it, but strange as it seemed, she felt the same, as if Castle MacLeod were a lodestone and she iron filings.

Why would a Highland castle be calling her?

Zoe had plenty of time to contemplate the question as she rode the stout Highland horse. The animals, hers along with the one Keegan rode, were lent them on the second night out, when they stopped, seeking shelter.

" 'Tis a friend of my father's lives here," Keegan had said as they approached the manse set from the back from the road. Unlike many of the houses they'd passed, Ramsey House seemed prosperous, fields golden, ready for harvest, and grounds in good repair.

Keegan had commented on it, pleased the English had spared John Ramsey. It wasn't until they were ushered into the dark-paneled library that doubt shadowed his expression.

Though recognition was immediate, Sir John was not pleased to see Keegan or his English guest.

"I'd a thought ye'd know better than t' come here, MacLeod."

"It wasn't as if I had much choice. I'd have thought to receive more of a welcome. 'Tis always been the case for ye at Castle MacLeod."

"Aye, and times have changed."

"Does that mean friendships are gone then?"

The older man, narrow of face and stooped of shoulder, darted his eyes from Keegan to Zoe and back. " 'Tis trust that died on Culloden Moor."

"Ye've reason not to trust me?" Keegan's voice was incredulous.

"Nay, not ye, but others that may see ye. See ye here." He'd settled his long, spare frame in a leather chair. "I kept my loyalty with the king . . . by outward appearances. 'Tis what saved my land."

"But what of Niall?" Keegan had fought with Sir John's son Niall, had seen him die at Culloden.

"We chose different sides in the rebellion. At least it appeared so. 'Tis the Stuart cause we both embraced with our hearts, but there were practical things t' consider." His small watery eyes lingered on the portrait of a handsome young man above the hearth.

"I was with him, standin' near shoulder t' shoulder, when he died."

The older man seemed to grow more into himself. "I've been told he died well, a credit t' his clan and name."

"Aye." Keegan nodded. "Ye'd have been proud."

"Aye proud." Sir John took a shallow breath. "And now I've this house and the fields, and tenants. Niall's sacrifice for the clan." His palms flattened on the polished desktop. "And I don't wish t' be squanderin' it by takin' in Jacobites. Especially those with a bounty on their head."

"Does that mean ye won't be helpin' me. You'll forget the years ye knew my da. The times the MacLeods came t' yer service." Keegan took one step toward him, then another.

"Ye needn't be remindin' me of the past . . . or me debts." He sighed heavily, then pushed to his feet.

"I'll help ye this once t' leave the Highlands."

"But 'tis to Castle MacLeod I go."

"Ach and why I would ask. 'Tis nothin' for ye there lad. It's been confiscated. There's been a factor named t' collect the rents from those crofters not killed or hidin' in the hills."

Both men seemed to have forgotten she was there, standing in the shadows, and for that Zoe was grateful. For she could think of nothing to say to either man to ease their discomfort. Keegan's expression closed, his eyes narrowed, and his jaw tensed.

"Are ye certain of yer facts?"

"Aye, ye'll find no friendly faces t' greet ye at Castle MacLeod, lad. For the sake of yer father . . . yer brothers, I say leave this place while ye can. Take yer fine Sassenach woman and go t' France, or the New World. There's no place for ye here."

Tough as his words were, Sir John bore Keegan no malice and showed it by having two of his best horses saddled and bags filled with oatmeal and tea. He even handed over a brace of pistols that had belonged to his son. But fear of English reprisal made him refuse the pair a night of rest on linens and goosedown.

When they left Ramsey House, riding out under a moon, muzzy in the night mist, Zoe wasn't certain where they were heading. Sir John's suggestions seemed to have merit.

But here they were, two days later, looking down from the drover's road toward a lush, green glen surrounded on two sides by hills, the third by an arm of the sea. At one end the valley narrowed, becoming little more than a ravine. A river tumbled over rocks, forming waterfalls, splashing its way toward the deep, blue loch.

On its bank, backed to the sea stood Castle MacLeod.

The sight of it, surrounded by the untamed beauty of the land and water, nearly took Zoe's breath away.

And she had only to glance toward Keegan, sitting so proudly astride his horse to know how deeply it affected him. The walls were thick, seemingly made from and part of the same rock on which it stood. Towers and chimneys thrust toward the sky. Windows sparkled in the sun. The castle stood in lonely splendor.

Defiant.

"They can't take this from you," Zoe mumbled, not realizing she'd spoken aloud till Keegan shifted his mount closer to hers.

"I fear they already have." Keegan calmed his horse with a pat before urging him along the only path leading into the glen. "But perhaps I can reclaim what is mine. What has belonged to the MacLeods for centuries."

The closer they came to the castle, the more desolate Zoe felt. The wind seemed to share her mind, howling through the mountains. They passed charred remnants of turf houses, bothies, empty and haunting.

But even that didn't prepare Zoe for the feel of the ancient castle when they dismounted and climbed the stone stairs. The door opened with a creak. Inside, dark shadows and cobwebs filled the high entrance hall with gloom.

At the base of the staircase stood a heap of charred wood. The unburned chair leg and paneled door identified the remains as furnishings.

"What happened here?" Zoe whispered. She walked about, as if afraid to move too quickly, staring around her.

"The English is what happened. Or the Royal

Scots. Same difference," he added his voice thick with scorn. " 'Tis punishment for all MacLeods to have their ancestral home burned."

"Where are they do you suppose? All the people who lived here." Zoe wrapped her arms about her waist, for there seemed suddenly a chill in the air.

"Gone t' the hills. I hope and pray." Keegan kicked at the charred end of a piano stool, sending a cloud of ashes into the air. "For if not, they're dead."

"They wouldn't have done that . . ." Zoe's eyes beseeched. "Would they?"

Keegan just stared at her, his mouth grim. Then he turned and strode through the open doors into one of the parlors. Zoe had no choice but to follow.

The view through the bowed windows of the churning sea below was spectacular, a cruel contrast to the destruction within. Ransacked and stripped of valuables the huge room echoed with the down-draft of wind through the chimney. Like the hallway it smelled of burned wood and wool.

When Zoe turned away from the window she noticed Keegan staring at the spot over the hearth where the paint was lighter.

"My mother's portrait was there. Da had her sit for it when they were in France. Not long before she died." He glanced toward the pile of rubbish in the center of the floor, then back at the spot where she'd once reigned over family gatherings. He turned abruptly away. "We need t' see if there be anythin' of value worth savin'."

It took them the rest of the afternoon to search the mansion. They found mice and bats in the abovestairs rooms, but no people. Most of the bedrooms had received the same treatment as the parlors and dining room downstairs. But in some of the lesser rooms, and in the servants' quarters, it was obvious the soldiers had grown bored with their destruction.

Zoe found clothing. Nothing so grand as her borrowed riding habit, but that outfit had been through shipwreck and bog and was sadly in need of replacement. Zoe gathered the shifts and petticoats, skirts and plaids and went in search of Keegan.

"There's bedding in the rooms upstairs," she said after finding him in the bedroom once occupied by his parents. When he only nodded, she stepped forward, grabbing his arm. "You can't let this defeat you."

When he turned on her his expression was every bit as wild as when he first broke through the window at her house. His eyes shone with an intensity that almost made her back away.

But she knew him now, and was not so easily quelled. "Do you think to scare me away, Keegan? You forget I haven't the option of leaving."

His face darkened, then he shut his eyes. When his thick lashes lifted again there was such pain and sorrow in their green depths Zoe couldn't stand to look into them. "I left," he finally said. "They didn't want me t'. But I'd had enough of life here." He walked to the window. As did the one downstairs this bank of leaden panes overlooked the Atlantic. " 'Twas too desolate for me." He lifted his shoulders. "And there were too many responsibilities."

"You can't blame yourself for any of this . . .

this . . ." Zoe sighed. What could she call what had happened here? She'd never seen anything like it.

"Who would ye have me blame, yer saintly brother?"

Zoe didn't look away from his stare this time. "Fox wouldn't do this."

"Nay?" His brow lifted. "And I suppose he wouldn't promise me my da would be taken care of, then watch while he was tortured?"

Zoe's eyes widened. "He didn't." Zoe straightened her shoulders. "I know Fox better than to ever accept that."

"The strange thing is, I thought I did, too." Keegan shook his head. "It sounds even more ridiculous when I say the words, but there seemed t' be something between us . . . I don't know. A bond, of sorts. Like I'd known him before." His expression hardened. "But as it happens ye're right about one thing. He didn't watch. He simply turned away." Keegan did the same now, walking across the room and out the door.

Zoe watched him leave, her mind struggling with his accusation. "He's hurt," she mumbled. "Trying to hurt me in return." And it did. Not that she believed any of it. Fox simply wouldn't break his word. He was too honorable for that.

But a small voice whispered in her ear that war made savages of men. Made them do things they wouldn't ordinarily do. "No." She refused to believe Fox could be anything other than the brother she knew and loved.

But there was one thing for certain. Keegan MacLeod believed what he told her.

* * *

The kitchen garden had resisted the horses' hooves bent on its destruction. Well, at least some of it had. Zoe knelt in the dirt, using a broken spade she'd found, to dig up potatoes. Even though a chill wind blew off the sea, the sun shone brightly, making her forehead damp with sweat.

Zoe leaned back on her heels, arching her back. Her muscles ached, and she had the strongest desire to tell someone about it. Perhaps it was more than just discomfort caused by working too hard. What if there *was* something wrong with her?

With a loud sigh Zoe bent back over the hole. There probably wasn't anything dreadfully wrong with her. And even if there was, nothing could be done. It wasn't as if there was a doctor about. She twisted her neck this way and that. Or anyone else for that matter.

Keegan had gone off to hunt or fish, she wasn't sure which. He'd been rather vague. But then he hadn't done much talking since their disagreement over her brother. He had grunted something about finding them something to eat, which had given Zoe the idea to do the same.

She glanced over at her small pile of wrinkled potatoes, pleased with her find. If Keegan brought back a grouse, or . . .

Zoe sat up, shading her eyes against the sun, and glanced toward the stand of trees off to the right. Was that the cry of a child? She listened, cocking her head, but heard only the rhythm of the waves and the howling wind. And occasionally the shattering scream of the gulls swooping over the rocks.

Shaking her head, Zoe lifted her skirts and pushed to her feet. She was beginning to hear things in this desolate— Twisting around, Zoe dropped the spade and headed toward the woods. There was someone there. A child. She was certain.

Zoe had almost reached the stand of trees when a man, looking as wild and unkempt as Keegan once had, leaped from the screen of leafy undergrowth.

The man yelled.

Zoe screamed.

And somewhere in the woods a baby cried.

"My goodness." Zoe clasped her heart with her dirt encrusted hand. "You frightened me." Actually Zoe wondered if she still should be terrified, but it was difficult to fear a man of his age. He seemed to be at least seventy, with long grizzled hair and more spaces than teeth in his mouth. He studied her with as much concern as she studied him.

"Who are you?" Zoe finally managed to ask. "And shouldn't someone see to that baby."

"Someone is, if it be any of yer concern. And I've a mind t' know who comes into the laird's garden t' steal potatoes."

"I wasn't stealing." Zoe was indignant. "My name is Lady Zoe Morgan, and I've come here—"

"With me."

Zoe whirled around when she heard Keegan's firm voice. She hadn't heard him return. And it was just as obvious the old man hadn't heard him either. When she looked back around the man's eyes were as big as saucers.

"Keegan MacLeod, be that ye, or am I seein' ghosts in me old age?"

"I'm no apparition, Donuld MacLeod, and don't ye ever think otherwise."

Zoe watched as the old man's toothless grin lit up his weathered face. Then he gave a high nasal call. As if materializing from thin air, three women, one holding a young child, moved into the clearing. They all appeared to have the same reaction when viewing Keegan. First surprise, then jubilation.

They ignored Zoe.

"So tell me all of it lad. We heard ye were more fodder for the Sassenach gallows."

They sat in the grassy area between the forest and the garden. Keegan leaned against an ash trunk, his long legs spread in front of him, his ankles crossed. One of the women had started a peat fire, the other washed the potatoes in a nearby rivulet. Since the third had a nursing child at her breast, Zoe was left to pluck feathers from the moor fowl Keegan caught.

Keegan gave an abbreviated version of his escape and flight from England . . . one that did not include kidnapping, and both men laughed and joked about the inability of the English to keep water in a pail.

But as the potatoes and grouse roasted, their talk grew more subdued. The old man was the father of the tacksman, apparently a coveted position among the clan. Of course the son was dead, a victim of Culloden Moor.

"Aye, we mourned them all, we did, what was left of us. The laird, sad we were at his passin'. And yer brothers, a brave and bonny lot they were."

" 'Tis true. They all are heroes, dyin' for a cause they believed in." Keegan took a bite of the fowl. "So are there any more of ye left or is this it?" He included all the group with a sweep of his hand.

"Nay, lad, there be more. Scattered for the most part the remainin' MacLeod are. When the English soldiers come, we took t' the hills. The lasses and me just wander down every now and then t' see if we can find a bit t' eat." He crunched into his meat with the few teeth left in his jaw.

"Can ye find them do ye think?"

"Find who?" Grease dripped down the old man's whiskered chin and he swiped at it with his sleeve.

"The others." Keegan bent his knees and leaned forward. "I've a mind t' see what we can do about unitin' the clan again."

"Unitin'?" Donuld swallowed. "Where? How?"

"Here." Keegan pushed to his feet. "Here at Castle MacLeod where we've been for hundreds of years. We'll raise cattle and oats and fish like we—"

"Dunn't ye know? 'Tis not ours anymore." Donuld jerked his hand through the air. "The castle. The land." He shook his head on a grunt. "None of it."

"I won't let them take it away."

"But they've already done it lad. 'Tis nothin' we can do."

"Is that it then, we just surrender all that's been ours for centuries?"

"But Keegan—"

"What have ye now? A place t' lay yer head at night? Enough food t' eat? Ye think I didn't notice yer salivatin' over the measly grouse as it roasted on the spit. This glen can support us and all the others as it's always done."

"They drove away the cattle."

"So we'll get more . . . as our ancestors did if necessary. There be more than one Loyalist clan I wouldn't mind strippin' of a couple dozen head of their finest cattle." Keegan looked from one to the other. Donuld was still shaking his grizzled head but Keegan could tell he was pondering the idea. The women, only one of whom he knew by name, stared at him, then drew back to whisper to each other. It was only Zoe whose gaze never left his. Her eyes were wide and as grey as the mist crowning the summits beyond the glen. He wished he could tell what she was thinking.

"Ye know they'll come," Donuld began. "The factor . . ."

"We'll turn him away."

"The English troops."

What could he say to that? He knew as well as anyone what well-trained soldiers could do. But the MacLeods of old had built their stronghold to stand against man's forces as well as nature's. There was but one land way into the glen. And the path was so narrow, the sides so steep, it only took a few well-placed men to defend it.

The seaside was well insulated as well, with offshore rocks and currents that deterred any large-scale invasion. Did he think a few score tenants and crofters could hold out against the power and might of the British army? Nay. But as he'd said earlier, what choice did they have?

Letting out his breath, Keegan stood, planting his

feet firmly on the ground. "We'll see about the soldiers when the time comes. There be more than one way t' fight."

"What is it you wish to tell me?" Lord Foxworth glanced up from the map of the Highlands he was studying. His eyes narrowed as they fell on the disreputable figure on the other side of the desk. He was short, a seafarer by the cut of his clothing, which was torn and in sad need of a washing. As was the man himself. His hair hung limp and greasy from a kerchief tied about his head. But it was the stub where his left arm once was that caught Fox's attention. He quickly pulled his gaze to the man's face.

"I've been waiting since yesterday to see you, goven'r."

And he wouldn't be granting him an audience now if he hadn't said one name that could gain it. Keegan MacLeod.

"Yes, well I apologize for the delay. Fox leaned back in his chair. When his aide first informed him of the civilian wishing to discuss something private with him, Fox had brushed the request aside. The Highlands were full of Scots wanting this and that from the government. But it was not his duty to give them any special privileges. He was here for one reason and one reason only.

"I hear you're looking for that rebel bastard, Keegan MacLeod."

"I am." His purpose was hardly a secret, and this was not the first person to come to him with wild tales of spotting the fugitive. He usually was described as near seven feet tall, with flames shooting from his mouth and eyes like burning peat. This damn MacLeod was becoming a folk hero among these people.

But Fox knew the true MacLeod. He was no mythical character, no superhuman being, despite the fact that he'd escaped from New Gaol. He was just a man. A despicable one at that. A man who would steal a poor sick woman from her deathbed and . . . Fox didn't want to think about what had happened to his beloved sister.

"Well I brought him to Scotland on my sloop, the *Sea Maiden.*"

The man's blunt admission focused Fox's attention on him.

"When did you do this?"

"A fortnight ago, maybe less. I wasn't well for a while. Time has a way of slipping by when you're gripped by fever."

"Can you tell me why you decided to transport a renegade, someone who'd been sentenced to hang? Or is your story that you didn't know?" Fox lost what little interest he had in interrogating the man and resumed his perusal of the map. How many had come to him since he'd made MacDonald House in Moirer his headquarters, with wild tales of smuggling the MacLeod into Scotland?"

"Oh I knew who he was. She told me."

"Who?"

"Your sister."

"My sister?" Despite himself Fox glanced up.

"That's who she said she was. Lady Zoe something

or another. I didn't believe her at first. She didn't look much like a lady."

"And she simply came up to you and told you who this man was and asked you to take him to Scotland." Both dark brows lifted in disbelief.

"She wanted to get away from him. Said for me to take her to you in Scotland. That MacLeod fellow followed her aboard, my men found him and put him in the hold."

Elbows on the desktop, Fox steepled his fingers. "Describe Lady Zoe to me."

The sailor shrugged. "A looker if you'll excuse me saying so. Short." He leveled his remaining hand near his ear to show Zoe's height. "A bit on the thin side, but enough there for a man to warm up to at night, if you get my meaning."

"I do indeed." Fox flattened his hands on the smooth mahogany and stood. "I would be across this desk to flatten your nose for using such words to describe my sister . . . If in fact you were describing her. However you are not." Poor frail Zoe had a certain beauty to be sure. But Fox was sure he was the only one to see it, so deeply was it hidden beneath the pale skin and sickly body.

"She called herself your sister." Holt took several steps back despite his attempt to sound persuasive.

"I'm sure she did. Now if you will kindly leave—"

"But I thought you wanted information about Keegan MacLeod. I heard you'd pay good money for it."

"That's true but frankly, I don't see you providing me with that information.

"But I brung 'em to Scotland I tell you."

"Guard." Fox called out for the soldier stationed outside. Abruptly the door opened and a burly soldier entered.

"You're making a big mistake here," Holt squealed as the soldier grabbed his good arm. "I seen who took them in after the shipwreck I tell you. I could take you there."

With a wave of his hand Fox motioned for the guard to remove the sailor.

"I waited in a copse of trees even though my arm was bleeding, and I seen them leave." Frustration over all he'd been through, over losing not only the ransom money and reward for turning both of them over to this haughty bastard, but now not even being believed. Being jerked around and manhandled. Holt's struggles only made the soldier's grip tighter.

"Fine with me, if you don't catch the bastard," he spat out. "And as for that bitch with her weak digestion, too good to eat—"

"What did you say?" Fox was around the desk now, his hands replacing those of the guard. "You heard me. Repeat what you just said."

"I don't care if you don't catch—"

"Not that." Fox's fingers tightened in the man's shirt. "What you said about my . . . about the woman."

"She was always complaining," Holt began. "The food . . . I don't know. Her weak heart . . ." Holt tried to pull away, but the major's hold wouldn't budge. "I don't remember."

"Well you better remember." With a shove, Fox sent the man into a chair. "You better remember all of it."

Fifteen

The low haunting tone of the sheep horn pierced the afternoon calm. Zoe stilled, as did the other women with her, their hands dropping to their sides, their faces lifted toward the narrow cleft in the hills leading into the glen.

"That's the signal," Mary whispered. Her fingers covered the mouth of the babe riding on her hip when he began to fuss.

"I know." Zoe shaded her eyes and watched, waiting to see something.

"Should we be gettin' t' the hills?" Anne's face was anxious.

"Keegan said we flee only after the second signal." Zoe left the semicircle of women who until moments ago were busy complaining about the mundane chore of washing linens. She strained to see . . . to hear.

"Well where is he? Maybe he's dead. Maybe the soldiers killed him and now they're coming here to kill us. But first they'll rape—"

"Hush." Zoe turned on Catriona. She was young and had experienced too much at the hands of the soldiers for Zoe to fault her hysteria. But panic was the last thing they needed. "Keegan is with the men, hunting. They're not dead." Zoe swallowed, hoping she was telling the truth. "And they wouldn't leave us vulnerable like this."

"Well now some of us aren't all that worried, are we?" This comment came from Seonaid, a tall buxom girl with eyes as green as Keegan's and a mouth that hadn't stopped making snide innuendos about Zoe since she first came down from the hills.

Zoe tried to ignore this remark as she had the others. No amount of explaining on Zoe's part appeared to quell the woman's tongue. Besides, what she said had an element of truth to it. Keegan hadn't told anyone who her brother was, and had warned her to keep it quiet. Still, Zoe wasn't one of them. And though there were times when she forgot to think about escape, she was a prisoner—even if no ropes bound her or bars locked her in.

What would happen to her if the signal had meant British soldiers were coming along the path? Would they fire into the glen killing everyone in their sight? Or would she be captured, be able to tell them who she was?

With that last thought came a twinge of hope, but it was quickly dashed by another notion, one that made her body tremble. If it was indeed British soldiers that caused the alarm to sound *where* was Keegan?

Zoe began walking before she realized what she was about. It was Seonaid's voice that made her pause, but only for a moment.

"Where are ye off to? The plan is to hide in the hills." Seonaid jerked her thumb toward the coppice of trees and the sheltering rocks beyond.

"I'm going to see what happened."

"To warn the British is what ye mean." The Scotswoman yanked her arm. "I've no understandin' of what Keegan sees in ye, but I know he don't want ye runnin' off."

"Let go of me." Zoe whirled on her accuser.

"Now ladies, this be no time for squabblin' betwixt ye." Mary tried to step between Zoe and the buxom girl.

"She's a spy. Probably got word t' the soldiers somehow, and planned t' have all of us killed."

"That's not true." Zoe's eyes narrowed and her gaze never left Seonaid's.

"Hmmph. Ye may have Keegan fooled with yer innocent ways, and smilin' lips, but I see right through ye I do. Yer a lowdown snake, a lying Sassenach, a—"

"That's enough Seonaid." Mary's voice had the ring of authority. " 'Tis no secret how ye feel about Keegan, so we'll all take that as yer excuse for being so rude. Zoe may not be one of us but—"

"Thank you but I can speak for myself, Mary." Zoe jerked her arm free of Seonaid's grip. " 'Tis true I'm not here by choice, but I'd never do anything to hurt any of you . . . including Keegan. Now I'm going up to the ridge to see what's happening. If I wave my arms, hide in the hills."

"So ye can lead them t' us?"

"Think what you will, Seonaid MacLeod. *Do* what you will." With that Zoe hurried off.

By the time she reached the path that twisted and turned its way skyward, Zoe was winded. Her heart pounded and she sucked in air through her mouth.

If worry hadn't driven her, Zoe was certain she would turn back, or at least find a rock upon which to sit and rest awhile. As it was she couldn't be certain she'd make the climb. What if her heart gave out? It *was* weak.

At least she'd always thought it was. But as she quickened her steps, Zoe realized her heart kept pace. And as gradually her mind became consumed with concern for Keegan, she forgot to even question whether her health was up to the rigors of the climb. She reached the summit, out of breath, but not hesitating to climb over the rocks toward the small group of men clustered there.

There was Donuld and his grandson, one too old, the other too young to be much help hunting and two others who apparently heard the horn and came back. They were huddled around someone or something, that Zoe couldn't see. No sign of Keegan. No English soldiers.

Lifting her skirts, Zoe marched forward. "What is it? Why did you sound the alarm?"

Donuld shifted and she noticed he held his dirk at the ready. She also got a look at a person crouched on the ground, his arms wrapped about two spindly legs.

"François?" Zoe nudged the old Scotsman aside just as Keegan's valet lifted his head. He stared at her, his eyes large. Zoe saw the moment recognition hit.

"Mademoiselle Zoe?" He started to rise, only to be pushed down by a firm hand on his shoulder. "Mademoiselle Zoe," he repeated. "I'm so glad to see you."

"Ye know this Frenchie?"

"Of course she does. Tell this barbarian who I am."

Zoe cringed. Though she'd used the description herself several times when referring to Keegan, she could tell the four men surrounding François didn't take kindly to it. And she could hardly blame them. Yet it seemed the sooner she defused the situation, the better.

"Gentlemen, allow me to introduce Monsieur François DeBerry, Keegan's valet."

"Ye're saying this little saplin' of a fellow is Keegan's man?"

"He is. Not only that. François is the one who arranged for Keegan to escape the noose." Zoe reached down, offering the Frenchman her hand. He rose with exaggerated dignity, brushing at his silk breeches and straightening a velvet coat that had seen better days. Then with a sigh he bent forward, grasping Zoe's hand and kissed it.

"What a pleasure to see you again Mademoiselle Zoe, and in such excellent health. This Scottish air, thin as it is, seems to agree with you."

"I suppose it must." Zoe gave his arm a pat. "For I've never felt better," Zoe said, realizing it was true. She was living most of her hours out of doors, eating whatever the men could catch and the women could scrounge from the garden and fields, and sleeping on a mattress in a large drafty room. She hadn't been bled in well over a fortnight, rested only at night, yet here she was smiling and laughing at François, feeling as if she could hike to the summit of the next mountain if need be.

It was a wonder.

". . . Monseigneur Keegan?"

Zoe forced her thoughts back to the present, realizing François had asked her about the Scot. "He's well, hunting with some of the other men, I believe." Zoe took his arm and started down the path. "I warrant he'll be surprised to see you."

After one last arrogant look at the men who'd captured and ridiculed him, François concentrated on his footing. His leather pumps were in sad repair to be sure. "Well, it's a miracle that I found this place. Have you any idea how out of the way it is?"

Zoe laughed. "Frankly yes. But wait a minute." She stopped, grabbing his padded shoulders and turning the little Frenchman to face her. "You didn't tell the English soldiers you were coming here, did you?"

"Please, give me credit for some intelligence." He brushed lint from his sleeve. "I keep my distance from English dragoons whenever possible."

"Good." Zoe let out her breath.

"Though I'm surprised by your question. I would have thought you'd be pleased by the prospect of a brigade or two swooping into this valley."

"Glen."

"I beg your pardon."

"Glen, it's called a glen, not a valley, and I'm not sure what I want." Zoe's smile was self-conscious. She shrugged her shoulders and walked on.

"It really is amazing," he said after a moment.

"What?"

"The change in you. Do you still have problems with your stomach, ma chérie?"

"No." Zoe shook her head." I'm much better now. But tell me of you. How did you know to come here?"

"Monsieur Keegan would hear of nothing else but coming here when he escaped, so despite his little setback . . ."

"You mean at the inn?"

"Oui. That was a close one for the two of you."

"It was my fault."

Zoe's admission earned her a shrug from François.

"Anyway, the inn's patrons were so busy planning what they should do . . . not doing it mind you . . . that I simply hitched the horses to the coach and followed you south. Unfortunately I reached Harmouth after the two of you had sailed."

Zoe bit her bottom lip. "That was my fault as well."

"Ah." He lifted his hands. "That does not matter now. I was surprised though to find Monsieur Padraic Rafferty still in the town."

"You saw Captain Rafferty?"

"Oui."

"But we heard he was dead."

"Non, he was very much alive, though I do believe he mentioned being late coming into the harbor. He arrived the day I entered Harmouth. But anyway when I explained my situation . . . and mentioned Mademoiselle Kate's name he brought me to Scotland."

"Goodness."

"Oui. We docked in a small cove near Fort William. And I came here."

Of course it was not nearly as simple as that. François's ordeal had been almost as grueling as Zoe's and Keegan's. He'd been forced to ford raging rivers and had climbed mountains that touched the sky, and eaten the most abominable food . . . François's words.

But he was delighted to be reunited with Keegan, and seemed equally pleased to see Zoe.

That evening, he delighted the Scots by taking the salmon they'd fished from the waters and poaching them with a divine cream sauce. One taste and most misgivings concerning the little Frenchman were forgotten.

But it was later, with just Keegan and Zoe present that François announced what would make him completely accepted by the Scots.

"I've had to spend some of it I'm sorry to say," he explained, after entering the room where Keegan and Zoe slept. With an apology for having it hidden in so many pockets and seams in his clothing, François produced gold coins. "It's the money Mademoiselle Kate lent you in London. I found it in the room you let in Harmouth. The proprietor of the inn hadn't even cleaned the room before I got there," he said with a snort of disdain. "Monsieur Rafferty kindly refused to take it for my voyage, suggesting instead it would be better used by you."

Keegan watched the pile grow. True, a year ago he'd have thought it a modest sum. But now it was a fortune. With an outburst of emotion, Keegan wrapped his arms around François, lifting him off the floor in a giant bear hug, that had the little man red with embarrassment.

"It is the least I can do for you Monsieur Keegan," he said, when Keegan thanked him for the second time. "After you saved me from those men and took me in."

"What did he mean by that?" Zoe asked after François left to spread a pallet in the main hall.

Keegan shrugged. "when I first went t' London I was by the docks and saw some bullies beatin' up on the little guy."

"So you jumped in and saved him?"

"I've always been too fond of a good fight for my own good," was all Keegan would add. He was more interested in the money François brought. "This means we can buy cattle. Start the herds up again. Perhaps—"

"The lookouts sounded the alarm today when François came into view," Zoe interrupted.

Keegan laughed. " 'Tis hard t' imagine him being much of a threat."

"I was with the women. We didn't know it was François. We thought it was English soldiers."

Keegan's expression sobered. "And are ye tellin' me this tale for any particular reason."

"They are bound to come." Zoe found herself hating that she was piercing his elation with a jab of reality. "If not today, then another day. You cannot hold them off with the men you have here."

"Perhaps other clans will join us. No one really wants the English here." His eyes, fiercely passionate one moment, disappeared behind a curtain of thick lashes. "I didn't mean to be insulting ye."

His apology warmed her heart, made what else

she had to say doubly difficult. "You know in your heart that I'm right."

Keegan strode to the window. The moon hung full and bright, shimmering fractured light over the black luster of the sea, limning the strong lines of his face in silver. "What would ye have me do, Zoe?" he finally asked.

The question was so poignant Zoe could do nothing for a moment but close her eyes. Then slowly, purposefully she joined him, wrapping her arms about his waist, leaning her cheek against his muscled back. She loved the smell of him, the feel. "What of the New World? I've read about places. The Carolinas. It would be a new start."

"I told ye, I don't want t' leave Scotland."

"I see." Zoe took a deep breath. She hated the response she had to give to that. "Then I don't know," she whispered. "I don't know what either of us can do."

He'd expected no other reply. Hell, there was no other reply. But hearing it, hearing the catch in her voice, brought reality crashing down on his shoulders. What was he to do? There was no answer. Keegan took a deep breath wondering if his father would know, wondering too if he'd stayed in Scotland, listened to his father, taken an interest in the clan's undertakings, would he be better able to lead. But he'd paid no heed to anything, anyone but himself.

His own amusement.

If his life had any goal before that misty morning on Culloden Moor it had been the impetuous pursuit of his own amusement. How much better it would have been for the clan had Angus lived, or Duncan, or even William, young as he was. Any one of his brothers would have known better what to do than he.

Unable to bare the direction of his thoughts, Keegan turned, folding his arms around Zoe, pressing her tightly to his body. She molded into his embrace willingly, holding him with the same intensity he held her. Keegan squeezed his eyes shut, allowing himself the luxury to think of nothing but her. Of her soft skin and gentle lips. Of the heat of her body, and the way she seemed to lose consciousness for a moment right after her passionate release. How she made him do the same thing.

He needed that sweet oblivion now. Needed to forget if for only a moment about all the people who depended upon him. All the lives.

His arms tightened. The kiss he gave, the response he demanded left no doubt to his purpose or the immediate nature of his desire. While his tongue invaded, his body pressed hers against the wall, pinning her with his hips.

Keegan's fingers found the laces of her bodice. With a yank the simple homespun fabric loosened. He caught her sigh with his mouth then nudged his chin down, rasping along the delicate skin of her neck. He paused to tongue the flutter of pulse, then nipped and soothed his way down to push at the simple shift.

Her breasts were small and firm and so responsive to his touch that Keegan groaned. He nuzzled, then bent, hands beneath her skirts and inched them up her thighs. When her knees gave way he lifted. "Wrap around me," he said, his voice husky.

Zoe managed to do as he asked, though her mind, her limbs seemed beyond functioning.

"Aye, that's it, lass." With hasty fingers Keegan fumbled with his trews, shoving them down to free his manhood. She was open to him, her womanhood a ripe plum waiting for his touch.

When he entered they both sighed, then caught their breath as the rocking motion began. She met each thrust, clutching fistfuls of cotton shirting at his shoulders, caught by the fevered crescendo. She soared, touching again that magic place where life seemed to end and heaven began.

Keegan brought her to peak once more, wanting to see the expression in those smoky grey eyes when they fluttered open. She always appeared dazed as if she was some fairy princess awakening from a long sleep of passionate dreams. He found the idea wildly erotic.

Gripping her bottom he surged into her, losing control, joining her in that special place where their souls merged.

When *his* eyes opened she was smiling, a cat-that-swallowed-the-cream smile, that Keegan couldn't help returning. She wriggled. He grunted. And they both laughed aloud.

It amazed Keegan how much better she could make him feel. When they made love he could almost forget everything, including that she was his captive.

* * *

"François said he barely recognized ye."

"He did?" Zoe was cuddled in his arms, not far from slumber. "That's silly."

"Do ye think?" Keegan combed his fingers through her curly hair. "Ye have changed ye know."

"Mmmm."

"The sun has put golden strands in yer hair, and brightened yer cheeks."

"Perhaps I should wear a hat," she said and Keegan chuckled.

He pressed his lips to the top of her head. There were more changes. Some noticeable on first glance; the softer, rounder figure, straighter carriage and brighter eyes. Others subtle, like the lack of any complaint about food or lack of rest. All were delightful. Keegan snuggled her to him spoon-like, her back to his chest. He didn't want to lose her. Even the idea made his chest tighten. But that was another worry he couldn't seem to shake.

Keegan declared a holiday—a time when everyone could come together to sing and dance and eat. Like in the days before Prince Charlie touched foot upon the Scottish shore. It would be the first break since Keegan and Zoe arrived, since the clansmen came back to Glen MacLeod.

True, they were all frantically doing what they could to fill the larder and make the castle livable before winter set in, but that was such a constant thing. And the pressure was taking its toll among the clan.

Arguments were breaking out with little or no

provocation and spirits were low. So one night, as they lay together Keegan mentioned his idea to Zoe. Her enthusiasm was all he needed.

So it was decided. Work would cease midafternoon, except for food preparation, of course, and by dusk, all would be ready for a night of fun and frolic.

Zoe, along with the other women, searched through the undisturbed wardrobes for any bits of lace and ribbon to add to their dresses. They took turns dressing each other's hair and sewing up gowns. The camaraderie was something Zoe had never experienced before and she loved it. Of course Seonaid sniped at her occasionally but Mary stopped her with a sharp word, then pulled Zoe aside.

"She had designs on Keegan, she did, though I don't recall him ever givin' her much notice. But 'tis jealousy greasin' her tongue, and ye mustn't pay her any heed."

"I didn't mean to take Keegan's affections . . ." Zoe wasn't even certain that's what she had. His desires, certainly. But though she'd long since realized it was love she felt for him, he'd yet to convey the same.

Zoe glanced at Seonaid, swirling about with her arms up to show off the extra petticoat she'd found. She was a pretty thing, with fiery hair and temper to match. Zoe felt pale and drab in comparison.

"Ach, and what are ye doin'?"

Zoe looked back at Mary who now stood, hand

on ample hips. " 'Tis ye the young MacLeod has chosen. Don't be worrin' none about that one."

Zoe smiled, thanking Mary and tying a red bow in her hair. But she wondered what the older woman would think if she knew exactly how Keegan had *chosen* her.

Simon had managed to save his pipes when the soldiers came through the glen. There was also a fiddle and tin horn, hardly the most elegant of orchestras, but enough to keep the revelers dancing. The sun had set, the moon was high and the flames of the bonfire licked into the air.

Reel after reel played, with much pounding of bare feet and swinging of skirts. To Zoe it was as grand as a coronation ball. She danced and danced, swirled about by Donuld and Andrew, Cawley and Adair, even François . . . and of course Keegan.

He looked wild and splendid in a snow white shirt with a plaid pleated about his trim waist then draped across his shoulder. A silver pin belonging to his father and found in a corner of the old laird's bedroom, kept the wool from slipping. His hair, combed neatly when the party began, now tangled about his shoulders, shining like an old copper penny in the firelight. He was handsome beyond belief, and Zoe's heart pounded whenever she looked upon him.

Though he danced with others and encouraged her to do the same, it was Zoe who sat with him when they ate, Zoe whose shoulders he squeezed, Zoe who stood with him as the moon waned and the last haunting strains of "Will He No' Come Back Again" echoed through the glen.

> Will he no' come back again?
> Will he no' come back again?
> Better lo'ed he'll never be,
> And will he no' come back again?

The song brought tears to her eyes, tears she couldn't quite hide when Keegan glanced down at her.

"What is it, lass?"

Zoe just shook her head and smiled. There was no explaining her feelings to him when she'd yet to decipher them herself. Had love for him expanded to include all those about him, his country . . . even his cause? Foolish thoughts, but Zoe knew she didn't want anything to threaten this glen or the happiness she felt.

As the night sky began to pale, most of the Scots lay sound asleep, some sprawled in the heather wrapped only in their plaids. Zoe turned in slumber, finding a warm pillow for her head in Keegan's shoulder. The first shrill blast from the sheep's horn made her snuggle deeper into his body. The second had them both sitting upright.

Keegan grabbed for his trews and the broadsword. Zoe scrambled to her feet. "What is it?" The horn sounded again and again.

"The hills Zoe," he shouted before racing from the room. "Get t' the hills!"

Sixteen

Still more asleep than awake, Zoe gripped her gown, staring after Keegan. Wanting to call out to him . . . saying nothing. It was a false alarm surely, as the other had been. But that other time when François came to the valley the warning blast had been short, not like the prolonged wails that screamed through the air now.

For an instant, panic paralyzed her. What should she do? What? Then with a surge of energy Zoe yanked the dress over her head. She grabbed up a plaid, tying it about her shoulders, stepped into her shoes and ran from the room.

Her foot missed a step when she heard the first report of a gun. Frantically she lurched for the banister, catching herself from tumbling down the wide curved staircase.

Below her in the great hall people were running about, mothers calling for their children, babies crying. Zoe spotted François just as he ran through the open door. The little Frenchman looked left then right. His coat flapped open, his head usually covered by a wig, was bald. He lifted his gaze, caught sight of Zoe and scrambled toward the staircase.

"Mademoiselle Zoe, thank God. Monsieur Keegan

sent me to see to you." He grabbed her arm and yanked.

"Do you know what is happening?"

"Non, but I can only guess it is the soldiers," he said with a shudder. "But do not concern yourself. Monsieur Keegan will not allow them into the valley. Come now."

They hurried down the stairs, then headed out the door. A veil of mist shrouded the path into the glen. Zoe arched her neck, trying to see, but only once did the tattered wisps part, and it was only Highlanders she saw.

"My God, chérie, come on with you." A stream of women and children were winding their way along the rocks to the north, climbing into the hills, disappearing into the fog. François was anxious to have Zoe join them.

"I should go to him. Perhaps I can help."

Lord save him from sentimental females. "Chérie." François tried to be rational but with the sounds of battle and the children's cries it was difficult. "You can do him no good this way. He wants you safe. He will escape and come to you." François held up his finger. "But you must be there."

Zoe whirled back toward the castle. Most of the provisions they'd managed to scavenge from the fields, the bedding they'd found, were there inside the grey stone walls. True, some people had been taken to the hills earlier. But what was left inside would do them no good. Yet there was no help for it. Sadly Zoe turned back to follow the other women and children.

François was already several steps ahead of her

along the path. "Come, come, Mademoiselle Zoe," he urged.

In front of him Mary was trudging along, Moia on her hip, her son Justin hanging to her skirts. Zoe quickened her pace, reaching for the redheaded girl as she drew abreast of Mary. "Let me help," she said while positioning the tot's legs round her waist.

Her burden lightened, Mary was better able to stay up with the others. They climbed higher, twisting around rocks, rugged and grim in the morning light. There were eighteen women and children on their way to hide in the hills and everyone of them was related in some way to the men they'd left behind to defend the glen. It was a somber group, but they knew their duty.

Their spirit seemed to penetrate Zoe who wanted nothing more than to turn back. But she trudged forward, and upward, only once stopping to look out over a dizzying precipice. Below, the loch cut through the valley, shimmering. She could see the dark shape of the castle, but nothing else.

It was near three quarters of an hour later when Zoe realized she no longer heard the crackle of gunfire.

Zoe tried not to think of what was happening below but she could not shake it from her mind. Was Keegan dead? Was her brother one of the British soldiers? If so, how did he fare? Unlike the other wanderers on the side of the mountain, she had loyalties to men on both sides of the sword.

The babe in her arms began to fuss, looking up at her with eyes that rivaled the blue of a summer sky. "I'm not your momma, I know," Zoe cooed. "But she's nearby and everything will be all right."

Zoe just wished she believed those words.

"They've retreated into this blasted mist and rain." The sergeant remembered himself and quickly added a "sir" to his remark. Fox dismissed the man with a salute, then strode to the cold stone fireplace. Carved mythical beasts graced the hearth that stood near two stories high. Fox smacked his palm against a serpent's head and cursed.

"Where is that bastard MacLeod?" More importantly, did he still have Zoe with him? He'd planned this predawn raid in hopes of finding them both . . . of getting to her before the damn Scots could hurt her. That is if she weren't already dead.

But he hadn't counted on the lookouts. Hell, he hadn't even known for certain there would be anyone here. But for some reason he almost felt as if he could read the Scot's mind. He was a proud one, and arrogant. He wouldn't take the confiscation of his estate easily. Or so Fox had thought. And he'd left word with Miss Phelps that he'd be here. So Fox had come looking. And he'd found them . . . MacLeod and what was left of his clan.

But he hadn't captured him. He hadn't captured any of them. Again his hand slapped the cold stone.

It wasn't over yet.

The caves were high in the hills, hidden from all but the stoutest climber . . . and the desperate. Zoe and the others reached them by midafternoon. The sun was a distant memory on this day when the mist seemed to swell, then drizzle down, as if the mountains were crying.

But the caves, if not free of dampness were at least free of rain. As Zoe entered one it reminded her of that other time when she and Keegan had escaped the storm. But this was no tempest, just the dreary constant drizzle of the Highlands.

At least there were provisions. Keegan and the men had not been blinded by their desire to stay in the glen of their ancestors. They'd been bringing food and supplies to these caves from the beginning.

Some of the women who'd lived here, after the first time the English soldiers burned and pillaged Castle MacLeod, settled in quickly. They started smoldering fires of peat to ward off the chill and cooked a great kettle of oatmeal.

Zoe ate with the others, taking her turn at entertaining the children, though all but the youngest seemed as stouthearted and resigned to their surroundings as their mothers. No one mentioned the men. There were no senseless questions asked, no weeping or wailing. But Zoe knew their absence prayed on every mind.

What had happened to them? It was evening now and the temperature, never warm this day had dropped till every shoulder was wrapped in plaid. But still there were no men except François. Zoe could see the unasked question in his eyes. But in the Highlands it didn't seem the thing to do.

So the women did what they had to. When darkness spread over them like a blanket they sought the solace of sleep. And perhaps for some it helped. But Zoe tossed and turned, dozing fitfully only to awaken from a nightmare that seemed all too real.

She awoke to find mist heavier than she'd ever seen, with no hint of sun. But by midmorning it shone weakly. By noon the first men came strangling into the clearing in front of the caves.

Some were wounded, all were tired and hungry, and Zoe worked with the other women to see to their needs. She bandaged wounds and spooned out gruel and all the while her gaze kept straying to the V in the rocks that led to the path.

"Aye, the MacLeod was with us. 'Tis him that gave the order t' retreat when the bloody bastards kept comin' at us." Donuld squatted in front of the fire, his gnarled fingers fisting. Zoe was beside him, a trencher of oatmeal in her hands, but he'd brushed the nourishment away, too churned up as he put it, to eat.

"Did he retreat with you?"

He looked her square in the eye, his expression sympathetic. "I wish I knew," was all he said.

So Zoe waited and pretended to be as stoic as the others. Talk was of the English soldiers, of their weapons and determination.

"We saw smoke too, risin' from the glen."

"They've burned us out again."

"Aye, but we'll be back. We're MacLeods and that land is our birthright."

But at what cost, Zoe wondered. Two men had yet to return. Two of eleven who had stayed to defend the land.

* * *

The wind was off the ocean and cold. Zoe sat, the plaid wrapped about her, staring into the white ash of the dying fire. The other women were in the caves, settled down for another night, as were all the men but two. Donuld and Cawley were huddled on a boulder that looked down over the side of the mountain. Keeping watch. Even here, one step away from the sky, they weren't safe.

With a sigh, Zoe stood. Arching, she stretched the aching muscles of her back. When she straightened, Zoe glanced one more time toward the hazy silhouette of the two men. They weren't there.

Without thought Zoe started across the clearing, her steps gaining speed as she went. By the time she reached the rocks, she was running. If it was the English they would have sounded the alarm. They must have seen something, someone, who caused them to leave their post.

Zoe let out a cry as she spotted the men climbing back up the trail, Keegan between them. They each had an arm around him, helping him across the rocks, but Zoe didn't care. He was alive and the relief that shot through her was near painful in its intensity.

He lifted his head when he heard her. Their eyes met and then she was there, wrapping her arms about his waist, sobbing against his chest. And Keegan felt as if he'd come home.

Zoe pulled away when she felt something warm and wet against her arm. "You're wounded." Something she should have realized when she noticed the men helping him, but hadn't. "We must get him to the caves."

" 'Tis fine I am. No more than a scratch," Keegan insisted. But he didn't object to a shoulder to lean on as he climbed over the rocks.

Zoe scurried ahead, rushing into the cave and spreading a plaid for him to lie on. She lit several fir branches to give her light, then filled a basin with water.

"This way," she urged as Keegan and Cawley came into the clearing, but Keegan shook his head.

"I've gotta be speakin' with Mary MacLeod first." Keegan straightened himself.

"Can't it wait?" Zoe saw the lines of pain deepen as he put forth the effort to stand on his own. "You need to rest."

"I need t' be seeing Mary," he repeated, his jaw tight. " 'Tis my duty." His voice softened. "But perhaps ye could come with me." He reached for Zoe's hand. "I fear 'tis a woman's touch she'll be needin' "

"Adair?" Zoe swallowed past the lump in her throat.

"Aye. He was bad off. Shot. I went back for him and dragged him along. But he could hardly walk." Keegan wiped the back of his hand across his grimy forehead. "But we managed t' move along till last night. We stopped t' rest." Keegan shook his head. "And there he died."

"You did what you could." Zoe stepped closer.

"Aye." Keegan nodded slowly. " 'Tis just that it never seems t' be enough."

* * *

He told Mary the terrible news she'd already prepared herself to hear.

"I knew he wasn't comin' back t' me but he died doin' as he pleased . . . defendin' his children and me . . . and the MacLeods." The woman stared at Keegan dry-eyed. "Ye do as well for the clan as yer cousin did and ye'll never have need to hang yer head." Mary settled down on a moss-covered rock, and stared up at the stars. "Now I'm thinkin' ye need some tendin'. I could do it, but I've a thought, Zoe might do best."

"Should I send one of the other women?" Zoe knelt down in front of her, taking Mary's chilled hands. "You shouldn't be alone."

"Nay, 'tis alone, I'd like t' be for a while. Now off with ye before yer man bleeds t' death." To Keegan she said, "Thank ye for doin' what ye could for my Adair. I'm grateful t' ye. Adair loved ye like a brother."

"Do you think we should leave her?" Zoe whispered as they entered one of the caves. "She seems so sad and lonely."

"Grief is a lonely thing," Keegan said with a grunt as he lowered himself to the ground. "But I'll go check on her again in a wee bit."

Which didn't happen, for as soon as the words were out of his mouth Keegan passed out.

"François," Zoe called to the Frenchman who slept a few rods away. He stirred, opened his eyes, then scurried to his feet.

"My God, what happened to him?"

"I'm not sure, but I need help turning him over."
Together they shifted Keegan to his side and
stripped away his blood-soaked shirt. When the
wound started oozing anew François turned away,
dropping his head to his bent knees.

"Please pass me that rag." Eyes on Keegan's side
Zoe stuck her hand out, wriggling her fingers when
she didn't feel anything. "François?" Twisting about
she saw the valet's position, then the paleness of his
face when he glanced up. "What's wrong with you?"

"The blood." François brought a hand to his
mouth. "I could never even watch if there was the
tiniest nick while shaving Monsieur Keegan." He bit
his lip. "It was good, he told me. Then I would try
my best not to cut him."

Fear of blood was something Zoe had never encountered. It certainly didn't affect her. As many
times as she'd been bled over the years she was used
to the sight of it. To the smell. A low moan brought
her attention back to Keegan.

For now she simply wished she could give to the
Scot all the blood that had been taken from her, for
he seemed to have lost so much. Zoe swallowed back
the urge to cry and reached across the rocky floor
for the supplies she'd gathered.

"I'm sorry." François took a deep breath. "Perhaps I can—"

"No, really, I'm fine now." Zoe dipped a bit of
cloth in the water and pressed it to Keegan's side.
When she rinsed the rag, the water turned a coppery
hue. She heard François gag. "But I would like you
to see to Mary if you don't mind. She's outside, all

alone. And Keegan brought word that Adair is dead."

"You need say no more." He pushed to his feet. "I shall comfort her." He hesitated. "But if you need any more help—"

"I shall call you," Zoe finished for him. With the Frenchman gone she concentrated upon washing away the blood. His wound seemed to be caused by a saber or knife, and probably wouldn't have been so serious if treated earlier. As it was, all Zoe could do was pack the wound and wrap it tightly. Then she covered Keegan with a plaid, cleared away the dirty water and sat down to keep watch over him.

She was sitting there, her hand pressed to the hot skin of his forehead when his nightmares began. Zoe jolted awake, grabbing a clean cloth and dipping it in cool water. But though she held this to his brow Keegan continued to call out and thrash about.

He was fighting again.

At first Zoe thought it the battle for the glen three days ago, but then she realized in his mind he was on Drummossie Moor near Culloden. Watching as his brother William died. Then Duncan. And Angus. Silent tears trailed down Zoe's cheeks as she heard the anguish in his voice as he cried out to the Fates.

"Hush, my love." Zoe tried to quiet him, but his movements became so violent she feared his wound would tear open again. "Keegan, you must calm yourself."

"My da. No. I'll save ye Da."

"Keegan, please, be still."

" 'Tis sorry I am Da. I trusted him."

"Keegan, you're bleeding again."

"I trusted him Da, I don't know why, and he lied t' me. The bloody English Lord lied t' me."

"Keegan, please." Zoe was sobbing now, her hands on his shoulders, the tears splashing onto his chest. "Please don't do this."

He opened his eyes then, but Zoe didn't think it was her he saw. But he did quiet, drifting into a calmer sleep, leaving Zoe to think on his words.

For two days and nights Keegan did little but sleep; Zoe did little but sponge him down with cool water. She tried to feed him weak gruel and dripped water into his mouth, declining offers of help from everyone. She did sleep for a few hours, falling into an exhausted heap when François promised to watch over his master.

But it was Zoe, Keegan saw when he first opened his eyes with any lucidity. He tried to smile but the effort seemed too much for him, so she smiled for him.

"You're awake. And I think . . ." She reached out to touch his cheek above the dark whiskers. "Yes, the fever is gone."

"How long . . . ?" His voice was rusty from disuse.

"You've been back two days. Do you remember coming to the caves?"

"Barely."

"It isn't important." Zoe reached for his hand, surprised at the strength he used to squeeze her fingers. "Nothing matters now that you're well."

But of course that was hardly the case. Life went on for the small band of renegades even as Keegan's side healed and he grew stronger. There were meals to fix, and weapons to clean and little more to do besides that, than sit and fret. At least that's the way it appeared to Zoe. The men were like a horse without a head, unsure of what to do next.

She mentioned this to Keegan one afternoon when he sat in the sunshine by a waterfall that splashed over the rocks.

"What would ye have them do?" Keegan picked up a pebble and tossed it into the water.

"Hunt. Build huts. Cut peat. We can't survive on oatmeal forever."

"Hell, Zoe. We can't survive forever period." Another stone arched into the stream.

"So that's it then? You're giving up? Just giving up?"

"Nay!" Keegan grimaced and clutched his side, then gingerly leaned back against the moss-covered rock. He hated being laid up, unable to move around as he wished. "But I don't know what t' do. They burned Castle MacLeod again."

"I know."

"This time I doubt there's enough grain left t' feed a titmouse."

"We don't have to go back to the glen."

"Where do ye suggest we locate? Here?" With a sweep of his hand Keegan indicated the untamed setting.

"I don't know. But these people look to you for leadership—"

"They best look somewhere else. 'Tis hardly a sterlin' job I've done so far."

"Do you think anyone could have done a better job in the glen? You and your planning saved us Keegan."

"Tell that to Adair."

"Yes, Adair died. 'Tis a shame, but look at all those you allowed to escape." Zoe shifted closer. "No one could have done better." She saw the hint of a smile and touched his cheek. His hand covered hers.

" 'Tis not the talk I'd expect from a fragile English rose like yerself, Lady Zoe."

"Perhaps I'm not so fragile." She leaned forward, pressing her lips to his.

Seventeen

"I don't think you should go."

"Am I t' assume from that, ye'll be missin' my company while I'm gone?" The words were spoken in a careless tone. It was only the intensity in the depths of Keegan's green eyes as he cupped Zoe's shoulders and turned her to him that gave him away.

Zoe knew the power that expression had over her. She knew the power *he* had over her. With a shrug she stepped out of his loose embrace. "You're not recovered yet."

"Is this Miss Phelps speakin' or her patient?" Keegan walked to the edge of the Highland plateau. The sun was bright, though the air, with a strong wind off the sea was chilled.

"You needn't bring up Miss Phelps. *Any* reasonable person would agree that your wound is not sufficiently healed for you to be . . . to be . . ."

"Raidin'?" Keegan tossed the word over his shoulder, grinning when he saw her eyes narrow. Despite her insistence that the men should do something to gain the clan food and provisions, she was not pleased by this plan.

But she seemed unwilling to argue that point at

the moment. She took a deep breath, squared her shoulders and stepped to his side.

" 'Tis less than a sennight ago you were delirious with fever."

"Aye and 'tis ye I have t' thank for seeing me well again."

"But that's just it." Zoe swiped a tangled lock of windblown hair from her face, looking up at him earnestly. "You aren't well. How could you be?"

"Zoe."

"No." She batted away the arm that reached out to drape her shoulders. "Don't try to make light of this." She stepped out of his reach. "Your wound is barely healed. What if it should reopen?"

"After the fine stitchery ye did in my flesh? I doubt it will happen."

"Don't jest." She'd never learned more than the rudiments of sewing as Miss Phelps feared such fine work was bad for her eyes. But after his wound continued to gape open she'd decided it needed to be sewed.

"Now Zoe, 'tis unfair, accusin' me of kiddin' with ye." He pulled his shirttail from the wrap of plaid, exposing the angry wound for her to see. Zoe ignored the uneven swatch of small scars crisscrossing the large welt.

"You're still weak," she said angrily, turning her back and folding her arms across her chest. Her eyes closed when the warmth of his lips touched the side of her neck. She felt helpless as his arms crossed over hers and he drew her back against his body.

"Ye wound me Zoe." His voice was low, a tingle

in her ear. "I thought I'd disproved that argument once and good, last night."

Zoe's head lolled to the side, memories of their lovemaking the previous evening still strong enough to elicit chills. They'd gone off for a walk in the moonlight, as Keegan called it. And he did have a point. His stamina had not been that of a man lacking strength.

Of course afterward, when they lay wrapped in each other's warmth beneath his plaid, Keegan told her of his plan to raid the stronghold of the Royal Campbells at Lochgreggan.

"There are too few of you." Zoe repeated one of her arguments of last night.

"We have surprise and stealth on our side." His defense hadn't changed.

"There's no need for you to do it."

"Zoe." Despite her initial reluctance Keegan turned her in his arms. His chin rested atop her head and he stared out over the sea as he spoke. "We'll die up here, starve t' death without more provisions."

"There must be another way." Her words were muffled by his shoulder.

"There isn't." Keegan took a deep breath. "We need horses and cattle, foodstuffs . . . ammunition if we're t' survive." Keegan shut his eyes, drawing her closer. For he feared even with those things there was little assurance the clan could make it through a Highland winter.

She opened her mouth to offer another argument, then let it slowly shut. Pulling away enough to see him, she said instead, "I don't want you to leave me."

Her words, the crystalline tears warmed Keegan's heart. He cupped her oval face in his hands, wiping at the moisture with his thumbs. He looked into her eyes. "I will come back t' ye my English rose. 'Tis a promise I'm makin' ye."

When his lips touched hers, Zoe leaned into him, accepting that this was the assurance she'd sought. Hoping his words would prove prophetic. She held onto him as if she'd never let him go. But in the end, of course, she had to.

Four days later he was in her arms again.

Keegan slid from the back of a shaggy Highland horse into Zoe's embrace. He tossed the reins to François before leaning forward and giving her a loud kiss. She was laughing and crying at the same time and Keegan thought she'd never looked lovelier. The sun had lightened her hair till the golden strands nearly equaled the brown. Her color was high, her eyes shining. The sight of her took his breath away.

He felt like a conquering hero, a crusader returning to his lady love, his saddlebags laden with treasures.

The women and children, the men too young or too old to take part in the raid, pressed toward him and the others. Reluctantly, with a last touch to the side of Zoe's neck, Keegan released her.

"What did ye bring us?"

"Did ye encounter the damn English?"

"What of the Campbells? Are there any of 'em left breathin'?"

Keegan laughed, drawing Zoe with him as he squeezed through the crowd. "Give us room here and we'll show ye, all of ye, what we brought. Is that not right, Cawley?"

"Aye, 'tis so." Cawley and the other men were busy unloading the packs off the "liberated" horses. The animals were taken away and tethered, as were the few cattle they'd herded up the mountain.

Then while the clan watched, the men unwrapped bags of grain, bolts of cloth, and wheels of cheese.

"How did you get these things?" Zoe asked when Keegan settled back to watch the women's faces as Cawley uncovered a cache of pins and needles.

"If ye're askin' if we slew the whole household, the answer is nay, dear Zoe." He grinned as she assured him she'd never thought him capable of such a bloodthirsty deed.

"I simply entered Campbell House by the front door, as brazen as ye please. They were more than willing to share what they had."

"You're fibbing to me, Keegan MacLeod. I don't believe a word of it."

"Now Zoe, love, 'tis hurt I am that ye don't take my word for it." Thick, dark lashes drifted down to cover his eyes. "Though t' be perfectly honest I think it more the pistol I had aimed at their dark Royalist hearts rather than my winning ways that gained us the most wares."

She couldn't help laughing. Not with him back safe. And all the others as well. And a pile of things they needed, growing on the trampled heather. It was enough to make one forget. How she came to be here. That she didn't really belong . . . everything.

But Seonaid was always around to remind her.

"I don't understand why she's in charge of dividing up the supplies." Seonaid's whisper was loud enough for all the women, including Zoe to hear. "She's naught but a Sassenach . . . and Keegan's whore."

Zoe's hand stilled on the pile of linens she was handing out. A quiet fell over the group, that moments ago had been chattering gaily about the goods Keegan and the men brought.

Abruptly Mary said something about the cheese tasting good after days of nothing but oatmeal, her voice too animated. Zoe glanced her way, silently thanking her for trying to shift attention away from Seonaid's words, but decided the best thing was to face the woman. Zoe straightened her shoulders.

"Keegan asked me to do this, Seonaid. As he asked Cawley to see to the cattle and François to store the food. I may be English, but I'm in the same situation as you at the moment . . . hiding away in these hills."

Seonaid's eyes shifted from one woman to the next looking for an ally against this outsider. When no one would meet her gaze she stiffened. "Well, 'tis not exactly the same as the rest of us now, is it? I doubt the soldiers will be killin' ye if we're found."

Hardly a point she could argue.

"And then the rest of us are either God-fearin' married women or we're without a man. We're not sleepin' with someone hopin' t' turn his head with our wide-eyed ways."

"That will be enough, Seonaid. I daresay you'd be a bit wide-eyed yer own self if the young laird would give ye a look. Ye can't blame Zoe that he don't."

"Thank you Mary, for your support, but I think this is between Seonaid and me." Zoe took a breath. "I didn't ask to come here, or to leave England for that matter. But I'm here now. And I . . . I love Keegan MacLeod."

"Aye, but does he love ye or the forbidden fruit ye give him?"

There was a sound like a large intake of breath and Zoe noticed every eye was on her, even Mary's. It was also a question she wanted more than anything to know the answer to. But one she didn't know.

Seonaid obviously sensed her reluctance to answer for she tossed her curls, a smirk spreading over her face. "Of course if he's asked ye t' marry him, or even handfast, I suppose it would show he does. Has he done that, Lady Zoe?" Her voice was sly.

She couldn't tell her the truth, yet lying seemed too difficult. Besides, by the look on the girl's face she, as well as the others, already knew the answer.

"The MacLeod has more on his mind these days than plannin' his nuptials," Mary countered. But it was obvious she spoke up because she was Zoe's friend.

* * *

"Ye seem a bit pensive."

It was evening four days later. Zoe sat with Keegan near the fire that burned continuously just outside the mouth of the caves.

"Do I?" Zoe drew up her legs beneath her skirt, resting her chin on her knees.

"Mmmm." Keegan traced a curl along her cheek then tucked it behind her ear. " 'Tis unusual for ye not t' talk a good deal."

Zoe turned her head and smiled. "Too much?"

"Nay." His grin showed white teeth in the twilight.

"I would have thought your answer different." Straightening her legs, Zoe looked up as the first star appeared.

"Ye mean with that 'Miss Phelps says' prattle?" When she nodded Keegan shrugged. "I can't say I've heard ye mention the old crone's name recently, let alone quote her." There was a pause when Zoe didn't respond. Keegan leaned forward, trying to see her face in the grainy light. "I didn't mean t' be insultin' the old hag."

Zoe's laugh was spontaneous. "I shall be certain to tell her." As soon as the words were out of her mouth Zoe's expression sobered and she looked away. How could she tell the woman anything when she most likely would never see her again? But then Zoe didn't even know that for sure. Though it seemed unlikely Keegan would decide to send her back to London anytime soon.

"Zoe?" Keegan's finger hooked her chin, bringing her about till he could see the silver sheen of her eyes. "What is it lass?"

"I was wondering what you planned to do?"

"About what?"

Her gaze met his. "About me."

He couldn't bring himself to hold her stare. Keegan picked a bramble from his plaid, then tossed it absently toward the fire. What did he plan to do about her? Holding her to lure her brother into the hills had seemed like a good idea at one time.

But no more.

He couldn't indulge his desire for revenge without jeopardizing the clan. And he wasn't sure he wanted to kill Fox Morgan anymore. Not that he didn't still hate him for what happened to his father. But Zoe loved him. And from what he could tell, the bastard had been the only one of her family who cared a fig about her. Keegan didn't want to hurt her any more than he already had.

So where did that leave her?

And where did it leave him?

Keegan hunched forward reaching his hands toward the heat radiating off the fire. It was cold tonight, and would get colder.

"I saw him."

"Who?" Zoe wrapped the plaid more tightly about herself and looked toward Keegan. The flickering light played upon the shadows of his face.

"Yer brother. Fox." Keegan watched as her eyes grew larger. She didn't speak at first and when she did he had to lean closer to hear.

"Did you kill him?"

"Nay!" Keegan shifted closer and took her hands. They were as cold as the winter wind. "No, Zoe." His fingers wrapped around hers. "It was the day we left Castle MacLeod. He was there."

"You didn't tell me."

"I know." Keegan bent forward till his forehead touched their joined hands. "I didn't want ye thinkin' he was near and runnin' off t' warn him." Keegan's eyes closed on that lie. He took a deep breath. " 'Tis not true. Was myself I was thinkin' of." Slowly he raised his head till he was staring into her eyes, lost in them. "I did not want t' lose ye, selfish bastard that I am."

He was so close Zoe could see the crystalline prisms of his eyes, feel the warmth of his breath on her cheek. Her mouth was dry. There was an ache in her heart that months ago she would have thought strong enough to kill her. Now she just wished it would last forever.

When she pulled her hands from his, Zoe noticed the twinge of doubt flash across his handsome face. But it disappeared when her palms cupped the side of his face. She pulled him closer, her lashes drifting shut when their lips touched.

The kiss was chaste compared to most they shared. But the emotions that flowed one to the other overpowered them. The night seemed to disappear, the stars and chill. The caves and clan. It was just the two of them, their souls uniting. Neither wanting to leave the other.

It was only later, when Keegan lay awake, Zoe curled at his side that he realized how true the second part of his admission was. He was a selfish bastard.

He'd stolen Zoe from her home and brought her to the wilds of Scotland. Soon the winter would come and despite his best efforts food would be scarce and the cold unbearable. The clan . . . he . . . had no choice but to bear it.

Zoe had a choice.

One that he must give her. Force her to take if necessary.

He tightened his arm around her and tried to come to terms with what he had to do. But even the thought of it was enough to break his heart.

"You're certain it was him."

"Ach, and ye think I don't know a MacLeod when I see one. Why the smell alone can signal their presence a mile away."

Fox stopped pacing. "Too bad it wasn't enough to give you some forewarning. Perhaps then he wouldn't have been able to march into your dining room, like the bold thief he is, and make his demands." Thomas Campbell's face turned as red as his hair, and the veins in his neck bulged. He didn't like being reminded of how his archenemies the MacLeods had swooped down on him, on foot, and robbed him blind.

If Fox knew what was good for him, he wouldn't do the reminding. It was the Campbell's cooperation he wanted . . . needed. But he didn't like their chieftain. He didn't like his pompous attitude, or the way he pandered to the army for favors.

But like it or not, that was the way of things in Scotland. There were the Jacobites who were either transported, dead, or well on their way. And the Royalists, fellow Scotsmen who were doing their damnedest to help the rebels get that way.

Thomas Campbell was one of the latter. Though Fox imagined it was more a strong sense of self-preservation rather than loyalty to the king that spurred him on.

"What are ye plannin' t' do aboot the MacLeods, Major? 'Tis not safe for decent people anymore." The Campbell had regained his composure. After ringing for a servant he offered Fox a glass of claret.

"I intend to catch him." Fox declined the proffered goblet. Sitting down in one of the chairs angled before the fireplace, he motioned for his host to do the same. "Now how many were there?"

"As far as I can tell aboot twenty-five." Thomas more than doubled the number out of embarrassment. "But I've told ye all this before."

"Tell me again."

Thomas puffed out his barrel chest. "It was late. Nearly a sennight ago. When the door burst open and there he was, dressed in his plaid, arrogant as ever, his broadsword catching the light and the dag-handled pistol pointed straight at me."

"And it was Keegan MacLeod?"

"None other." Thomas took a quick swallow of wine. He could still feel the panic that coursed through him when he recognized the bastard. He didn't like it.

"What did he do then?"

"Threatened t' kill me, and my wife, he did. Swore he would, if we didn't do exactly as he commanded."

"And his commands were?" Fox asked with a lift of his brow.

"Food. He wanted cheese and oatcakes. Turnips. He came close t' wipin' us out."

Fox couldn't muster even a pittance of sympathy for the Campbell who looked as if he hadn't ever missed a meal. "So they must be hungry," Fox said more to himself than the other man.

"Needin' clothin' too, I'll wager. He took pins and cloth."

"So there are women with him." Despite the small amount of hope Fox held that his sister might still be alive, his spirits rose with the thought.

"He's probably gathered what's left of his clan about him. That would be my guess."

"Where would you say he's hiding with them?"

"Could be anywhere. Ye'll have a hard time of it searchin' these hills. Especially with winter on its way."

Fox leaned back and steepled his fingers. "That's why I don't intend to chase him into the mountains."

"But I thought ye said ye intended t' catch him."

"And I do." Fox's eyes were hard. "Yours isn't the only house he's raided. I've had word from two other Royalist Scots. He hit Jamie MacNabb at Glenrubin and Dugald Chisholm at Skinettle. Their descriptions of what happened are similar to yours. Though either Keegan MacLeod has lost most of his men or they can count better than you."

"I never said I was certain of the number."

"True enough." Fox stood. "But he will be coming out of the hills again. He has women with him, most likely children too. He'll need more food. As you say, winter is coming. When he comes down to raid again I will catch him. Him and his band of renegades."

Eighteen

"They be comin' back!"

Zoe glanced up from the sleeve she was hemming. The sound of the lookout's voice heralding the return of the men never ceased to make her smile. This was the fourth raid Keegan and the others rode out on. Stockpiling for winter he called it, when Zoe asked why they had to go so often. But they were back now, and perhaps there were enough supplies to last them awhile. At least she hoped so.

"Sounds as if they're ridin' their ponies hard," Mary commented after biting off a length of thread. "I hope there's naught wrong."

"Anxious to be back, I imagine," Zoe said, but Mary's words sent a chill racing down her spine that had nothing to do with the biting wind. She rose, brushing dirt and wrinkles from her skirt and folded the fabric she was painstakingly fashioning into a shirt.

She told herself that naturally Mary was apprehensive, seeing ghosts where there were none, and hearing trouble in the clip-clop of horses' hooves over rocks. Her husband was dead, and it was at a time very much like this, when the men returned, that she discovered Adair's fate.

That didn't mean there was a problem this time, Zoe reminded herself, but her step quickened as she made her way toward the crevice in the rocks.

Zoe knew the moment she saw Cawley's face come into view over the rise that something was terribly wrong. And it wasn't only the blood seeping through the hastily wrapped bandage circling his head. His eyes were wild, his expression terrified. As the riders thundered into the clearing Zoe half expected a regiment of English soldiers to pour in on their tail.

But there were no cavalry. There was also no Keegan.

As soon as Cawley jerked his mount to a halt, Zoe grabbed the reins. "Where is he?"

"Weren't nothin' we could do." Cawley slid to the ground, his knees wobbling. Zoe reached to help support him, but her own knees felt weak. All around her, loved ones were rushing forward helping others who were wounded or simply winded from the hard ride.

"Keegan? Where is he?"

"They got 'im, Zoe." Cawley took a few steps away and Zoe hastily shoved the reins toward François who'd come up behind her. Part of her felt sorry for Cawley. He was tired and had obviously been through a lot, but she couldn't stand not knowing.

"Tell me." Zoe grabbed his shoulder, turning him.

"Mademoiselle Zoe." François covered her hand with one of his own. The other held a tankard. He handed it to Cawley. "We should give him a moment to catch his breath, oui?"

Zoe swallowed, tilting her head so he couldn't see the shine of tears and nodded. "I apologize Cawley." Zoe knelt beside where he'd slid to the ground. "Let me look at your head."

"Nay." His hand stilled hers. "Not till I tell ye, what ye want to know." He took a deep drink, back-handing his mouth of the liquid. " 'Twas a trap. Musta been." He paused, shutting his eyes. " 'Tis a miracle any of us escaped with our lives."

Zoe twisted to look around her. It was obvious all had not. She wasn't the only one begging information from the survivors. Wails of grief echoed off the mountain cliffs.

"They was waitin' for us, hidin' in the barn." Cawley took a deep breath. "We opened the doors and 'twas like they exploded out at us." His eyes clouded. "I saw Donuld fall, and Andrew. 'Tweren't nothin' I could do." He looked at her then. "The MacLeod, he's yellin' for us t' get out of there. His horse was twistin' and he was shootin'."

"Did they kill him?" Zoe steeled herself for the answer.

"I don't know. Not that I saw. But he stayed behind, drawin' his broadsword and chargin' at them." Cawley dropped his head into the crook of his arm. " 'Tis because of him, I got away."

"He was alive the last I saw 'im."

Zoe looked around to see Will at her elbow. He appeared unharmed but his eyes, like Cawley's, wore that same anxious expression.

"But they'd caught 'im."

"He's a prisoner?"

Will shrugged. "Don't rightly know if that be the

case. But I stopped at the top of a rise t' see if they was followin' me. I saw Keegan standin' on the ground, surrounded by soldiers."

Zoe pushed to her feet. "If he's still alive there's hope." She glanced around. "Were there any others who were captured?"

"Didna' see any. Most were either shot straight out, or got away."

"I see." Zoe paced a few steps. "Then it is clear what we must do."

The hair on the back of his neck bristled.

Keegan MacLeod stood as he was, refusing to turn around, but he knew who'd just entered the small stone out-building. He flexed his fingers, the desire to have a broadsword in his hand almost painful.

"Tell me what you've done with her." Keegan heard the swoosh of steel. "Tell me, or so help me God, I'll run you through like the dog you are."

Keegan's stare was hard as he shifted about. "Will I be disemboweled first, or do ye reserve that for helpless old men?"

Fox's eyes narrowed, then he hefted the sword higher. " 'Tis my sister we're discussing, and I'll give you two minutes to tell me where she is."

"What makes ye think she's still alive?" No sooner had the taunting words left his mouth, than the English major was across the room, grabbing Keegan's shirt with one hand. The other held the sword point against his exposed ribs.

"You're a dead man, Keegan MacLeod."

Their faces were very close, their eyes dark with

hatred. Yet as tense as the moment, as filled with hostility, neither man could dispel the odd feeling that swept over them. It was hardly kinship but its roots seemed buried in the same soil.

Fox loosened his grip. "She's not dead, is she?"

As tempted as he was to keep up the ruse, to hurt the English bastard any way possible, Keegan couldn't do it. His mind filled with Zoe, her grey eyes shining, her smile . . . "Nay," he finally said, and jerked out of the major's grasp.

Relief swamped him. Knowing what he did of Zoe's health, Fox had assumed that his sister had died long ago. But now, for the first time in months, he believed she was alive. And as strange as it seemed, he believed it because Keegan MacLeod said it.

He sheathed his sword. "Where is she?"

"Go t' hell, Sassenach."

A nerve in Fox's jaw jumped as he stared at the man he'd been pursuing for over a fortnight. He was tall, with skin browned by the weather, with those green eyes that he remembered well.

"Why did you do it? Why Zoe? She never did anything to you."

Keegan's head whipped around and he speared the Englishman with a look. "Do not pretend ye don't know."

"I'm pretending nothing. I know we've crossed paths before."

"Aye, we have."

"On Drummosie Moor."

"Right again, Major. 'Twas there that ye encountered me and my father."

There was little about the battle and its aftermath that Fox hadn't relived in his mind hundreds of times, including his meeting with this Scot. "That still doesn't explain why you'd hurt Zoe."

"It was ye I was aimin' t' hurt, ye bastard, not Zoe."

Fox kept his gaze steady. "I did what I could for you at Culloden."

"Ha! I'll be believin' no more of yer lies. I listened t' ye then and handed over my broadsword only t' see it used on my da."

"I ordered your father taken prisoner."

"But he wasn't. And it was yer men that killed him." Keegan's jaw tightened as the horror of that day played out in his mind. "And it wasn't just killed. It was tortured, and left t' die layin' in his own blood."

The impact of the Scot's words . . . of his anger shook Fox. "What did you do to her?" he asked, his voice low. When Keegan said nothing, Fox continued. "If you hurt her so help me—"

"I didn't hurt her!" Keegan wondered if part of his own vehemence was the niggling question of whether or not he had. True, she hadn't been tortured or hurt physically. Not yet. If truth be known she seemed in much better health now than when he broke into her house.

But there were other wounds, wounds no one could see.

"She's fine," Keegan added before turning away. It was the sound of a pistol cocking that made him look back.

He wasn't surprised to be staring down the barrel of the major's gun.

"You're a lying son of a bitch. Zoe isn't fine and we both know it. Her heart—"

"Is stronger than ye think. She survived a cross-country ride, a shipwreck and a raid by yer soldiers."

"Tell me where she is."

Part of him wanted to. Keegan stared at his tormentor, feeling the same eerie sense of déjà vu as last time they met. He knew him, yet didn't. It was the kind of foolishness that played with his mind that time too.

Keegan wanted to hold onto his hatred yet felt it slipping away. He had no reason to believe this man innocent of ordering his father's death, except his word. The word of an enemy.

Keegan sucked in a deep breath. He kidnapped Zoe to hurt her brother. It was the only leverage he had. And he would give it up. Give it up for Zoe's sake.

As much as he wanted her with him . . . as much as he loved her . . . she was much better off with her brother. She belonged in London, not the wild hills of Scotland. She had no future with him. Hell, he had no future period.

But if he told Lord Foxworth where Zoe was, he'd give away the hiding place of the clan. He'd seen and heard of too many atrocities against the Jacobites to chance that.

So he continued to defy, to stare steel-eyed at the major. Keegan watched as the other man's finger toyed with the trigger, and he didn't flinch. But his thoughts were of Zoe, and as he took what might be his last breath he prayed she would forgive him for what he'd done to her.

* * *

"It will never work."

Zoe threw up her hands in exasperation. "It will I tell you."

"There be too many of them," Cawley said, adding his nay-saying to Will's.

Zoe tried to calm herself. There was too much at stake and she'd already learned that the MacLeods didn't respond well to hysteria. "Of course, I agree with you that there are many more soldiers at Moirer than we have men." An understatement to be sure. Since the ambush there were barely a half-dozen men able to ride, and that number included François.

"However, we will not be counting on strength but stealth." She ignored the subtle shake of several shaggy heads and continued. "We will go in at night. Free Keegan, and be gone before the English know what happened."

"Strange words they are, comin' from an English-woman such as yerself."

Zoe closed her eyes briefly. The last thing she needed was to spar with Seonaid, but the woman clearly decided to enter this particular fray. Zoe twisted around to face her. "I'd have thought you eager to endorse any plan to rescue Keegan."

There was a flash of anger in those green eyes, then a swish of her head that sent red curls flying. "I do wish to bring the MacLeod back, but I do not trust ye to do it." She glanced around, including everyone who sat around the fire in her audience. "I do not trust her."

There was a general buzz of agreement, though

it was by no means unanimous. Mary raised her voice in Zoe's defense as did François. And there were others who seemed undecided. But trust or no the important issue to Zoe was rescuing Keegan. For she had no doubt what awaited him at the hands of the English . . . if they hadn't already hanged him.

But she couldn't allow herself to think that way. Pushing to her feet, wrapping the plaid, Keegan's plaid, more tightly about her, Zoe faced what was left of the clan.

"Whether you trust me or not, I'm the only one who can help you rescue your chief."

"What does she think she can do?" one of the old men said above the crackle of the fire.

"It is not what I can do. But who I am."

"Mademoiselle Zoe." François scrambled to his feet and rushed toward her. "Do not do this. Monsieur Keegan would not want it." He grabbed her hand in both of his. "Please, think of yourself."

He made a comical figure, dressed in silks, a wig—Keegan had stolen it for him—askew. But it was his imploring eyes that Zoe stared into. "I have to," she said, then immediately focused back on the group. "I am Lady Zoe Morgan," she said, her voice clear and strong enough to carry over the wind's howl. "My brother is Lord Foxworth Morgan. He's most likely the man who captured Keegan. He is the major that led the attack on Castle MacLeod."

She expected their shock, but not the vehemence. Almost as one they began shouting and cursing. Zoe reminded herself that her brother was responsible for the death of loved ones, the loss of their livelihood. Of course she knew it wasn't Fox's fault, but these people couldn't see past their grief.

It wasn't until someone suggested that she be bound that François gave her a push and yanked a pistol from his jacket.

"François."

"Stay back, Mademoiselle Zoe. I shall protect you."

"But I don't wish—"

"Monsieur Keegan would wish it," he said while brandishing the pistol about, swerving its aim this way and that across the group. "He charged me with protecting you."

"Perhaps he would have thought more of it had he known who she was," Seonaid said, then scooted back as François aimed her way.

"Don't . . ." Zoe reached around covering the hand that gripped the gun's handle with her own. "Please François, let me tell them." He studied her a moment, then on her nod, lowered the gun. To Zoe's relief no one rushed forward to grab it from him.

"Keegan does know who I am." Zoe took a deep breath. "He knows because he kidnapped me from my London home right after he escaped from New Gaol."

"She's lyin'. "

"It's the truth," François blurted out, then stepped aside again.

"It is," Zoe said her voice calm. "It was night. He broke into my house and spirited me away."

"Why would he do that? Seems t' me he'd be headin' for home."

"Because of my brother. He believed . . . believes Fox is responsible for his father's death. At least for the horrible way he died."

"He was tortured," came a cry.

"An insult t' us all," said another.

"I know." Zoe held her hand up and was surprised the the protests stopped. "Keegan told me about it. And I told him that my brother would not do that. But the fact remains," she said now over the grumble of voices, "that Keegan is in their grasp and I am the one who can free him."

"Turn the lot of us in t' yer brother ye mean."

"That's not what I intend." Zoe was yelling now to be heard. "If that were the case why didn't I simply stay at Castle MacLeod? My brother would have rescued me. Or I could have taken one of the horses and headed south. It doesn't make sense that I would tell you who I am, simply to betray you now."

"I'll tell ye what doesn't make sense. That ye'd help us."

"Aye."

"Aye."

"That's what makes no sense."

Several of the men started to rise. François fumbled with the gun and Zoe saw any gain she'd made with the Highlanders crumbling. She stepped forward.

" 'Tis because I love him," she said then watched as her words impacted each Scot. "I didn't plan to. But then I didn't plan to be kidnapped either. But I do." Her voice was low. "I love him." Tears glistened her eyes. "And I can't bear the thought of him dying all alone."

Zoe scrubbed at her eyes. "Now, I don't know about the rest of you, but I plan to go to that town and do what I can to free Keegan MacLeod."

The silence lay as thick as the mist on the mountains. Zoe waited, then accepted that they would let her go, but go alone. So be it. With a nod of dismissal she shifted to turn away.

That's when François stepped forward. "You can count on me, Mademoiselle Zoe."

"And me." Pushing on her neighbor's shoulder Mary hefted herself up.

"Ye can't go, woman. What good would ye be?"

"I can shoot a gun, or hold a horse, or do whatever Zoe asks of me." Mary edged her way through the group to stand by Zoe.

Then came Will. Cawley and Anne stood. They all did, till there was only Seonaid sitting. Slowly, her gaze never leaving Zoe, she rose, but it was to turn her back and walk away from the puddle of light spilling forth from the fire.

Zoe grasped the reins and prayed the horse could find his way along the road. The town of Moirer loomed before her, twinkling lights in windows surrounded by misty darkness. She was alone, but the others weren't far off. At least she hoped they weren't.

Not everyone had come. In the end it was decided that the best plan called for the fewest people. Cawley and François to care for the horses. And Zoe.

She was to be the distraction. The catalyst that would free Keegan.

The army had taken over several houses. Anne had stolen into town earlier in the day to discover which one housed her brother . . . and where they held Keegan.

He was still alive, thank God, but there was to be a trial on the morrow. On what charges Zoe didn't know, for he'd already been sentenced to death. Whatever the case, Zoe imagined the punishment would be swift this time.

She glanced about her as she entered the town. It was late and the streets were deserted. She imagined everyone snug inside, protected form the damp chill that penetrated her plaid. It wasn't until she reached the front of the house where Fox was staying that her progress was slowed. A soldier stepped forward, the light from the window gleaming on his bayonet, and demanded to know her business here.

"I've come to see my brother," Zoe said as she slowly slid from the horse's back. She ignored the soldier's demand that she halt. "Please tell Major Morgan that I'm here."

"Miss." The soldier was backing up as Zoe approached. "You can't go in there."

Zoe stopped very near the man. "Please announce me. I'm Lady—"

"What's going on out here, Sergeant?" The door opened and light spilled onto the street. Fox stood in the doorway, his jacket open, the neck of his shirt loose. He held a pistol in one hand, a branch of candles in the other.

Ignoring the soldier, Zoe stepped forward into the light. "Hello Fox," she said smiling, for despite the circumstances she was thrilled to see him.

"Zoe?" Fox stepped onto the stone porch, then thrust the candles toward the soldier. The next minute his arms were around his sister.

Nineteen

"Are you certain you're all right. He didn't . . ." Fox loosened his embrace. "Never mind. I'm just glad you're safe now." Taking her hands, Fox led Zoe to the settee. "You look . . . so . . . so full of good health. I've never seen you like this before."

"I feel wonderful." Despite her reason for being here Zoe couldn't help being excited by the sight of her brother. "And you. So tall and handsome." Zoe squirmed a bit under his continual gaze. "I've missed you."

"And I you."

"Fox."

"Zoe."

They spoke each other's name at the same moment.

Fox tightened his grip on her fingers. "I don't know how you got here but I want you to know we have the man who kidnapped you locked up."

"Yes." Zoe took a deep breath and continued. "That's why I'm here." Fox's brows lifted, and Zoe felt a moment of panic. This wasn't part of the plan. At least not the plan that Cawley and the others agreed to. But now that she saw Fox again . . . She didn't want to hurt him. And she didn't want to betray his trust.

"Fox." She hesitated only a moment. "I want you to set him free."

"You what . . . ?" Fox let out a bark of laughter. "If this is a joke it's not very amusing."

"It's no joke. I want you to let Keegan MacLeod go."

"So he can terrorize the Highlands again."

"He would stop. I'm sure of it." At least she hoped she was. "He would live in the mountains, off the land, grazing sheep, I don't know." Now it was Zoe clutching his fingers. "I just know he wouldn't cause you any more trouble."

"Zoe."

"Fox, please."

"Are you mad? Did he do something to your mind?" The question came too easily. It was his own mind that seemed tampered with whenever he encountered the renegade. Fox shook his head. "What you ask is impossible, Zoe."

Leaning back against the cushion Zoe nodded. "I see."

"You know I would do anything for you."

"Yes, of course."

"Zoe, the man was tried by a court in London. Convicted. He's a rebel. And as you should know for yourself a dangerous man." When she looked away from him Fox continued. "It isn't in my power to do this, Zoe."

"I know." Zoe reeled in her scattered emotions. She'd been foolish to even suggest this. She knew her brother and his sense of duty, but even if that were not so, the very idea of allowing Keegan MacLeod to go free was ludicrous. To everyone but her.

Leaning forward she touched her brother's cheek. "You look tired. And I know I am."

"Of course. Zoe, I was just so shocked to see you here. And looking so different." Fox stood, helping Zoe to her feet. "There's so much I want to know."

"But it can wait till morning, can't it Fox?" Zoe deliberately leaned on his arm as he led her from the front room.

"Yes, Zoe. We'll talk more in the morning."

Except she wouldn't be here in the morning.

Zoe waited in the room Fox gave her. He'd awakened a servant to help Zoe get ready for bed. The woman was a Scot, understandably surly about the interruption to her sleep, and obviously not pleased about the English soldier in the house. As soon as she left, Zoe quickly dressed again, then sat in the dark.

The minutes crawled by.

But she forced herself to be patient, waiting until the house was quiet, then waiting longer. Finally she judged it probable that Fox was asleep. Praying it was so, she crept from the room, feeling her way to the head of the stairs.

The third tread from the top squeaked. Zoe had noticed it on the way up. Now she did her best to balance her weight on the side near the banister.

Once downstairs she moved carefully toward the library they passed earlier. Inside she shut the door and fumbled in her pocket for a flint. With a candle lit she began her search.

Desk drawers. Shelves. She scoured them all, her desperation mounting with each second. "They must be here someplace," she whispered, standing on tiptoe and running her hand across a ledge. Her brow furrowed in concentration, so absorbed in her search she didn't hear the door open.

"Are you looking for these, Zoe?"

Her eyes closed, Zoe took a deep breath, then she slowly turned to face her brother. He stood just inside the door. The light was dim, his face in shadows. It was only the ring of brass keys he held out in front of him that caught the light.

Zoe's gaze locked there, then shifted upward. She couldn't see his expression, though she knew full well his dark brows would be lowered in anger . . . and disappointment.

"I hoped you were asleep," she said, taking a step toward him. "I wanted you to be asleep."

"Why, so I wouldn't know of your betrayal till the morn?"

"That's not the reason." Hesitantly Zoe reached into her other pocket. When she grasped the carved handle she withdrew it slowly. She knew the moment her brother saw what was in her hand. His body stiffened. Zoe swallowed back tears.

"For God's sake, Zoe."

"Fox." She was having a difficult time aiming the pistol at him. "Try to understand. I love him."

"Oh, Zoe." Fox took a step forward and the trembling in her hand grew worse. "You don't know what you're saying . . . or doing."

"Don't come any closer Fox. I don't expect you to believe me. But one day you will feel about someone the way I feel about Keegan and then you will understand."

"I hope to God that day never comes if it means I would hold a gun on my own flesh and blood."

"Don't be angry Fox, please. Give me the keys." She motioned toward where they dangled from her brother's finger.

"They won't do you any good. There are guards." Fox tossed them onto a nearby table. The rattle jangled Zoe's already frayed nerves. "Damnit Zoe, you're just going to end up getting yourself killed."

"Move away Fox."

"I won't."

"Don't make this more difficult for me, please." He folded his arms over his open shirt and held his ground.

"Fox." Zoe leveled the pistol.

"I don't think you'll shoot. You won't hurt me, Zoe."

Her name was barely out of his mouth when Fox grunted. The next moment, before Zoe's startled eyes, he crumbled to his knees and then onto the floor.

For one horror-filled moment Zoe thought she'd actually fired the gun. Then she saw Cawley standing behind her brother in the doorway.

"Aye, Sassenach, but I'd hurt ye in a heartbeat."

"Oh God." Zoe dropped the pistol and lurched forward, falling onto her knees beside Fox. "What did you do? Fox."

"Don't get yerself in an uproar lass. I only tapped 'im on the head. He'll be all right."

Needing more convincing than Cawley's dubious testimony, Zoe moved her fingers to her brother's chest frantically feeling for a heartbeat. When she found it her breathing began again. "What are you doing here? The plan was for me to bring you the key."

"And ye were takin' yer own sweet time about it, ye were. We decided t' see what was keepin' ye."

"I had to wait till Fox was asleep. Now help me get him to his bed." As she stood Zoe tried to lift his upper body . . . Without any assistance from Cawley or Will. They were busy scooping up the key and pocketing the pistol.

When she looked around, it was Will's eye she caught.

"Are ye daft lass? For yer sake we won't be killin' the bastard. But I won't be puttin him t' bed like no nanny neither. Besides." He stepped over Fox. "We need to be gettin' the MacLeod."

"What . . . what are you doing?" Zoe asked as Cawley jerked her brother onto his side.

"I'd think that obvious."

Zoe watched as he yanked Fox's hands behind his back and bound them with cord. "He's unconscious."

"And could wake up any moment. Do ye want him comin' after us? Or callin' out?"

"No, but . . ." Zoe stopped arguing when Will stuck a gag in her brother's mouth.

"Come on with ye." Cawley hooked his arm about

her waist and pulled her toward the door. "We've Keegan MacLeod t' think of now."

With one last look toward her brother, Zoe obeyed.

Ten minutes later she was huddled in the misty cold on the outskirts of the village. François stood nearby, wrapped in a plaid, his wig drooping in the moist air. He held the horses' reins and occasionally whispered something soothing to them.

"What's taking them so long do you suppose?" Zoe tried to peer through the thickening fog.

"We must be patient Mademoiselle Zoe."

"But what if—" Zoe stopped in midsentence when she heard a rustling sound. Almost immediately three men materialized, running toward her. Even in the darkness she recognized Keegan's form and let out a little squeal of delight.

Keegan stopped in his tracks, then whirled toward the sound. "Zoe?" In five strides he was by her side, cupping her shoulders. "What in the hell are ye doin' here?"

"I . . ." This wasn't exactly the welcome she expected.

"It was her plan, damn the man. Her brother with the keys." Will grabbed at Keegan's arm. "Now come on with ye."

"Wait." Keegan shrugged off his hand, keeping his firmly on Zoe. His fingers tightened. "I want ye to stay here."

"What? No, I won't." Zoe shook her head so hard the plaid draped over her hair slid down.

"Listen, Zoe." Keegan ignored the hushed suggestions that 'twas no time for discussions. "This is the best place for ye . . . with yer brother."

Zoe could hardly believe what he was saying. "With you," she countered, reaching out to grasp his coat. "I want to be with you."

"Zoe, livin' in the hills as a fugitive is no life for ye, and 'tis—"

"What's that?" Will hissed, continuing as the sound of voices grew louder. "We need t' ride, and ride now." With that he swung into the saddle. Without further comment the others did the same.

They rode off toward the hills, Cawley and Will, François, Keegan, and Zoe. If any soldier followed, they were soon lost in the wild Highlands.

By late the next evening they were back at the caves, filling their stomachs and relating their adventures. Telling of sneaking up behind the soldier guarding Keegan's prison and knocking him flat. Of unlocking the door and riding for the hills. No one said anything to Zoe about her brother, no one questioned her loyalty. And Keegan was the only one to question her sanity for her part in the rescue.

He pulled her aside, asking her to take a walk with him. It was late, dark, with only the moon to light the way as they followed winding footpaths between high, craggy rocks. But they knew the way well. Zoe was certain she could find the spot she thought of as their own with her eyes closed.

High above the churning waters of the sea, the ridge was secluded, padded with moss and bracken, and large enough for two people to sit . . . or recline. Zoe had no doubt they would be doing the latter before they retraced their steps to join the others. She could tell Keegan was annoyed with her for her part in his rescue, but he must understand she could do no less. Not loving him as she did.

"I saw the wild swans flyin' south today as we rode."

They had settled, their backs against the rocks, and Keegan's words were not what she expected to hear. "Did you?"

"Aye." He took a deep breath and drew his knees to his chest. "The heather is dried up, the rowen berries fallen." He touched her cheek. "Even the wild roses are gone. All sure signs that winter's close."

"Mmmm."

"We'll never make it through a Highland winter, Zoe."

His words were bad enough but it was his tone, flat . . . defeated, that tore at Zoe's heart. "Of course we will," she countered. "If we all work together."

He shook his head. "Doin' what? Not harvestin' t' be sure. Nor fishin' either from up here."

"Then you'll have to raid some more Royalist Scots." Zoe had never been in favor of that particular enterprise. But to keep Keegan's spirits up she would suggest just about anything.

He seemed to realize her tactic, for he smiled, that smile that sliced through the bitter winds to warm her heart. "T' my chagrin I fear my raidin' days are done." He took her hand, bringing it to his lips. "Ye shouldn't have risked yerself t' rescue me, Zoe."

"Don't you know I'd do anything for you?"

The question was stated simply and though he couldn't see her well enough to tell, Keegan knew her pure grey eyes would be sweet and honest and totally sincere. But he didn't want her willing to do anything for him. Despite the fact that the reverse was true. For he knew in his heart how very much he loved her. And that, yes, he would do anything for her.

"Zoe," he began, for he enjoyed the sound of her name, "none of ye should have come. Ye should have left me there."

"To be hanged?" Zoe clutched his hand. "I couldn't bear that."

"Ye could, sweetling. Ye're much stronger than ye think. I've come t' see that ye can do . . . bear, most anythin'."

"Don't talk so," Zoe leaned into his shoulder, listening for the steady beat of his heart. "It frightens me when you do."

"It's sorry I am t' frighten ye." His palm curved along her scarf, then slid beneath the wool to the silky hair beneath. Keegan took a deep breath and pulled her closer. "Will told me what ye did, holdin' a gun on yer brother." He shook his head. "I'm sorry it ever came t' that." Zoe only shrugged, but Keegan knew how difficult it had been for her—knew how much she loved her brother. He was counting on that love being mutual, and strong with forgiveness.

Deciding it best to change the subject, else he become maudlin, Keegan began, "I've been thinkin of somethin' ye once said t' me."

Zoe's laugh was swept away by the wind. "I've said so much to you."

"Aye ye have, and some of it even made sense."
He kissed the tip of her nose when she looked up
at him, her expression indignant. "Do ye want t'
know what's on me mind or not?"

"Tell me."

"Ye once said that I should let go of the past.
Look toward the future."

"Yes and you said Scots didn't do such things, as
I recall. It was in their blood to cling to the past."

"I may have been exaggeratin' a bit," Keegan said
with a chuckle. "I've come t' think that it may be
best for the clan to leave Scotland. Yer idea of the
New World sounds appealin'."

"Do you really think so?" Zoe squirmed about till
she could see his face.

"I do. There's land t' be had, and trees, rivers full
of fish, did ye say, and even mountains?"

"So I've read."

"Aye, that seems t' be the best solution."

"Then you wouldn't have to raid, or worry about
the soldiers." Zoe sat up. "We could build a house,
and plant crops. Oats. I can help you."

Keegan pulled her back into the crook of his arm.
"I don't think yer hands were meant for pushin' a
plow." He lifted one and kissed the palm.

"I'm strong, Keegan. You showed me that I am.
I'll always be grateful for that."

Keegan shut his eyes, " 'Tis not yer gratitude that
I want, Zoe Morgan." It was a blatant invitation and
one Keegan was not especially proud of. But he'd
made a decision, the hardest he'd ever made in his
life, and he needed the warmth of the woman he
loved.

He needed Zoe.

Her arm swept around his neck, her upper body molded to his. When their lips met Keegan knew he'd never wanted anyone more. Never needed anyone more.

His hands brushed aside the plaid covering her head and he dug his fingers into her thick hair. When the wind caught her curls he pulled the scarf back up. " 'Tis cold tonight. I don't want ye catchin' yer death."

"Then 'tis up to you to warm me," Zoe whispered into his neck.

Keegan wriggled down till he lay flat, Zoe snuggled by his side. "I think we can manage to heat up the night a bit," he said, then preceded to do just that. Though he wished they could be naked, wrapped about each other, the weather *was* a consideration. So instead of seeing her, Keegan relied on his other senses.

His hands worked their way beneath her bodice, finding and skimming across her breasts. The nipples puckered tighter with his touch. He buried his face in her hair, loving the sweet fragrance, muttering to himself, and perhaps to her, how she smelled like a rose.

He drank of her lips, kissing and probing with his tongue, drowning in her.

She was wet, writhing in his arms when he lifted her skirts and found the delta of tight curls. His fingers pressed, her body arched, and Keegan heard the sound of her ragged breathing above the wind.

"Zoe." He said her name because he couldn't stop himself.

When he settled atop her, she opened for him, offering her body in sweet surrender. Her legs wrapped around him and Keegan reached behind to draw the plaid over her. His hair, loosened by the wind, hung around them like a curtain, and Keegan felt as if there were only the two of them snuggled together in a forgotten cubby in the rocks, sheltered from the world.

They were joined, and Keegan wished for one foolish moment they could stay like this, hidden away. Just the two of them.

But life was not like that, and even as his hips began the ancient rhythm, even as she arched with each thrust and clung to him, Keegan knew it was not to be. He clutched her bottom, lifting her up, demanding as much as she could give, pressing deep within her body.

Each surge brought her closer. He could sense her hovering on the precipice. Then his fingers skimmed down between their bodies and like a spark to tinder, she ignited, pulling him into her, making them one.

And letting him forget just for a moment what he must do.

"Mmmm, Keegan," she sighed when her breathing had steadied enough for her to say anything. "Do you suppose we can find a place like this in the New World?"

Keegan's throat tightened. " 'Aye," he managed, rearranging their clothing to conserve their warmth.

"I want you to promise me that we will." She settled her arms around his neck. "And even though we have a giant bed with a thick down mattress, we'll still sneak away to our special spot now and again."

When he said nothing, Zoe lifted her head. In the dim light she saw his profile. With her finger she traced the straight nose and the firm lips she adored. "Keegan?"

"What? Oh . . . aye." He looked at her, at the guileless face that stared at him with such love. "Whatever ye say, Zoe."

He wanted so much at that moment to give her everything she ever wished for. And he knew he couldn't. So he held her close and dreamed along with her, pipe dreams in the mist.

In the morning he called François to his side. While Zoe and the others broke their fast he gave the little Frenchman a message. Despite the valet's protests Keegan insisted he take it to Major Fox Morgan.

"I am counting on ye, François. We all are."

"But Monsieur Keegan, there must be another way."

"There isn't."

"Perhaps Mademoiselle Zoe can—"

"Ye are t' say nothin' t' her. Nothin' t' anyone except Morgan."

"But—"

"Nothin', François. Will ye do this thing for me?" When the Frenchman nodded, albeit reluctantly, Keegan clasped his shoulder. "Now go."

Keegan watched François scramble down the path before turning toward the rest of his clan. Then he joined them, ready to plant the seed of an idea in their minds.

Twenty

"What was his answer?"

"Oui."

Keegan let his head fall back. He took a deep breath then straightened and nodded toward François. "Not a word of this t' anyone. Do ye understand me?"

"Oh, I understand all right." François slid from the horse's back. Keegan had grabbed the reins as soon as he entered the clearing. "I understand you're going to get yourself hanged."

"Hush that talk." Keegan glanced back toward the caves where what was left of his clan was huddled about the peat fire trying to stay warm. Zoe emerged from a cave, wrapped from head to toe in his plaid. She glanced up and waved, smiling at Keegan and François and started toward them.

"I mean it François. Ye are t' follow my lead and say nothin' more." If François answered Keegan didn't hear before Zoe was beside him.

"Where have you been François? Keegan wouldn't tell us a thing. Goodness, aren't you cold. Here." She began unwrapping her own shawl but Keegan stopped her.

"François can go warm himself by the fire." His

arm draped around Zoe's shoulders. "He's brought good news."

"What is it?"

"Come, we'll all hear it together."

They were leaving Scotland.

Despite that she'd suggested this course weeks ago, and that Keegan had talked of the possibility, Zoe was surprised. "How did you manage to find a vessel to take us to the New World?" she asked him more often than he liked. She could tell he grew annoyed by her questions, even though he did his best not to show it.

His answer was always the same. He had his ways. No one else questioned their chief. They were all excited about the prospect of starting new lives in a place called Carolina. Zoe had read of it, and told them any bit of knowledge she could remember. They were all so eager.

All except François.

The little Frenchman grew more morose the closer the day of departure came. They were to return to Castle MacLeod. The schooner was to meet them there, in the bay.

"Is it that you do not wish to leave Scotland?" Zoe asked him one morning. François was sitting on a rock, staring out toward the sea. He was alone, and Zoe realized that in itself was unusual. He and Keegan were always together lately.

He turned to look at her, his large nose twitching slightly as he glanced past her. "Where's Monsieur Keegan?"

Zoe swirled around to see if he was behind her. "I don't know. Why?"

"I was just wondering."

"Oh." Zoe sat beside him on the rock. "Are you going to tell me what's wrong? You've hardly said two words to me since you returned."

"Everyone's so busy." François peeked about nervously for Keegan. He didn't want to talk to Zoe alone. He was afraid what he might say.

"There is truth to that," Zoe laughed. "Everyone seems thrilled to be leaving . . . except you. I thought you disliked the cold. And the mountains. And the fog. Or was I wrong?"

"Ah, Mademoiselle Zoe, I am a great complainer. You should pay no attention to me."

"It does grow on you, doesn't it?" Zoe looked about and hugged herself. "This land. Its people." She glanced toward François and smiled. "When I first met Keegan he seemed so wild and untamed. A barbarian," she said and laughed. "Now I've come to see that it's not entirely a bad thing to be uncivilized . . . to a point." She breathed in the salt-tinged air. "There's a freedom here, along with the wildness, that's . . . Well, that I admire very much."

"I think it is Monsieur Keegan that you admire very much."

"I think you're right." She gave her friend a quick hug. "Now don't fret about going to the Americas. It will be fine. The important thing is, we shall all be together."

* * *

It rained the day they started down from the caves, icy arrows of water that penetrated to the skin. The land, the mountains and rocks, were concealed in a blanket of grey. Despite their destination it was a somber group that wound its way along the path. Each person carried on their back what they would take from their homeland. No one's pack was heavy.

It took them two days to reach the glen. By then a weak sun was shining and the air held the promise of winter.

Keegan hadn't seen Castle MacLeod since the second fire. He could only shut his eyes and look away. Zoe was by his side, and she wrapped her arms about his waist and held tight. It was all Keegan could do not to cry out to the heavens.

Three days later a sail was spotted on the horizon. By twilight the schooner was docked in the bay. The captain sent a message ashore. Keegan read it, then nodded his agreement. The sailor returned to the longboat and was taken back to the schooner.

"What is it?" Until the moment Zoe saw the vessel she could hardly believe that they were really going. Now it seemed strange to her that there was a delay.

"We'll board on the morn," was all Keegan said before turning away.

She went to him that night, for it was obvious he wasn't coming to her.

Zoe found him outside the castle, sitting on the ground, staring into the night. He didn't look her way even when she settled down beside him.

"Ye should be inside, where 'tis warmer."

"It's cold in there too."

"Aye." He could easily recall a time when the castle was warm. When the fires were lit in the great hearths and music and laughter filled the rooms. Now there was naught but the howling wind. The castle was desolate. After they left, it would become even more so. In a few years Highlanders would come and quarry the stone. The factor would protest, but he was far away in England. If he ever did return it would be to find only a pile of rubble where there was once the seat of clan MacLeod.

Keegan shook off that dismal thought. He had other worries to keep his mind occupied.

He turned toward Zoe, lifting her chin with an icy finger. "I want ye to promise me you'll be strong tomorrow."

"What are you talking about? Strong about what?"

Keegan shook his head. "Just promise me, Zoe." Before she could say anything he leaned forward, brushing her lips with his own.

"You're to set up camp here." Fox strode toward his horse, his second in command, Captain Monroe, by his side. Fox and his men, twenty strong, had stopped near a placid loch, fringed by saffron weeds. On every side hills rose, as if piled one on top of another. It was a lonely place, but one that held a haunting pull to Fox. He tried to ignore the mood drifting over him. "If I haven't returned by morning . . ." Fox hesitated. What should he have his company do in that case? "Ride for Fort William." He paused. "Then continue to hunt Keegan MacLeod." Though in truth if he didn't return, there was little chance the renegade would ever be found in Scotland.

"Are you sure you wish to go alone, sir?"

"I've no choice, Captain. I've given my word." Fox pulled on his riding gloves.

"Sir, if you don't mind my saying it, I question whether the MacLeod can be trusted. You could very likely be walking into a trap. He doesn't seem the type to give himself up."

"I appreciate your concerns. And believe me, they echo my own. But in a strange way, that I can't explain, I believe Keegan MacLeod will do what he said he would."

"Are you telling me you think him an honorable man?"

Fox took the reins from the corporal. "Is that what I'm saying?" He gave his head a shake. "I don't know." He mounted on one fluid motion. "But we will see, Captain Monroe, we will see."

From his vantage point on the ridge he could see the whole like a miniature scene. The shimmering loch, the gently sloping hills, the bay, the castle. Anchored off the craggy shore was the schooner, *Irish Pride*, just as he'd arranged.

Just as Keegan Macleod had asked.

Fox lifted the spyglass to his eye, squinting till he could focus on his sister. She was there, among the others, waving toward the longboat heading toward shore. Keegan MacLeod was there as well, standing a bit apart as befitted his role as chief of his clan.

A role he would soon relinquish.

Fox watched as the renegade glanced about toward the hills, his hand lifted to shade his eyes. He could tell he'd been spotted when the Scot moved to Zoe's side. He bent down, saying something to her, then took her arm. Together they started toward the path that led to the hills.

"I don't understand what's so important that we must see it now," Zoe lifted her skirts and quickened her pace, rushing to keep up with Keegan. "What of the longboat? It's almost to shore. We don't want to miss it. What if it doesn't wait for us to return? Keegan!" Zoe grabbed at his arm in frustration. He appeared not to hear a word she'd said. "Will you stop a moment and listen?"

"Damnit, Zoe, there's no time." Keegan halted his headlong press up the side of the mountain. He turned to face her, softening his tone when he saw her expression. She didn't understand. And who could blame her? He'd lied to her. For all that he told himself it was a necessary lie, it was a lie all the same.

He didn't want to hurt her. But he would. And his only consolation was that someday she would see it was all for the best.

"What is it Keegan? What aren't you telling me?"

He had started walking again, but not before she'd seen the regret in his eyes. Zoe hurried her steps, racing around in front of him. She was breathless now, from running, from fear. A quick look behind her, down toward the bay showed the longboat nudging the shore. Everyone was huddled on the beach waiting to embark on their new life.

"Keegan." She batted at his chest, but still he wouldn't stop. Tears were streaming down her face now. She couldn't seem to stem them. "Why are you doing this? What of our house in the Carolinas? What of—"

"Stop it, Zoe." Keegan reached out, cupping her shoulders. He leaned back against the rockface that formed one side of the gorge. His eyes closed for a moment, then opened, revealing a tortured soul "Ye must not carry on so, lass. Ye promised me ye'd be strong today."

"But how can I, Keegan, when I've no idea what you're doing. What we're doing." Zoe's head whipped around, the wind catching her golden brown hair. "Look, they're climbing into the longboat, Keegan. They're going to leave us."

Keegan took a deep breath, letting the air escape slowly. "Aye."

"But why? We're going with them. We're going to the New World." Zoe tried to control her sobbing, tried to stop the tears, but it seemed as if her life was disappearing into the mist that was drifting down from the hills.

"Nay, Zoe, we're not." Keegan watched her face and cursed himself for bringing her to this. "I've been playin' myself the fool, Zoe. Wantin' what I cannot have. This land. A new life . . . ye." He lifted his hand, letting his fingers skim her cheek before jerking away.

"Morgan!" he yelled, his voice carried by the swirling wind. Then he grabbed Zoe's arm and pulled her along over the rise and around the bend in the path. And there he stood.

"Fox." Zoe took a step toward her brother, then stopped. She glanced back at Keegan, still not certain what was going on. Neither man had a weapon aimed at the other. And for the first time she realized that Keegan had no weapon at all. No pistol. No broadsword. "Someone tell me what is happening."

"What was destined to happen from the beginnin'. I'm givin' ye back to yer family."

"But I don't want . . ."

" 'Tis for the best, lass."

"No, no it isn't. I want to stay with you."

"Well, ye can't."

"But—" Zoe looked from one man to the other. They both stood tall and straight.

"Ye can't go with me, Zoe, for I'm . . . I'm turnin' myself over to the authorities."

"But they'll hang you."

Keegan tried to shrug. "As I said, 'tis what was destined from the beginnin'."

"I don't believe that. What did you do—trade your life and me for safe passage for the clan?" Keegan said nothing, but she could tell by his expression that she was right. Zoe dove toward her brother, pounding his chest. "You can't do this. I won't let you take him from me. I won't."

"Zoe." It was Keegan's voice that sliced through her hysteria. "We both knew this was t' be the end of it. Ye were my captive, and that was all. And now I'm handin' ye over t' yer family and doin' the only thing I can t' stay in Scotland."

"What are you saying, Keegan MacLeod, that you never loved me? That I should look upon this as an . . . an adventure and go off with my brother and pretend it never happened?"

Keegan stared at a spot over her head. "Aye, that's what I'm sayin'."

Zoe's voice was calm. "I don't believe you."

Keegan turned toward Fox. "I'm turnin' myself over t' ye but I'd just as soon get this over with if ye don't mind. Have ye soldiers nearby?"

"Over the ridge."

"And are they expectin' me?"

"They are."

Keegan nodded. "Then with yer permission I'll be goin' off t' meet them."

"Go on then." Fox motioned him along the path with his hand. Perhaps he was being foolish, allowing the renegade to go off. He could disappear again, hide in the hills and never be found. Except Fox didn't think he would. He trusted him, irrational as it was, he did. And he admired him. He wished things could be different. For like Zoe, Fox didn't believe for one moment that the Scot didn't love his sister.

He loved Zoe, and he loved his clan and he was willing to sacrifice himself for the good of both. Fox wondered if given similar circumstances he could be as noble.

For long moments after Keegan walked away Fox didn't look at Zoe. But he could feel the icy prickles of her stare, feel her pain. And he could feel the Scot's pain. Almost as if it were his own.

Fox tried to fight it. He was a soldier, sworn to do

his duty. "Zoe, someday you'll understand this is for the best."

Their eyes met then, and he could read the truth of her words in hers. "I've always loved you Fox, and I always will. I'll learn to forgive you for this. But I will never . . . never think this was for the best." She straightened her shoulders. "Do not expect that from me, brother."

Her words seemed destined to be etched in time, time that Fox saw sprawling out in front of him. Zoe was right. She'd never think this was for the best. And he'd never truly believe it was either. The knowledge would haunt them both.

"Go to him."

"What?" Zoe scrubbed her hands down her face. She would cry and carry on no more.

"Go to him. Bring him back." Fox let his breath out. "I want you both on that schooner and gone from here. No, don't hug me. Get that damn Scot back here."

Fox watched as his sister ran along the path, calling out Keegan's name. It was still hard for him to reconcile this beautiful woman with the sickly girl he'd always known. But he imagined he had the Scot to thank for the metamorphosis.

She was telling him now, and though Fox couldn't hear from this distance, he could sense the other man's reluctance to believe. He shook his head, and squared his shoulders. But Zoe persisted, and when the Scot finally glanced toward him, Fox signaled for him to come back.

Now that he'd made his decision Fox was anxious to be done with it. But he didn't begrudge the time it took the Scot to lift Zoe off her feet and twirl her around. Or the kiss they shared.

"I could have told you he wasn't to be trusted."

Fox stood at attention. "Yes sir."

"The very idea of taking one of these damn Scots' word for anything, let alone a renegade like MacLeod was ludicrous. And I hope you learned your lesson Major Morgan."

"I have, sir."

Upton leaned back in the leather chair. There was nothing he enjoyed more than being agreed with . . . unless it was proving one of his officers, especially an arrogant bastard like Morgan, wrong. And this time the righteous son of a bitch had screwed up royally.

"Well, at least he's dead. But it could have just as easily been you, or one of your men who met that fate. You wouldn't wish to inform some hapless widow that her husband died at the hand of a Highland brigand that you trusted to surrender peacefully."

"No sir . . . but as you say, it was Keegan MacLeod who took the bullet and fell from the cliff."

"Into the sea."

"Yes sir . . . into the sea." Fox noted the tinge of disbelief coloring the colonel's voice. But he kept his own firm. Upton could think what he might, but proof was another story.

Colonel Upton folded his hands. "What of your sister, Major? Rumor has it she was with the Scot. Did you find her?"

"I fear not. Another of his lies I suppose." Fox relaxed his shoulders. "If you'd known Lady Zoe, you'd know she would never have survived long at the Scot's hands."

"So you assume she is dead as well?"

"Yes, another casualty of this rebellion."

"Indeed."

There were more questions. More answers. And then Fox's announcement that he was resigning his commission. To do what, he didn't know. He was a younger son. His brother, the Earl of Warwick, despised him, and the feeling was mutual. But he couldn't stay in the army. He couldn't stay in Scotland where the hills and lochs, the glens and even the mist seemed to call to him.

Fox left Colonel Upton's headquarters and took a deep breath. Unable to stop himself his gaze turned toward the Highlands.

Then with a firm step he headed south, toward England.

Epilogue

"You're thinking about Captain Rafferty, aren't you?"

"Aye." Keegan slipped his arm about Zoe's shoulders. She'd come up beside him as he stood on deck, staring out at the gentle swells of the grey Atlantic. "How did ye know?"

"Call it wifely intuition," she said, smiling up at the handsome man at her side.

Keegan chuckled and shook his head. "You've developed that skill after but one day?"

"I'm a fast learner."

Keegan leaned down and kissed the tip of her nose. "Are ye feelin' any better?"

"Some." Zoe leaned her elbows on the polished wood rail. "I don't want to complain . . ." She slanted him a look through her lashes. "At least not too much," she added when he laughed.

"Ye needn't think I doubted yer illness this morn." He'd awakened to find her bent over a pail. "The sea was a bit rough last night."

"Mmmm," was all Zoe said.

"I had a talk with Padraic . . . Captain Rafferty." Keegan played absently with his new wife's hair. "While ye were sleeping."

"Was he the man you remembered from Culloden?" Yesterday as they boarded the schooner, Keegan thought he recognized the vessel's captain. But there was little time to discover the truth, for there was much excitement about Keegan and Zoe's arrival.

François had told the clan about Keegan's deal with the English major. Their freedom and transport to the New World in exchange for Zoe's return to her brother, and Keegan's surrender. So it was with a great deal of enthusiasm that the pair was greeted. And when Keegan, after a quick word with the captain, announced there would be a wedding that night, the celebration escalated.

It wasn't until less than an hour ago that Keegan had a chance to question the captain. "Aye, he was there. And he remembered both my father and me."

Zoe hesitated. "And Fox?"

"Aye, him, too." Keegan took a deep breath and cuddled his wife closer. "As it happens I came close to killin' the good captain, and he doin' the same t' me."

"He was in His Majesty's service?"

"Nay, but the scoundrel was garbed as if he was. Wore a red tunic, he did." Keegan chuckled. "But he was in disguise, hopin' to find the Bonnie Prince and carry him off before the British could capture him. But he was wounded, and found shelter near where I took my da."

Keegan paused and studied the horizon. "He saw it all. My fight with the British troops, yer brother, the killin' of my father."

"Keegan, I know how you feel about Fox, and that nothing he can do will ever make up for the horror but—"

"I may have been wrong, Zoe."

"What?"

"All this time I've been blamin' yer brother." He shrugged. "Perhaps I was askin' more of him than any man could give."

"I don't understand."

"I'm not sure I do either. But after talkin' t' Captain Rafferty I have a better idea of what went on. The horror." Keegan shifted to look down at her. "I know that sounds ridiculous, for it was nothin' but horror for me. 'Tis just that's all I was seein' . . . what was happenin' to me and mine."

"You can't be blamed for that."

"Maybe not. But I think perhaps yer brother did try t' stop the killin'." He shrugged. "Captain Rafferty believes as much."

"He does?"

"Aye, and 'tis sorry I am t' have doubted ye all this time when ye tried t' tell me about yer brother. I think . . . I don't know but when I saw him, there was this odd feelin' that came over me. The same strangeness happened when I set eyes on Captain Rafferty." Keegan shook his head. "Now I wish I could talk t' yer brother. Thank him again for lettin' us leave."

"I think Fox knew how you felt. How I felt."

"I still can't believe he let me live."

"Well, in the strictest sense he didn't. He did kill off the renegade."

"Aye, he did." Keegan started to laugh but his

good humor ended quickly when he saw his wife's face. "What is it, love, ye look a bit green."

"Do I?" Zoe tried to smile. "I . . . I'm not really feeling very well." The deck rolled on a swell and Zoe groaned. But before she could say another word she was scooped up in her husband's strong arms.

"What is it, Zoe?" True, Keegan had felt at one time that Zoe had a penchant for exaggerating an illness. But this was no figment of her imagination. He hurriedly crossed to the hatch and made his way down the ladder to their cabin, wondering where Miss Phelps was when he really needed her.

As carefully as he could, Keegan lowered his wife to the bunk. "Can I get ye anythin'? Do anythin'?"

Zoe shook her head. "I'd say you've already done your part. At least for the next couple months or so."

"Ye're not talkin' sense now, Zoe. What have I done t' make ye so ill?"

Zoe couldn't help laughing. Her hand grazed his cheek. "Keegan darling, it isn't what you did exactly. More what *we* did." She paused, but could tell by his expression he was too agitated to understand her meaning.

"And I'm not ill," she continued. "Though truthfully it does feel as if I am. But the other women say it will all be better in a month or two. Of course it won't be completely better until the babe is borne, but—Keegan!"

Zoe sat bolt upright, her eyes big in her face and stared at the floor. Where her big, rugged, renegade husband lay, having swooned dead away.

TO MY READERS

Writing about a kilt-clad Scottish hero has long been a dream of mine. And Keegan MacLeod exceeded even my expectations. Of course, like Keegan, I adored Lady Zoe Morgan too. Their love was a delight to put on paper. I hope you enjoyed reading *The Renegade and the Rose* as much as I enjoyed writing it.

And *The Renegade and the Rose* is only the beginning of the *Renegade, Rebel and Rogue Series*. In mid May, 1997 Zebra will publish *The Rebel and the Lily*. You met the hero of *The Rebel and the Lily*, Padraic Rafferty, in *The Renegade and the Rose*. He's a charming Irishman, a smuggler and chameleon of sorts. While masquerading as an effeminate dandy (not an easy task for our hero) Padraic uses his sword to wreak havoc with the English overrunning his homeland. Of course this charade is made more difficult by the presence of his father's young widow, a woman Padraic finds difficult to resist.

The *Renegade, Rebel and Rogue Series* continues as we return to the Highlands for *The Rogue and the Heather*. Lord Foxworth Morgan, a man haunted by memories of Culloden, travels through time and space, meeting Grace MacLeod, and learning the secret that binds him to Keegan MacLeod and Padraic Rafferty.

Thank you all for your kind and supportive letters. I'm so glad you enjoyed *Splendor* and all my other books. I can't tell you what a thrill it is to write these romantic stories for you. For a newsletter please write me and send a SASE care of:

Kensington Publishing Corp.
850 Third Ave.
New York, NY 10022-6222

And visit my homepage on the World Wide Web at http://www.infokart.com/dorsey/christine.html.

To Happy Endings,
Christine Dorsey